Afterworld Series

AlibiZ

Book Two

KARICE BOLTON

ACKNOWLEDGMENTS

Cover Art: DepositPhoto Image ID:35160069 ©feedough, Image ID: 12337811 ©oblickstudio, Image ID: 41875547 ©VBaleha

I want to say a simple thank you to Amazon, iBooks, Barnes & Noble, and all of the other avenues available for the indie publishing world. It allows the art of storytelling to continue to flourish in unexpected ways!

Chapter One

"Stay where you are. You're completely surrounded on all sides."

I froze and looked around the forest. I didn't see anyone until I looked up into the trees where several sets of eyes watched our every move, shotguns and rifles centered on Preston and me. It seemed like they'd converted deer stands into people-watching stands. It was creepy and clever at the same time.

My heart rate increased as I slowly lowered my rifle to the ground. Preston did the same. Did we stumble upon some leftover militia members or survivalists or something?

"We don't do visitors. We haven't survived the outbreak this long to welcome strangers and the virus into our lives," the man said, motioning for one of his men to pick up our weapons.

I glanced at Preston as the realization dawned on both of us. The woods held a madness I hadn't felt since the outbreak.

"The outbreak is over," Preston said, his arms still raised.

"Don't give me that garbage," the man replied. "Get on your knees. Both of you."

How could he not know?

My knees hit the hard surface, a sharp rock digging into my skin. I hoped my ankle holster didn't peek out.

"It's true. There's a vaccine," I said, staring at the men in front of us. "We've been vaccinated."

"Sure you have, doll," the man said, his brown eyes dulled by exhaustion and hunger. "But there's no room at the Inn."

I let out a sigh and held back a laugh at the craziness of our situation.

"Take them to the barn." He pointed at the two men who took our weapons. "I'll be there shortly to deal with them. Ron, come with me. We need to cover their tracks so no others find their way here."

"Yes, sir," a young guy yelled, as he climbed down the tree and jumped to the forest floor. He wore a ratty flannel and a pair of well-worn jeans. There was a strong resemblance between Ron and the man barking orders. Both had dark hair and very sharp features, accentuated by their lack of nourishment. The older man's hair, however, was speckled with silver.

One of the men pulled zip ties out of his pocket and told us to put our hands together. We both complied as he first tightened the plastic around my wrists and then Preston's. I really disliked being put in this situation. We didn't have time for it. The plastic tie dug into my skin, and the more I moved, the tighter it became. The moment we were left alone, Preston would cut us out of these in no time.

"Get up," the guy in front of me commanded.

I watched Preston who gave a slight nod as I stood up.

"You gonna give us trouble?" the guy asked.

I shook my head. "No need to."

"Jay doesn't like visitors," the guy said, pushing me forward to walk.

"I kind of got that," I said.

Preston stood up and hid a smile as I walked by.

Looking around, I noticed the men up in the trees were no longer interested in us. They were busy scanning for more intruders. I wondered how many intruders they actually got.

The men led us over to the river that we'd followed into this area.

I ignored the biting cold as we traversed the rocky riverbank. The gushing river below did little to calm my nerves as the rocks crunched beneath my hiking boots. Every so often, pieces cut loose and tumbled to the water below. Not my idea of a fun hike, especially when my hands were tied.

I spotted smoke off in the distance and assumed that was where they were leading us.

"I love the smell of wood smoke," I said, taking in a deep breath. "It always reminds me of fall."

"No talking," one of the men ordered. His

breathing was heavy as we trudged along the river's edge, and I hoped he wouldn't keel over before we got to wherever we were going. It would be a shame for him to live through the outbreak to die of a heart attack before finding out it was all over.

Letting them call the shots for now, I nodded and walked in silence for what seemed like an eternity. The trail along the riverbank became less severe the longer we hiked, but I still had my worries about slipping into the ice-cold water.

"This way." The man climbed up an embankment, his foot slipping slightly at the top. I noticed the soles of his hiking boots were completely trashed and worn down.

If any of these people took the time to really examine us, they'd notice that neither Preston nor I were starving, and our clothes and shoes were in excellent condition. Unfortunately, if they thought the outbreak was still active, they weren't in their right minds. They were still in survival mode. They'd only see what they wanted to see, hear what they wanted to hear, to ensure they'd come out breathing on the other end. It was a tricky situation, but one I wasn't too worried about. We got past the first part. We were lucky they didn't blow our heads off when they first spotted us. Now we only had to convince them that the outbreak was over.

A hemlock branch, brittle from the cold, snapped back from the guy hiking in front of me and hit my face. I spit out the grime and wiped my mouth with the crook of my elbow as we hiked through the woods. I spotted a clearing through the trees and looked over my shoulder at Preston who flashed me a quick grin before I darted my gaze away. They had a little encampment set up with one large building and a few smaller outbuildings of some sort.

"Over here," the guy said, glancing over his shoulder at us.

I remained silent, following the man's lead as he hiked us over to a large shed. To call it a barn was simply overstating things. I saw another structure that would qualify as a patchwork residence, new sections built as the need arose. I wasn't sure how it would last through another winter in the mountains. I doubted it would.

While I stared around the property, the man fumbled with the lock on the shed. The clearing provided a beautiful vantage point of ancient Douglas firs and cedar trees that covered the surrounding mountains. No power lines were visible, which would explain their lack of information.

"You got it, Josh?" the other man asked, just as the lock popped off in Josh's hand. He swung the door open to reveal a cluttered mess of odd finds, ranging from old saws to rusty metal teapots. I spotted an old, stained mattress propped against the back wall, and a couple of plastic buckets placed in between the piles of junk.

I examined the man I could now call Josh and noticed his breathing was still labored.

"Asthma okay?" the other guy asked, looking

noticeably worried as he shifted his weight from one foot to the other.

Josh mumbled an answer I couldn't grasp before he pushed us inside the cobweb-filled building. The musty smell was so thick in the air I could taste it. Preston let out a few coughs, and I pushed the tickle down. Several rays of light poked through the roof of the building, making it clear why it smelled so stuffy. Must be what the plastic buckets were for.

Josh snatched a bucket, dumped out the smelly water, and flipped it over for me to sit on. He did the same for Preston.

"Ron and Jay will be here soon," Josh said, turning quickly on his heels and leaving us alone in the shed. The click of the lock being fastened on the door made me chuckle.

"They do realize we could just kick out the walls of this place, right?" I whispered to Preston.

He smiled, leaning over to release the knife that was strapped around his ankle.

"Apparently not." Preston flipped the blade open and motioned for me to move closer. I held out my hands, and he cut through the plastic tie in under a second. Handing me the knife, I did the same for him.

"So do we waste our time trying to explain the outbreak really is over?" I asked. "Or do we get out of here?"

Preston pressed his lips together and nodded. "I think we should give it a try."

I stood up and stretched, noticing some of the

items this group had collected. Most of the found objects had probably been left over from camping trips before the outbreak. There were tent poles, skillets, netting, tarps, and even a car headlight. It was an eclectic assortment, but I recognized the mentality. Grab anything and everything a person could get their hands on. It was the *MacGyver* method that got most of us through the outbreak.

Preston leaned over my shoulder and pointed out a tennis shoe. "Clothing always creeps me out."

"I don't know why in the world it never occurred to me that there could still be people that didn't know it was over. I thought our government did a better job of notifying everyone."

"It's a big country," Preston said.

I nodded. "True. I wonder how many more pockets of these guys exist?"

"Probably more than we think."

Footsteps crunched outside the shed, and we both took our seats on the buckets again.

"Did they give you any trouble, Tim?" Jay asked.

Tim must have been Josh's buddy.

"Not at all, sir. But Josh's asthma is flaring up. I sent him inside."

I heard a sigh and then a whisper, "We only have enough medication for another month, and that's if he uses it sparingly and suffers the rest of the time."

"Yeah, and that will only work if he doesn't

have any big attacks that could kill him."

The door creaked open, and a blaze of light shone through the opening. I looked away to let my eyes adjust, hearing Jay's footsteps circle around us.

"Who freed you?" Jay asked.

Neither of us answered his question. Instead, we were focused on getting him to listen so we could get out of here.

On the drive up here, we passed through several small, vacant towns that still showed signs of the outbreak. Merely convincing them to go to the nearest town would do nothing. They'd see the devastation, sense the isolation, and would assume everything was as it had been. There was no sign of life in those towns, only death. The horrors of the outbreak lived on in rural America, and it hadn't occurred to me what that meant for people who were still in hiding. We had to convince him to go to a bigger city, and the closest one was over four hours away.

"We aren't here to cause any trouble," Preston said. "Let us go, and we'll forget we ever saw you."

"You've already caused problems for us. Giving my people false hope. I'm sure what you said has already gotten back to everyone at the house. I can't let you go because others will follow and then they'll die. We'll keep you in the shed for forty-eight hours, and if you aren't infected, you'll join our community."

I shook my head and turned away. Jay's odor was really strong in this small space. I covered my mouth and nose with my hand. "We don't want to stay here. That was never our intention. We hadn't expected to come across anyone out here. Since the vaccine most people have centered around—"

"Enough," Jay shouted, taking a step back.

"We can get Josh new medicine." I tried a new tactic.

Jay's eyes flashed with anger. "I can take care of my people."

"They aren't your people," Preston said. "People aren't property. Maybe you should let them decide what they'd like to do, see, or hear."

The anger I felt rolling off Jay made me nervous. I didn't want to get shot trying to do something nice for someone. No good deed goes unpunished and all that.

"What can we do to make you believe there really is a vaccine?" I asked, softening my voice.

"Dad, maybe we should listen to what they have to say?" It was Ron. He took a step into the shed, but none of the tension dissipated. Instead, it heightened.

"Nothing could stop those creatures," Jay said in a clipped tone. I couldn't tell if he was annoyed with his son or us.

"You are *absolutely* right," Preston replied. "It's a vaccine, not a cure. Those who were infected weren't saved, but people like us, we've been vaccinated."

"We need to hear them out," Ron said, his voice more urgent. "We're running out of food and snow hasn't even hit. If we're out here for no reason..."

"Don't be foolish," Jay replied. "I will not put my people in harm's way."

"You are doing that very thing," Preston said. "Honestly, what would we have to gain by telling you the outbreak's over?"

"He's got a point, dad."

"How dare you." Jay's anger was getting too volatile. It was the hunger. I recognized it from when Gavin and I were on the run. When days had turned to weeks without a substantial meal, our comprehension became faulty and our tempers flared for no reason. He probably did mean well for his community. In fact, he probably ate the least, giving his son and others his rations, which would explain why his son was willing to listen to reason and he wasn't. Unfortunately, the instability of his father made me nervous.

"Did you forget we killed two zombies last week?" He turned to his son.

Shoot! The stragglers. I hadn't counted on how to explain those away.

Preston let out a deep sigh. "Which is exactly why we need to get you all vaccinated—"

"Is it really over?" a woman's voice cried outside, distracting Jay.

"Praise the Lord," another woman sobbed.

A crowd was congregating outside the shed.

Jay's eyes connected with mine. "See what you've done and you..." He turned to face Preston pointing a shaking finger.

A few children began singing as men's voices

cheered outside the shed.

"Let them feel the happiness, Jay. It's true. It's over," I whispered. "We can help."

I glimpsed a few of the women standing outside the shed. Their hands and faces were caked with dirt as they firmly held onto baskets of freshly picked roots. This had to stop.

"Let us talk to them," a woman shouted.

"Look at what you've started," Jay growled.

"Stop it, dad. They're here to help," Ron said, placing his hand on his dad's shoulder to calm him down.

"They're liars. There's probably more of them hiding in the woods... ready to strike, ready to steal everything we have. Don't you trust them for a minute. You hear me, son?"

Ron took a step back and looked us both over. His eyes narrowed on Preston, and my heart sunk, realizing he'd succumbed to his father's suspicions.

"Then why are they so well dressed?" Ron asked, surprising me.

Jay wasn't going to let his son or anyone tell him what to do. Not now. Not while his stomach was empty.

I watched through the doorway as the crowd of men, women, and children grew. The collected sounds of excitement, anger, and worry filled our tiny space, and it was clearly getting to Jay.

"Send the group back to the house. All of our supplies are ripe for the taking. We're falling perfectly into these two's plans," Jay yelled at his son. "Don't you see it?"

"I won't, dad," Ron said. "It's time we all got to hear what they have to say."

A small hum outside turned into a chant, "Cure. Cure. Cure."

My heart pounding, I glanced at Preston who was studying the two men in front of us.

"I will not be responsible for my family's death," Jay said quietly to his son.

"We can get your family vaccinated. This can all be over," I tried one last time, hoping the energy of the group congregating would persuade Jay to give us a chance to help.

I noticed a few of the women's expressions suddenly change just as the chants turned to screams, shattering my hopes of delivering the truth. My blood chilled as I heard the familiar grunts of the undead—the stragglers, but I wasn't scared of the undead. I was frightened of what Jay's fear and delusion would push him to do.

The crowd scattered completely, leaving only the undead in view. Ron spun around and aimed his shotgun at the first of the three stragglers. Taking down the first, second, and third within seconds, I glanced over at Jay whose eyes were filled with an unyielding fury as he reached for his pistol.

"You brought them here. They followed your scent," he snarled.

I heard the click of the trigger, but it was too late.

Chapter Two

Ron tackled his father, and I ran to Preston who quickly removed his shirt. The bullet had grazed Preston's upper arm. There was quite a bit of blood, but the wound was only superficial. I tore his shirt and wrapped it around his arm.

"You two can get out of here," Ron said, through his father's grunts as he held him down.

Preston shook his head and picked up some rope off the floor. He kneeled down next to Ron and his father. "Do you mind?"

Ron shook his head, and Preston began tying the man's wrists together and then bound his feet.

"This wasn't how I wanted to go about things," Preston mumbled, pulling Jay up to his feet.

Jay began shouting and hollering warnings, but Preston quickly put a stop to it by stuffing a glove in his mouth.

"I'm really sorry about this," Preston said to

Ron, while he hauled a half-hobbling Jay with us.

Six guys were walking over to the three undead.

"Don't let any of your people dispose of them. We can handle it. We're vaccinated. You guys aren't," I told Ron.

Ron nodded and hollered for the men to stop and to follow us to the house. They appeared somewhat relieved about not having to dispose of the bodies and quickly caught up with us.

The sound of the gunshot brought a large group of people to see what was going on. Fearful they would attack Preston since he was hauling a tied-up Jay to the house, I was relieved that Ron was on the other side of his father calming the fears of those milling about. The expressions dotting everyone's faces ranged from concern to anxiousness. I stayed close to Preston and Ron, fielding questions here and there about why he was tied up, and my simple answer was that he shot my friend.

A couple of logs pounded deep into the earth acted as steps to the front door, and the inside was just as rustic. The main room was large and expanded into another room behind. No doubt the first of many expansions. Tables and chairs had been made out of twigs and logs. Rugs woven from tattered clothes and rags were spread across the floor. There were a few people sitting on the window ledge, gauging our every move, and several more people had slowly congregated in the front room, staring at us with a mix of hostility and hope. Word had traveled fast that we'd tied up their leader.

A woman holding a bowl of sudsy water came up to Preston. "Please sit," she told him, pointing with her free hand at the closest log seat. She was wearing a smock that consisted of several different pieces of rags sewn together. Her blond hair was pulled on top of her head, and she was quite beautiful. I glanced at Preston's bare chest, and a twinge of jealousy erupted, which I had to internally laugh off. We were both too broken to pursue much of anything between us. At least that was what I'd been telling myself recently.

He shook his head, kindly refusing treatment and, instead, sat Jay on the log stool.

More people were trickling in from the front door and through the back room.

"How many people live here?" I asked Ron.

"Thirty-nine people live in our community."

His father only scowled at his son.

I began quickly counting and came up with thirty.

"Do you know where the other nine are?" I asked.

"They're on watch duty. If you don't mind, I'd like to keep them there. We can fill them in later."

"Sounds good to me," I agreed.

I looked at the woman who was eager to help with Preston's wounds. She was almost clinging to him, and I turned away. It wasn't my business. We'd both thought about going down that road together, dabbled a little, but decided it was best to stick to finding answers right now.

Ron quieted everyone down, and a few people began sitting on the floor while others pulled more log benches into the main room. A few of the children roamed the room, not paying attention one way or another. Once we'd gotten most everyone's attention, Preston glanced around the space and then over at me before beginning.

"First, I apologize for subduing Jay. We didn't see eye-to-eye about some of the topics we wanted to discuss with you. We didn't want to cause problems for any of you. We didn't come here to hurt or to steal from you. In fact, we didn't expect to find anyone out here in the woods, and we certainly didn't expect to find unvaccinated people."

I nodded in agreement as some of the women glanced at me, their minds trying to make sense of things.

"A vaccine has been developed and administered to the majority of the population. Zombies are no longer a threat to those who are vaccinated," Preston continued.

Nervousness turned to excitement in the room as this revelation soaked in.

"There is no cure yet, but the vaccination stopped the spread of the disease. The vaccines have been given out worldwide. The outbreak was declared contained, and order is slowly making its way back into civilization."

"When did the outbreak end?" one of the men questioned.

Preston seemed uncomfortable. I doubted

anyone else caught it, but I did. He didn't want to make these people even angrier with Jay. After all, Jay did the best he could under the circumstances, but the outbreak had been over far longer than anyone here would want to know. We didn't need to incite anger.

"Several months ago," I lied, trying to mix a nice amount of vagueness and honesty together. They'd figure out soon enough once they acclimated back into society.

"If the outbreak is over, why do we still get zombies all the way up here?" a woman asked. She placed her hands on her hips and arched a brow while waiting for our response.

I nodded, acknowledging that was a fair question. "The CDC came up with a vaccine, not a cure. The National Guard rounded up the bulk of zombies in our country, and private security companies have also helped, but the initial numbers of undead was staggering, overwhelming really. There's a system in place now to gather up the stragglers, like the ones who've been pestering you, but the undead are still roaming around here and there." I eyed Preston to take over for me.

"The difference is that in the cities, we have a number to call and the undead are scooped up and hauled away to be taken care of. If we encounter an undead creature, we are protected. We are immune from the virus. Right now, the government is trying to bring back normalcy as best they can. Living out here puts you in jeopardy, especially unvaccinated," Preston explained.

Or at least that was how it was supposed to work.

Whispers could be heard in the room as Preston and I looked at each other. We hadn't discussed how to get these people off the mountain. We hadn't expected to find these people on the mountain.

"How do we know this isn't a ploy?" a man asked, standing up so abruptly he knocked his log bench over.

"Yeah. How do we know you don't just want what we have?" a woman asked.

I was trying so hard to be sympathetic, but it was beginning to grate on me.

"Listen, we're going back down the mountain. In less than an hour, we're going to hop in our truck and carry on with our lives. Either two of you can come with us and see for yourselves or you can all just stay up here—paranoid—for the rest of your lives. We have nothing to gain by wasting our time trying to convince you to come off the mountain," I said.

"I'm sure this is a shock. Finding out that you've been up here, starving and cold long after you needed to be, but now is the time to get back to living the life you want to live." Preston glanced at Ron who nodded his head in agreement.

"There's no reason not to have one or two of us ride back to town and check out what they're saying," Ron said.

"How long has the vaccine been out there?"

someone asked again.

Ron stepped in, answering on our behalf. "They said a few months. Now is the time to concentrate on the future. Not the past."

A few of the women began to wipe away tears of joy. Excitement displaced the nervous tension in the air as hope became contagious.

"How are we all going to get off the mountain? I don't want to spend another minute here," a woman laughed.

"We'll get a bus as close as we can, and you'll just have to hike down the mountain a little ways," I replied, smiling at the woman.

Looking into her eyes, it was as if I was reliving the moment I had found out that the government had a vaccine—that the outbreak was over. The worst was over. Or so I thought. I shifted my gaze away from the woman and swallowed back my disappointment. Now wasn't the moment to think about everything Preston and I had discovered.

I heard Josh's breathing from behind and turned to observe him before speaking to Ron. "How about Josh comes down with us? I think he could use some current medication before his asthma gets worse."

Ron nodded. "I'd like to come too."

"Absolutely. I think that makes sense," Preston agreed.

We announced our decision to the group, and I glanced at Jay, who appeared completely defeated. His head hung low and his shoulders were hunched over. I got Preston's attention and nodded toward Jay. He took out the gag but kept him tied up.

"The first thing we need to do is to get you to the clinics where you can get vaccinated. That's the most important thing," I began.

"What will happen once we get there? We have no place to live. We have nothing but what's here..." a woman asked, holding her child.

I nodded, but I didn't want to scare them. The Afterworld looked nothing like what our world had once been. "The government has programs in place and there are temporary shelters."

I wasn't actually sure how many of those temporary shelters were still open considering much of the search and recovery had happened so long ago, but I remembered seeing a few scattered around Seattle.

The woman seemed relieved, and I smiled back at her, wishing I could take them all right now.

"Spend the next twenty-four hours gathering anything you think you want to take off the mountain," Ron instructed.

"Try nothing," a man in the back laughed from the pit of his belly. "Have you seen what we've been dealing with around here?"

The group began breaking into smaller groups, discussing their fate. It was the oddest feeling to be in a room full of people who only thirty minutes ago thought they were fighting the world to stay alive. Now as I examined the room, I saw the glimmer of hope begin to grow among the people. It was exactly what I needed to see because what Preston and I had been dealing with this week had been anything but pleasant.

"I'd like to show you something," Ron whispered.

I nodded and motioned for Preston to follow. We walked through the backroom to a door that led outside. Several wooden tables dotted the area in the back, and laundry hung from two lines between cedar trees. An intricate community had been built here.

As Ron led us deeper into the forest, I began to get slightly nervous about where he was taking us. Barely any light sprinkled through the dense woods, and the temperature had dropped at least ten degrees. I spotted large boulders in front of us just as Ron stopped hiking.

"My father's a good man. He's tried his best for us all," Ron whispered.

"I don't doubt it," Preston replied, sliding his arm around my waist.

My breath caught, but I hoped he didn't notice.

"This is where my mother and sister are buried."

I stared down at the forest floor and realized the dark soil had been recently exposed. My chest tightened, and I brought my gaze back to Ron's. He wiped away a tear and cleared his throat.

"They were attacked two weeks ago," Ron said. "My father will never forgive himself. I knew that's why he didn't want to listen to what you were saying. If he let himself believe that we could have gotten off the mountain and had a vaccine pumping through our veins..."

"My God," I whispered, shaking my head. "I'm so sorry."

Ron nodded. "I am too. I want to get them off this mountain. I want them to have a proper burial."

I looked away from the soft, mounded dirt of the graves and leaned my head against Preston's good arm, wondering how many more communities like this one were out there. How many more unvaccinated people were living off the land in fear? With everything we'd been focusing on, this certainly wasn't something I'd thought of. Preston's fingers softly circled my hips as we stood trying to comprehend even a sliver of the grief Ron felt.

It definitely explained why his father was so against hearing the possibilities. Scanning the ground in front of us, I counted twelve graves with forest debris in various stages of decay marking the holes that held loved ones, all because they weren't vaccinated. A shiver ran through my body and I pushed away the anger.

"We should get on the road," Preston said, as Ron picked up and tossed aside a few branches that had fallen onto his sister's grave.

"Agreed. I'd like to get your arm checked out before—"

"It's fine," Preston said, as we retraced our steps out of the woods. "Just a flesh wound."

"That doesn't make it any less worrisome," I

said, under my breath.

We walked back into the home, and the energy was completely different than when we'd left only a few moments before. The pulse of the room had quickened. A buzz of exhilaration allowed everyone to dream of a future that didn't involve hiding.

Preston jogged over to Jay and I felt a tug on my sleeve. I looked down to see a little boy staring back up at me. My guess was that he was three or four. I was never very good at that.

"Were you sent by the visitors?" he asked.

I bent down as I glanced around the room, wondering who he belonged to.

"Visitors?" I questioned.

He nodded.

"When was this?" I asked.

He shrugged and smiled.

"Do you know what they wanted?" I asked.

He shook his head.

"How many were there?" I asked.

He held up three fingers on each hand just as a woman came over and hugged him.

"Sorry," she laughed, pulling him with her. "My son isn't the least bit shy."

"No problem at all." I followed her toward where Jay was tied down. She took a seat on the floor and anchored her son on her lap. I knelt down, whispering so only she could hear.

"He mentioned visitors?"

She shook her head. "Toby's got a wild imagination. We've had no visitors besides you two and the occasional zombie."

She avoided eye contact, and I knew I wouldn't get any answers.

"That's a good trait for him to have," I said, standing back up.

I was surprised to see that Jay was still restrained, but I suspected no one in the house wanted to do anything to jeopardize their own ability to escape from this commune.

I watched Jay slowly raise his head as Preston neared. His mouth moved, but I couldn't hear what was said.

Preston began freeing the man's arms and shook his head.

"It's not your fault. No need to apologize," Preston replied.

Very few could understand the guilt and pain that Jay experienced. It would haunt him until the day he died. Ron came over and hugged his father while Preston and I walked over to the front door.

Josh said his goodbyes to his little sister and mother, promising them that he'd be back the next day. I looked away not wanting to invade their privacy. Instead, I surveyed the rest of the room full of eager eyes and nervous expressions. A gnawing feeling attempted to spring to life in my gut, but I ignored it. We didn't have time to get caught up in an emotional upheaval because of this new discovery of unvaccinated.

"Let's go dispose of the bodies," Preston whispered.

I nodded and followed him outside. I hated dealing with the undead in any way, shape, or form. The irony wasn't lost on me as I glanced at the three stragglers. The smell of their rotting flesh was something I'd never get used to. Preston had wandered into the shed and came out holding some canvas tarps and one glove.

"We'll just use this to drag and burn," Preston said, pulling the tarp.

"Zombie potholder. Nice." I nodded and caught the glove he threw in my direction.

Preston laid the tarp over the first body. I grabbed the slippery material, finding ankles to hold onto, and carefully hauled the creature toward a clearing that would allow us to create an intense fire. I dropped the zombie's ankles and removed the tarp to start the process again. Glancing at the undead's face sent a shot of disgust through me. My stomach churned as my eyes grazed the tattered clothes clinging to its body, and the cloudy, grey eyes still open and staring toward the sky. Its mouth was slightly parted with rust-colored crust dripping down its chin, which made the nausea come in full force.

"I got it," Preston said, taking the tarp from me. "Take a break. Doing these things on an empty stomach is never a good idea."

"Did I turn green?" I asked, but didn't have the strength to argue. Instead, I worked on keeping the nausea at bay.

"Guess we need to add another thing on our to-do list," I mumbled, swallowing the bitterness back down.

"What's that?"

"Find as many of these encampments as we

can before anyone unsavory does."

"Yep."

Preston dragged the other two bodies and piled them on top of the first. An ankle snapped off on the last one so I snatched the elusive foot with my gloved hand and tossed it on top of the zombie mound as Preston placed tinder all around the undead. I shook the glove off and let it fall on top of the pile and walked away as Preston began to light the fire. I jogged quickly toward the house to avoid the smell and looked through the door, hoping Josh and Ron would meet us outside soon.

The smartest thing to do was to alert the authorities and get everyone off the mountain and vaccinated as quickly as possible. These weren't the only stragglers in existence, and this many unvaccinated was an accident waiting to happen. If I could, I'd take them all now, but cobbling together a rescue attempt deep into the night would only delay and possibly complicate the effort. The government was prepared for this type of evacuation. We weren't.

Preston came running up, his nose buried under his shirt and his eyes watering.

"Pretty horrid stench," I grinned.

"Always is."

Josh and Ron met us outside. I looked toward the sky and saw the threat of a storm thrashing above us. With the weather shifting and the breeze picking up as the clouds rolled in, I just wanted off the mountain before the rains hit. Slipping down wet moss and even wetter rocks wasn't my idea of a good time. Judging by our travel partners' footwear, I was uncertain they'd even make it without injury in those kinds of conditions. We started our trek back to civilization, and I couldn't be happier.

Preston was busy explaining to the men that as soon as we were back in an area with cell service, we'd make the call to find out the closest place to take them and get the process started. My mind drifted away from their conversation as I thought about the visitors the little boy had mentioned. Who were they? Did they even exist?

We moved down the mountain through the dense forest. The dangerous terrain became more evident with every step. Uneven ground made for a treacherous journey even in solid hiking boots so I couldn't fathom how Ron and Josh managed to stay upright most of the time.

The sound of Josh's breathing concerned me, but this was his best hope to get some medicine that actually worked. He assured us that it wasn't one of his severe attacks, but his breathing didn't sound good to me.

The conifers spread out as we descended, and I spotted the trail we used to hike in. The truck was only about a half-mile away.

"Is there anything we should know about this new world?" Ron asked.

Oh, so many things... But now wasn't the time to worry them.

"You'll settle in very quickly. Everyone seems to," I assured him.

Our pace had picked up on the more stable

ground, and when I spotted our truck, relief spread that I wouldn't have to talk to him about the Afterworld. Sure. The vast majority of the population had been vaccinated, but the tendrils of evil still managed to caress and taunt human civilization. The outbreak was over, but what Preston and I knew could threaten us all again.

"I held onto the hope that there was life on the other side of all this," Josh said, through low wheezes. "But I started to have my doubts."

He climbed into the back of the truck and sat down, his back leaning against the cab as Ron took a seat next to him. Bursts of vapor emitted into the air with each of Josh's short breaths. We needed to find him medicine quicker than he was willing to recognize.

"The one thing I've learned so far in the Afterworld is to never give up hope. No matter what we might face," I said, slamming the truck gate shut.

"The Afterworld?" Ron asked.

An unexpected chuckle left my lips, and I shook my head. "Yeah. Don't ya love it? That's what the academics and media's been calling life after the outbreak."

"Guess it's kind of catchy," Josh laughed.

"True." I smiled and caught Preston's gaze.

I wanted to be sensitive to the losses Ron and everyone in his community faced, but something had been troubling me.

"So there were only ten other community members who became infected?" I asked Ron and Josh, thinking back to the twelve graves we'd seen earlier in the afternoon.

"There weren't ten infected," Ron said, shaking his head. "Besides my mother and sister, we only had four others who'd been infected."

"Then who did the other six graves belong to?" I asked, my heart pounding.

Chapter Three

"I was afraid you'd ask that," Ron sighed, smoothing his hand across his whiskers.

Josh appeared uncomfortable as he sat next to Ron, but I was pretty confident Josh's anxiety had more to do with what Ron was about to reveal than with his breathing issues. Preston rested his arms along the truck bed, leaning over slightly as we waited for Ron's response.

"We had some unexpected visitors," Ron began.

"Like us?" I asked.

Ron and Josh both shook their heads.

"No. They came as an armed force on some sort of mission. There were three groups of three," Ron said, his body tensing.

"Past tense. Not comforting." I crossed my arms and waited for Ron to finish.

"They came barging onto our land. We had to protect what was ours. We had to protect our people. They were heavily armed and didn't mean well. I can assure you of that," Ron said, his jaw clenching.

"How so?" I shifted my weight.

"They immediately took shots at some of us... tried to round us up like cattle. They weren't expecting that we were ready for such an attack."

I thought back to the men hanging out on the deer stands and had to conceal a chuckle. So far it sounded like self-defense, and it also explained why they weren't exactly welcoming when we arrived.

"So you had to protect yourselves," Preston stated.

Ron nodded.

"When did this happen?" I asked.

"A few days ago."

A chill ran through my bones.

"The math still doesn't add up. You had nine people attack you, but six graves?" I asked.

"Three of the men escaped," Josh replied. "We've been on high alert ever since."

"You're sure they meant to cause a problem for you? Because I vaguely remember what almost happened to us." My eyes stayed on Ron and he nodded.

The breeze picked up, and I eyed the rowdy sky as the storm clouds moved in quickly. No matter how many details I wanted to get from these two, we had to get off the mountain.

"Did they seem well organized?" I asked. "Or give you any clues what they wanted?"

Ron gave my questions some thought and threw a look toward Josh. "To be honest, I can't imagine what they'd want from us. We were in a much different place when this happened. We didn't know the outbreak was over. Hopefully, they weren't..." his voice trailed off. He had no intentions of continuing.

I took in a deep breath and watched Josh as his chest heaved. We needed to get off the mountain. The answers could wait until we got to town.

I tapped the truck bed. "Time to get out of here."

I turned away from the truck bed and opened the door, hearing Josh and Ron quietly arguing about something.

Right when I climbed onto the seat, Josh spoke up, "They were all wearing black uniforms."

My body tensed, and I glanced at Preston who was thinking the same thing.

"We thought they might have been government officials," Josh continued, ignoring Ron's harsh stare.

I leaned the back of my head against the glass and waited for Preston to ask the question we were both thinking. Preston climbed out of the truck. His feet crunching a few steps before he stopped and watched them.

"Was there a name or any identifying information on their uniforms?" Preston asked.

"After our men had taken their shots, that's when we saw it," Josh continued. "At first, I thought it was a SWAT team or something. But it wasn't."

"What was it then?" Preston pressed.

Josh shrugged. "I don't know. I'd never heard of it before. TRAC. I think that's what it was." He turned to Ron who seemed aggravated at Josh's admission.

"Yeah. Each of them had large, white letters emblazoned on the back of their uniforms... TRAC," Ron confirmed. "Does that mean something to you?"

"More than you can imagine," Preston said.

"Are they government? Are we going to get pinned for downing agents or..." Josh's voice trailed off.

"Nothing of the sort. It's..."

I looked behind me through the glass and raised a brow at Preston.

"It's a long story," he finished. "Time to get out of here before the rain hits."

Preston hopped in the truck, and we were met with the large roar of the engine, which was oddly comforting. The thought of being stuck on this mountain any longer wasn't appealing. He clicked on the CD player, and we were off for the many-hour drive back to civilization. If that was what it could be called.

Even though the head of TRAC, Marcus, was no longer in the picture that didn't mean that his organization wasn't functioning. In fact, it was thriving. All of TRAC's government contracts had rolled over to Barrell security once the media got wind of TRAC's checkered past. The media didn't even know the half of it, and we intended to keep it that way until we learned the extent of the organization. All the media was concerned with reporting was the government waste and the lavish lifestyle that Marcus enjoyed, and that was plenty. The less focus on TRAC from the media, the more we could uncover.

However, taking away the government contracts didn't disband TRAC. It only made them stronger and drove them deeper into the underbelly of the Afterworld. Instead of TRAC having to be bothered with the façade of acting lawfully, they were now able to act like the thugs they truly were. It also made it more difficult for us to determine what they were doing, which was why what we'd originally planned to do today was so important.

True to her word, Dr. Falino went into hiding. I'd hoped once she learned of Marcus's death, she would've re-emerged to help expose the true intentions of this thriving underworld that we'd just barely been able to piece together. But she didn't, and I couldn't blame her. She had a daughter to keep safe.

My body shivered as the truck hopped along the old forestry road. The mountain storm continued to gain momentum, with the branches bowing down to us as we made our way off the mountain. With each gust, branches snapped and flew through the air, and thunder cracked in the distance.

"You're pretty quiet over there," Preston said, angling the heater vents toward me.

"I think I'm tired."

"It's been a long day," he agreed.

"I mean tired of everything," I said, looking

out the window. "I heard from Abby this morning before we headed out. All is going good in their world."

Preston caught the bitterness in my tone. I hadn't meant for it to come out that way.

"We live in the same world."

"Do we?" I asked.

"We do. It's just that some choose to see what's going on around them and others don't. You know that more intimately than most."

"Your arm okay for the drive?" I questioned, hoping to change the subject. I wasn't sure what had come over me, but there was definitely a cloud hovering low.

"Now you ask?" he teased. "Yeah, it's fine. Besides, I wouldn't want you behind the wheel right now."

"What's that supposed to mean?"

"Nothing."

"Nothing my ass. What are you getting at?"

"You're a naturally aggressive driver and when you're in a mood..."

"I'm not an aggressive driver. I'm a defensive driver."

"Who says?" Preston attempted to hide his grin.

"My driving school. And I'm not in a mood. I'm just annoyed that we're running behind. We had things to do today. No. Correction. We had *one* thing to do today and we blew it."

Preston nodded. "But at least it wasn't for nothing. Knowing TRAC is out scavenging is an interesting bit of news."

"My only hope is that it isn't for the same reason as us."

"Doubtful."

I checked my cell phone for service and wasn't surprised to see zero bars. It would probably be a couple hours before I'd pick up service.

"What do you make of TRAC being out here?" Preston asked.

"Maybe they were scouting for a new place for the zombie pits or training..."

Neither of those answers felt right, but it was all I had to offer. I was too wiped out to come up with anything clever.

"You okay?" Preston held the wheel tightly and tossed me a quick look. "Those were pretty weak guesses. You usually love this part."

I felt a pinch at the base of my neck. I attempted to massage it out, but I was left with a dull ache that spread to the bottom of my skull, threatening to radiate to the rest of my head.

"Just a headache coming on."

"There's some aspirin in the glove compartment."

I opened the bin and several things came tumbling out, dropping to the floor. I spotted an old tech magazine, a knife, and a pack of .22 caliber bullets resting against the top of my feet. As I leaned over to pick up the items, a small gold-foil packet fell out of the pile. I tried to contain my laughter and chucked the pack of condoms at him and smiled. "Seriously? The woods bring it out of you?"

"I didn't know those were in there," he

laughed.

"Right." I rolled my eyes.

"Check the date."

I lifted the foil packet from the seat and scanned it for a date just to call his bluff. I burst into laughter as soon as my eyes landed on the expiration. He wasn't kidding. These suckers were old.

"Well?" he asked.

"They expired three years ago." Heat rose in my cheeks, and I stuffed the whole lot back in the compartment and shut the bin, too embarrassed to look at him.

"Jeffrey's become a very rich man now that all of the TRAC contracts rolled over to him," I said, determined to change the subject.

"He wasn't doing shabby before that."

"True." Silence settled between us as I thought about Jeffrey. He'd gotten us out of a bind when Preston set the building on fire, but I still wasn't sure how much we could trust him. It was everyone for themselves in the Afterworld. It wasn't just survival of the fittest. From my perspective, the ones who would survive in this new world needed to be smart, cunning, and inventive. My fear was that self-preservation in the new world also demanded a seed of evil to thrive, and that wasn't something I was willing to accept. Not yet anyway.

"Why do you think Jeffrey didn't hand over the goods to the government?" I asked.

This was something that had been bothering Preston and me, but neither of us wanted to face the obvious answer.

"You mean bodies?" he laughed and I cringed.

I didn't like associating anything human with these modifieds.

"I think he knows at some point, he's going to need leverage," Preston continued, glancing at me out of the corner of his eye. "And who's to say the government can be trusted?"

I nodded. We'd managed to find some very loose ties to the CDC when we found the room full of modifieds that Preston had blazed up. The more we dug, the more we realized that a few bad seeds didn't make for a completely corrupt agency within the government, but it made for a dangerous one. We couldn't yet risk bringing the information to light. Whoever was tied into the government could make everything including us disappear. If that happened, the truth—whatever that was—would be a thing of the past.

"On one hand, it worries me that Jeffrey was so quick to move all the modifieds into new facilities, but on the other if he hadn't, they probably would've all fallen back into TRAC's hands."

"As it is, TRAC managed to nab more than I'd like to consider." Preston pressed his lips together. "And the fact that none of us, Jeffrey included, can find out where TRAC is hiding them all is beyond frightening. He's found countless empty buildings with remnants of modifieds left behind. Whoever wants this research conducted and an army built is a ticking time bomb. We need to find out who in TRAC is driving things now and what their main goal is."

"An army of undead. A weapon like no other..." I nodded and glanced out the window, watching as the trees and blackberry vines whipped by. "And Jeffrey has been more than willing to share where he's put the modifieds," I acknowledged. "But you know the old saying, keep your friends close and your enemies closer? What if that's Jeffrey's mentality? He might just be letting us feel like we're in the know when he's as corrupt as the rest of them."

"Listen. We can't assume everyone's an asshole."

"Have been so far."

"Present company excluded, I hope."

"Of course." I gave a faint smile.

"In this instance, why don't we wait until Jeffrey proves that he can't be trusted rather than the other way around? So far he's done everything and more to show that he's on the up and up. Neither of us wanted to deliver our findings to the government, so we shouldn't be suspicious because he didn't want to either. There is too much unrest and uncertainty to let this information get into the wrong hands... anymore than it already has. Jeffrey's still uncovering sites where the creatures are being held."

I nodded in agreement. Preston was right. One thing at a time. Marcus was out, but TRAC was still thriving. At the moment, Jeffrey's organization was handling everything as discreetly as it could, while still trying to mend the MHA. So far, it appears the government wasn't aware of the atrocities at the MHA. Or so their story goes.

"Let's not talk about this until my headache's gone. As of now, it's getting worse." I threw two small aspirins into the back of my throat and took a swig of water to wash them down.

He looked over, and his eyes held mine for a heartbeat before replying. "Certainly. You know, I think you're more fascinated with what you found in the glove box than anything else."

"Yeah. That's it." I rolled my eyes.

The grin plastered on Preston's face was far too telling. It would only be a matter of time before what I found came back to haunt me. I should have just shoved them back in the bin without saying a word, but I always managed to stick my feet, not foot, in my mouth. I was certain my only salvation was the fact that there were two men in the back of our truck.

"Do you think they'll manage to get everyone off the mountain and vaccinated tomorrow?" I asked.

"I do. I think the government's so worried about mutations and things like that, they'll drop everything to get them vaccinated. The less in the chain, the better."

"True," I said, rubbing the base of my neck. "I wish we could've gotten done what we intended today. Now we have to wait until everyone's evacuated and there's no chance of getting caught. I can't wait to get back to base and check in. See what the groups have come up with. How rude is that? We stumble on an entire group of people who didn't know the outbreak was over, and all I care about is getting back to business."

"It's understandable, considering…"

I nodded, feeling the tension begin to release from my body. "I know."

The truck continued down the long, winding road, and I rested my head against the window.

"It's okay if you fall asleep. Nothing's going to happen with the cell phone reception for another hour or so."

"Maybe I will. I can't promise I'll wake up any more pleasant though."

"Would never expect you to," he chuckled.

I closed my eyes, listening to the soft hum of the CD player, and the tires pounding over the rocky terrain bringing us closer to the civilization we'd left only hours before.

It wasn't until the car stopped and a hand caressed my cheek that I realized not only had we reached cell service, we'd managed to drive all the way to the social service building that handled integration back into society.

The Human Integration Agency had been instrumental in administering the vaccines. No one was allowed to obtain any of the subsidies, acquire home ownership, or claim property until they went through the HIA and were vaccinated. Not that there were many citizens who didn't want the vaccination, but there were a few.

There were always a few.

I wiped the sleep from my eyes and glanced at the large, concrete building. A handful of cars dotted the parking lot, but the building appeared to be open. Lines used to be commonplace at these buildings. Now, I suspected Josh and Ron wouldn't even need a number.

Josh and Ron had already climbed out of the truck bed by the time I opened the door. Their eyes held a glimmer of hope as the idea of the Afterworld settled around them.

"Things appear so similar but so..." Ron's voice trailed off.

"Different," Josh finished.

I nodded. "Take this in case anything comes up." I handed Ron a piece of paper with my contact information on it. "Do you want us to wait?"

"You've done enough," Ron said, smiling. "I just... You won't mention—"

I shook my head. "We won't mention a thing."

Preston shook their hands and wished them luck before we climbed back into the truck. We watched Ron and Josh climb the steps to the entrance and walk through the glass doors. It was a nice sense of closure, something we hadn't felt for a long time.

"At least one story has a happy ending. It feels good to do the right thing sometimes," I said, as we pulled out of the parking lot.

"But?"

"But something seems really off kilter, and I'm glad it's out of our hands now," I laughed.

"Always the optimist."

The hours-long drive back to the compound was uneventful, and I was pleased to see Braden and Emily's car around the side of the building. It was nice to have them back. I slammed the truck door harder than I'd intended and spun around to see one of my least favorite people standing on the porch, waiting.

"Where the hell have you been?" Charlotte asked. She was a new addition to our group, and I wasn't sure she added much. There was a fine line between being assertive and a pain in the ass, and I was pretty sure she was teetering on the latter.

"We stumbled upon a little discovery that derailed our original journey. It couldn't be helped," Preston replied, unfazed by Charlotte.

"Just what kind of discovery would do that?" She scowled at the two of us, and I couldn't help but chuckle as a crowd gathered behind her to see what the ruckus was about. Emily pushed Braden's chair next to Charlotte and parked it. She gave me a quick wave even though her expression looked concerned. I rolled my eyes to reassure her it was just another one of the newcomer's tantrums. Emily got the message and dropped her gaze to hold in her chuckle.

"We came across an entire community that hadn't been vaccinated. They thought the outbreak was live and that the undead were still roaming and infecting," I replied, not bothering to glance in Charlotte's direction. I honestly didn't care what she thought one way or the other. She'd joined the Believer's Network in Idaho because her sister had been targeted and killed by a horde of undead, or so the story went.

Braden stretched his arms into the air and smiled. "Wow. That's huge. Boy, it's good to be back in the game."

Preston nodded and walked over to Braden, smacking him on the shoulder. "It's good to have you back."

Emily wrapped her arms around Preston and gave him a squeeze as the others wandered back inside. "You're half-naked and you're bleeding." She took a step back and gasped as her eyes fastened on his wound.

Preston shrugged. "It's just superficial. Bleeding stopped a long time ago."

"Doesn't matter. We need to clean it off. Get you bandaged," Emily said, glancing at me. "How'd it happen?"

"Thankfully the guy was a terrible shot." Preston grinned. "We've gotta fill you in, but it sounds like some interesting people paid this community a visit out in the boonies."

"Is that so?" Braden's brow arched.

"Indeed."

Preston was always so good at changing the subject when it came to his injuries. "We'll have to go back out in a couple of days. We weren't able to accomplish our mission. Hopefully everyone else was."

"Sounds like everyone managed to get the job done," Emily confirmed.

"Good." Preston nodded, as Braden wheeled himself through the door.

"It makes me wonder how many more of these places exist," I mused, as I followed the group back inside.

The air in the house was warm, almost sticky, signaling just how many people were packed into the old house on this cold winter day. A row of metal hooks and shelves lined the wall, and I hung my jacket on the last empty hook. Kicking off my shoes felt like a gift from above. The hiking boots weren't broken in yet, and my toes felt as if they'd died a long, cold death up on the mountain. I wiggled them, pleased to find out that they still worked.

Recognizing the wonderful aroma of sage, onion and garlic as we walked down the hall, I knew immediately that stew was on the menu.

"Dinner's warm in the crockpot," Emily said, catching me take a deep breath in. "We ate when we arrived earlier."

"Where's the pooch?" I asked.

"We left him with my sister. More stable and Izzy loves him."

I walked into the kitchen and waved to a few people who were huddled around the table. If I remembered correctly, Amy was wearing the pink, knit cap. Next to her was her boyfriend, Brad. Next to him was Caitlyn, whose curly red hair was woven into a thick braid, and next to her was another guy, but I didn't remember his name. Darn it. What was his name?

Not realizing that I was staring at him while trying to jog my memory, Preston handed me a bowl of stew and whispered in my ear, "Sam."

"That's what it is," I said, louder than I planned. They all looked up at me as I slid onto the bench, bowl of stew in hand.

"What's what it is?" Caitlyn asked.

"Nothing. I'm just babbling." I took a bite of the stew as Preston took a seat next to me.

Sam glanced over at Braden, "Any of our insertion points come online yet?"

Braden shook his head. "Not yet, but any time now."

I nodded and continued to eat dinner as chatter picked up all around us, and I thought about when we should go back out to finish what we'd started today. We needed to give the HIA time to get in and get the people out before we went back to complete the mission.

Our goal had been to install an IMSI catcher on a cell tower that was near the community we'd stumbled upon. I hated the fact that we were the only ones who didn't complete the task. Today, our entire organization began installing the devices all over, centering them near the hot beds of illicit activity.

Braden had been building and shipping out these wonderful contraptions while he was supposed to be taking it easy in Idaho, but there was no stopping him. Emily had tried countless times.

The purpose of the IMSI was to exploit the weaknesses of our country's cell towers and allow us to intercept text messages and content of cell calls. The idea was genius and would hopefully give us the information we needed against TRAC and anyone else who might be involved.

Ever since the world tried to get back to normal, the vulnerabilities of our infrastructure grew more apparent by the day. Since the government had been so preoccupied with the outbreak, it hadn't had much time for upkeep of our infrastructure, cell towers included, which provided Braden with the exact weakness and point of origin to gain access.

"Since you're about as good as Braden when it comes to these things," Emily chuckled, coming up behind us with a bowl of sudsy water, an antibiotic ointment, and gauze.

"Thank you, Emily," I said.

Preston grunted in mild protest, but he had a soft spot for Emily. We all did. She dabbed the washcloth on his wound, cleaning the dried blood off before applying the ointment and gauze. Preston continued to eat the entire time.

Braden rolled his wheelchair up to the end of the table. He set a bowl of stew on the table and glanced at Emily. "I guess I was hungrier than I thought."

"Whoever made this deserves to be on cooking duty every night."

"Thanks," Caitlyn said. "But honestly that's all I've got. That and scrambled eggs."

I ate another spoonful and watched Caitlyn eye Charlotte as she sauntered through the kitchen. She caught my gaze, and her eyes dipped to the table. She must not have been a fan either. It was difficult to hide my smile.

Since it was a pretty hectic day for everyone, the group around the table said their goodnights and left the kitchen.

"So tell me who these interesting characters were." Braden's mouth twisted downward.

Preston pushed his empty bowl away and sighed. "TRAC found the community."

"What? You've got to be kidding? They wouldn't have been able to keep that a secret..." Braden threw a nervous glance to Emily.

"Well, six of the nine will definitely be keeping the secret. I couldn't tell you about the other three." Preston scratched his chin.

"It only proves our theory."

"Which theory is that?" I asked.

"That we've got to find whoever is controlling TRAC now and destroy the organization before it's too late."

Chapter Four

My heart pounded as I shot up to the sound of an air raid siren. I glanced around the bedroom and saw my phone lighting up on the dresser. I was going to kill Preston. He changed my ring tone, and I'd almost died of a heart attack because of it. Unfortunately, he was so damn cute that no matter how hard I'd tried, it was impossible to stay mad at him.

I shoved off the blanket and darted toward my cell, answering it just in time.

"Rebekah speaking."

"They're gone."

I didn't recognize the man's panic-stricken voice on the other end of the line.

"Pardon me? Who is this?"

"It's Ron. They're gone. They're all gone," he repeated.

I leaned against the wall as I tried to absorb what he said. Who exactly was gone? I tapped the wall to Preston's room while I attempted to calm Ron down.

"Take a deep breath and start from the beginning. Who all is gone, Ron. Tell me exactly what is going on."

Preston ran into my room, shirtless and only in his boxers. Not what I wanted to see this morning, but I couldn't help but give his body one more sideways glance. He looked amazing even fresh out of bed with his dark hair matted against his head, and his eyes still groggy.

"What's up?" Preston asked, before he saw that I was on the phone.

"I'm going to put you on speaker," I told Ron. "Now tell us exactly what happened."

"We met with the agency last night. The caseworker who'd been assigned to us was extremely helpful. We gave her all the information, expecting the extraction would be today. As we were leaving, she caught us outside. She'd arranged for immediate extraction and requested our presence since we knew exactly where the encampment was."

"Keep going." Preston was less than a foot away. It was nearly impossible not to be distracted by the way his torso stretched, revealing the definition along his stomach. I snatched the blanket off my bed and threw it at him. A faint smile lined his lips as he draped the blanket over his shoulders, barely covering his exposed skin.

"We rode up last night on the bus and hiked in."

"In the dark?" I asked.

"Yes. They felt that having that many unvaccinated was a public health and safety issue, especially since we'd encountered stragglers recently. It took us a little longer to hike in since it was pitch black, but there was a group of eight of us. When we got to the place, it was deathly quiet. No one was standing watch, and as you know, there were always people on the platforms."

My stomach knotted as he continued talking. Noticing the tension, Preston rested a hand on my shoulder and squeezed it softly.

"The home didn't even have a flicker of candlelight in the front room, and there was always someone designated each night to stay up so that concerned us. When we reached the front door, it was splintered and busted in. Someone had torn through the front door, and it had been ransacked inside, even though there wasn't much in there to go through."

My pulse raced as my mind imagined the scene Ron laid out. It made no sense. Who would've done something like that and why?

"Benches were upside down and tables had been overturned. What few pots and pans we had in the kitchen area were thrown about," his voice broke.

"It's okay. We'll find them," I said, wishing I hadn't. I hated lying.

"They put up a fight. I could tell."

"What did the agency say?" Preston asked, his expression grim.

Ron was silent for several seconds, and I stared out the window rather impatiently. The sky was overcast and mist hung in the air. Not a great day to go into the mountains, but we might not have much choice.

"There was blood everywhere in the back of the house—smeared on the floor, scraped across the walls, and pooled near the door. Our flashlights bounced from one deep crimson puddle to the next. Once we spotted the blood, it was only a matter of minutes before the guns that were drawn to enter the premises immediately turned on Josh and me. I think they thought we brought them to a murder site—that we were the murderers."

"What changed their mind?" I asked.

"I don't know. I honestly don't know. Maybe nothing did. Maybe they still think that."

"What do you mean?" I glanced at Preston.

"They haven't let us go yet. I'm calling you from inside some facility."

Shit. Was this his one phone call and he called us? We didn't need to be put on anyone's radar.

"Some facility?" I questioned. "Did they arrest you?"

"No. Nothing like that. It looks like some sort of hospital or research facility. I couldn't really tell when they drove us in. It was still dark."

My heart sank. Had they taken them to an MHA facility for evaluation? I never imagined this scenario. Anyone who went into the Mental Health Agency never seemed to come back out. I hoped it would change in the future, but so far it hadn't seemed that way.

"Is there a phone number where you can be reached? Do you have your caseworker's information?" I asked.

I handed Preston the phone, our eyes locked for a split second before I grabbed a pen and notepad.

"Her name's Shannon Flynn. I don't have her contact info. They wouldn't give me any information about this place." He let out a deep sigh. "I don't have a good feeling about this. I'd kill to be in the mountains again, believing the outbreak was still active. I've got to find my dad, everyone. What happened to them?"

"That's enough, Ron. Phone privileges have ended," a female's voice could be heard in the background.

Fear slinked through my consciousness as the call ended without a goodbye. This never would've happened if we hadn't tried to help.

Preston put the phone down and took a step forward, touching my chin gently. "It's not your fault. No one could've predicted this."

"Do you think they're alive?" I asked.

"I don't know. With the amount of blood that Ron described…" He glanced toward the door. "It could be that some of the intruders were injured as well."

I knew he didn't even believe the words that came out of his mouth.

"Do you think it's TRAC? Payback for what they did to some of their colleagues?" I asked, taking a seat on the bed. I was in a skimpy T-shirt and thermal bottoms and felt very exposed. I wasn't sure why it didn't worry me a few minutes ago, but now it did. I clutched a sheet and wrapped it around my body, only to have Preston smile to himself as if he enjoyed some private joke.

"That's my hunch." His eyes locked on mine.

"But what would they do with that many people and why?"

"Not sure, but I think we better find out." Preston started toward the door.

"Where are you going?" I asked.

"Gonna start to fill everyone in while you get ready."

I reached for a pair of jeans off the floor and pulled them on. "I'll get ready later. I don't want to miss anything."

He grinned and tossed the blanket on the chair before leaving my room to get dressed, and I had to force myself to look away from his bare, broad back and shoulders. There was something that just screamed sex about this man, and I knew just sex was impossible with him.

I ran a brush through my hair and pulled a sweatshirt on. I heard the kitchen faucet turn on as everyone readied for their morning. Preston stopped at my door, already changed into a pair of jeans and a shirt.

"Ready?"

I nodded and followed him downstairs.

Emily was making oatmeal and Braden was stretching. It would only be a matter of time before he'd be able to walk again. I was sure of it.

"We've got some unexpected developments," I said, sliding a mug out of the cupboard. Pouring myself a cup of coffee, I grabbed a granola bar and took a seat next to Preston.

"You want any?" I asked.

He shook his head. "Not yet."

"We got a call from Ron. He's one of the guys we took to HIA yesterday."

"Yeah? Are things going okay?" Braden asked, wheeling over to where we were.

"No." Preston pressed his lips together and glanced at my coffee. "Maybe I'll take some after all." He stood up and walked over to the coffee pot.

"Care to expand?" Emily probed, arching her brow.

"HIA wanted to get there right away, so they didn't even wait until daylight for the extraction. They went last night and what they found was nothing and everything," I replied, taking a sip of coffee.

"Nothing?" Braden's expression puzzled. "And everything?"

"Everyone was gone. The structure was intact, but everything inside had been ransacked. And according to Ron, there was blood everywhere in the back of the house leading outside," I continued.

"Who would've found them?" Emily asked, stirring the oatmeal.

"We're guessing it's TRAC. But if they were going back for revenge, why not just do everyone in and leave the bodies there?" Preston said, sitting back down.

"That's why I'm thinking they weren't killed, just severely injured," I replied. "And captured."

"Hopefully the ones who fought are only injured," Emily said, reaching for a stack of bowls.

"Whatever's going on, our hunch is that Ron and Josh are either being treated as suspects or loonies."

"Oh no." Braden nodded, as Emily set the oatmeal down in front of him.

"Ron called us from what he described as *some facility*, and there was a lady in the background who made him end the call. He had no idea where he was, but my gut says..." I glanced at Emily and she nodded.

"Sounds like it."

"I still don't trust Jeffrey completely, but maybe he's far enough along in the transition to be able to help," I said, my eyes resting on the scratches on the table.

Jeffrey's company, Barrell Security, was in the midst of taking over all of MHA's facilities so it wasn't a guarantee that the transition was complete. It was worth a shot. He might at least have access to their databases.

"For what in particular?" Braden asked.

"One of the main functions of TRAC was to vet admissions for the MHA. I'd imagine Barrell Security would be assuming that role as well. Maybe he has access to new arrivals. Maybe Ron and Josh would show up on a roster or something, if they were put in the institution." I watched Preston. "And if it's one Jeffrey's taken over completely…"

Preston let out a deep breath and slowly nodded. "I guess it could be worth a shot, but I'm with you. I'm not sure how much we can trust him."

"He made the entire Marcus situation disappear without even a finger pointed anywhere," Emily countered. "He didn't have to do that. There's a high chance that Marcus's death could've been tied to you, and the ensuing ordeal would've dragged on, self-defense or not." Her eyes locked on mine.

I nodded.

"True, but think about what Jeffrey gained by covering it up for us," Preston replied.

"For me," I corrected. "But yeah. Jeffrey was already doing well, now the amount of wealth he'll obtain by having TRAC out of the picture…"

"True," Emily said, taking a bite of the oatmeal. "But I still think it's a good idea. If he has access to the information and can let us know one way or the other, why not try? We don't want to waste time barking up the wrong tree."

I couldn't hide my smile when I realized Emily had turned over a new leaf while they'd been in Idaho, recovering.

"You're right. It's a better option than calling their caseworker. I don't want anything else leading HIA or any agency back to us. Our group's fragile as it is," I agreed. "It wouldn't take much to dismantle it. I'll give him a call right after my shower."

"Need any help with the shower?" Preston asked, turning in his seat to watch my exit.

I rolled my eyes and laughed, taking off for the stairs. "Nice try."

"I'm not giving up," Preston muttered under his breath, as I climbed the steps quickly.

"Just give her time," I heard Emily whisper.

If only it was as easy as time.

I walked through my bedroom into the bathroom and flipped on the shower water. I wanted to get my thoughts organized before calling Jeffrey. It seemed like a logical question to ask Jeffrey. Plus, any other dirt we offered on TRAC might make Jeffrey more inclined to open up.

As soon as the steam rolled out of the shower, I stripped out of my clothes and stepped into the tiled basin, feeling the warmth roll down my skin. My mind raced from one topic to the next as I focused on needing to find out why TRAC targeted the encampment, and how they found it in the first place.

The longer I was in the shower, the more hope I pinned on Jeffrey. My nerves ignited with anxiety at the thought of obtaining the information any other way than from him. If there was one thing I understood more than anything else, it was that I didn't want to get on any government agency's radar. It was bad enough that Ron called my number.

I rinsed out the conditioner, and my mind drifted to Preston. We'd both decided not to pursue anything between us, but he wasn't playing fair, and I intended to talk to him about that soon. The attraction was undeniable, but the situation was filled with nothing but obstacles, and I had to focus on the tasks at hand, not on him. I'd already lost one man I loved, and I wasn't about to let myself do that again. I wouldn't be able to handle the heartbreak for a second time.

I turned off the water and reached for the towel. Drying myself off, I wrapped my hair in the towel and quickly dressed, putting on a sweater and jeans. Moving a chair, I took a seat before I dialed Jeffrey's number. I took a deep breath in as he picked up on the second ring, which surprised me. I'd actually expected that I'd have to leave a voicemail.

"Rebekah, how's everything going?" he asked, his tone friendly.

"Pretty good. Still sorting things out."

"Aren't we all?" he laughed.

"True."

"So to what do I owe the honor of this call?"

"Well, we encountered something we hadn't planned on."

"That's not too unusual in this world."

I couldn't help but laugh. Jeffrey had a way of making me feel at ease, but I was smart enough not to let my guard down.

"Have you completed the takeover on admissions and security details for the MHA's facilities?" I asked.

"That's a loaded question. Completely

confidential, but I suspect you know that already."

"I suspect you know who you can thank for obtaining the contract on those facilities, but you already know that," I replied, not saying another word.

"What is it you want to know?" he asked at last.

"Does Barrell Security receive a report on all new admissions?"

Jeffrey let out a deep sigh. "We do."

"Would you be able to tell me if a Ron or Josh was admitted this morning in our area?" I asked.

"Are you going to tell me why you're asking?" he questioned.

"No."

"What are their last names?" he asked.

"I don't know."

"You don't know, but you want me to risk things by—"

"Don't give me that, Jeffrey. You and I both know finding the answer is as quick as a database. You're not risking anything. It's important. Really important. I doubt more than one would show up anyway."

He was silent for a few more moments.

"I think TRAC is already on the move. I think they set these two men up, possibly kidnapped their families."

"Can you prove this?" he asked.

"Not yet, but give us time. We'll be adding it to the list of things to pin on TRAC."

"All right. I'll see what I can do, and if I find

anything I'll send it along."

"Thanks Jeffrey. It's for a good cause."

"I'm sure it is." He didn't sound amused.

"There's also something else I was hoping you could do."

"Of course there is," Jeffrey replied. "What is it?"

"Since you have access to the patient lists, I was hoping you could check on another person."

"Let me have it," he replied.

I brushed aside the worries about asking him to do this and gave Jeffrey the very few details I had about Preston's mother. My hope was that she was still alive, but I hadn't survived this long by pinning my life on hope.

Chapter Five

"Look, I know we'd planned on going to the ring tonight, but are you still up for it?" Preston asked.

"I'm fine." That wasn't completely true. I felt uneasy, and I wasn't a hundred-percent sure why. I didn't like that I'd gone behind Preston's back to find out about his mom, but if the information wasn't good, I didn't want him to find out. If it turned out she was alive, well then, we could deal with that when it came up so I didn't think that was the source of uneasiness. An unsettling feeling that there was something else under the surface taunted me, but I didn't have time to puzzle over it.

I glanced at the clock in the kitchen. "We'd have to leave in a few minutes to get there in time. It's not a place that I'd want to make a grand entrance at. Do you think that tonight's a good time to go with everything that's happened?"

"They might be preoccupied enough that tonight is the night to go." Preston had been working with Braden on retrieving some of the data from the cell towers. He stood at the entrance into the family room where several people still congregated. Most of the people had left today to go back to where they lived.

"It would be helpful to see how they're running things now," Braden said.

I nodded. "Something tells me just fine. They probably stuck another busty hustler in Brenda's place, but it would be interesting to see who filled Marcus's shoes."

"It's odd that we haven't been able to figure that out," Braden said.

"It is," I agreed, knowing that we'd be heading to the newest zombie pits tonight. No question about it. "I'll go change, and I'll meet you down here in ten."

"Sounds good." Preston and Braden exchanged glances, and I knew those two were keeping something from me, which never sat well.

Trading out my nice sweater for a ratty sweatshirt and my jeans for a pair I didn't care about, I felt as prepared as I could for tonight's adventure. Not that I planned on standing in the front row, but I certainly didn't want to ruin what few things I had left. I'd never really gotten around to filling my closet again. Securing my holster on the inside of my waistband I was set for the night. I glanced in the mirror and everything looked fine. No hint of a pistol.

I met Preston downstairs, and we headed out the door with barely a grunt to one another. There was definitely something going on.

"Do you know where the pit is?" I asked.

"Yeah. I've never been to this one before, but I know the area," he replied, with barely a glance in my direction.

"Mind telling me what's going on?" I turned to see Preston.

"I could ask you the same thing."

"What's that supposed to mean?"

"I think you know very well what I'm referring to."

I considered what to say next very carefully. Jeffrey promised he'd send me the information directly and wouldn't involve Preston. Yet, it didn't seem like that's what happened, and the tension between us was beyond palpable. My intention had been to protect Preston, not hurt him.

I sighed and looked out the window. "You're right. I'm sorry. It wasn't my place. I just thought—"

"What do you mean it wasn't your place?" Preston asked, shooting me a skeptical look. "You always like to call the shots. That's the pattern you've established with everyone who comes into contact with you. Believe me. Anyone who spends any amount of time with you knows that's how it rolls. I'm not asking you to apologize about it. I just don't understand why you didn't say anything to me of all people."

I wasn't sure whether to be flattered or insulted. I didn't see myself quite like that. I was silent for a few seconds, watching the peaceful scenery go by, worried that anything I said next would create a war zone in the small cab of the truck. What had I been thinking asking Jeffrey to snoop around for me? I felt the speed of the truck increase, and even though it was a country road, it felt a little too fast for the curves ahead.

"I wanted to protect you," I finally said.

"Why in the world would I need protecting from that?"

"I didn't want you to get hurt in case it turned out that something happened to her," my voice almost hoarse.

"Well, I would be sad, but I'd make it. I mean I'd imagine we'd all be sad if something happened to her or anyone. But it's not like I have a special attachment to her."

Huh?

I glanced at Preston. His brows pulled together as he continued to focus on the road while waiting for my response.

"What do you mean you don't have a special attachment to her?" I questioned, completely bewildered by how cavalier he was acting over this possible revelation.

"Is that why you've been so standoffish with me recently? You think I'm into her?" he asked, a hint of a smile touching his lips.

"What are you talking about?" Saying I was confused was putting it mildly. I lifted my foot and tucked it under me as I turned to watch

Preston. There was no hiding his smile. In fact, he seemed gleeful. We obviously weren't talking about the same woman.

The truck hit a large pothole, and if it hadn't been for the belt, I could've bounced right into his lap. Talking about my aggressive driving seemed rather comical compared to what I was experiencing with him at the wheel right now.

"I understand why you might think that. I guess some people might consider her attractive, but I'm more into the type sitting next to me."

I shoved my hair out of my face and continued to watch him, hoping to figure out who he was talking about without asking.

"But that being said, I still don't think it was the best idea to send her off into the woods to do our job. We aren't even sure if it's safe yet. She might get caught, which would only complicate things."

Oh, my god. He was talking about Charlotte. She had begged me earlier to go out to place the IMSI on the tower. I got so tired of her whining I finally relented. She promised she'd take one of the guys with her.

I started laughing as the realization settled over me. "Charlotte."

"Yes. Charlotte," he repeated. "I don't have a thing for her."

Never in a million years did I think he did. Preston had made that clear as day, but I had to admit it was kind of nice to hear him clarify it.

"I didn't actually send her out. It was her idea and she wouldn't shut up about it. She said she'd take one of the guys."

"Well, she didn't."

I sighed. "Great. Nothing like having a reckless know-it-all join the team."

Preston chuckled.

The tension between us immediately dissipated, but I realized I needed to tell him about what I asked Jeffrey to do. On the way to the zombie pit definitely wasn't the moment, but I'd tell him as soon as we got back.

"Glad you cleared that up about what's-her-face." I flashed him a grin.

"Somehow I feel like the joke's been turned on me."

"Now you're just being paranoid," I scoffed.

"You know that's a dirty word in our line of work."

Preston slammed on the brakes, and my entire body flew forward. My hands braced the metal dash so I didn't fly into the glass. I brought my eyes forward to see a horde of undead in front of us, standing in the middle of the road, staring at us. Fear thundered through me as my mind flashed back to Gavin trapped in the car. We had to nowhere to go. We had no way to fight them.

Heat rose through my body. It felt like the cab was twisting and contorting, closing in on me. The air was stuffy, becoming thicker with each breath in, and all I wanted to do was escape. My breathing became labored, and my pulse quickened as I watched the horde take slow, deliberate steps toward us. Only a slight mumble or grunt could be heard over the engine of the ancient truck.

One of the undead, wearing a blue flannel shirt, slowly raised his arm as he sluggishly made his way to the truck, pointing with his knuckle. His fingers were missing. He wasn't a new zombie, but it didn't matter.

There were more of them than us.

We needed to get out of here.

The clouds that held the thick mist in the air all day, darkened and a heavy downpour drained from the heavens. A crack of thunder in the sky stopped the undead in their tracks, their heads angling toward the noise above. They were unable to reason. The noise intrigued them, drew them toward it, but there was no way for them to go up so they stood still as the rain continued to pound down on them; their clothes drenched within seconds, their hair slicked with wetness as they awaited more.

My hands were moist from fear and apprehension. I needed to focus, but I couldn't. Images of Gavin continued to scroll through my mind at a rapid pace. The last time we held hands before he was taken—the fear in his eyes—the zombies' hands reaching and grasping at him, *for* him. It was as if my mind stopped living in the present. There was no focusing on the beasts in front of us. My breathing quickened as sweat trickled down my back.

There was no escape.

There was no saving Gavin.

He wasn't who I thought he was.

I clenched my eyes shut as I tried to slow my breathing down. I had to focus, stay in the present.

"Rebekah, you're okay. We're okay. It's just a group of stragglers. I'll take care of them. It's no problem. You're here with me now. Stay with me," Preston's voice centered me, calmed me—only slightly.

My eyes flashed open and coolness began drifting over me.

It was okay.

I was okay.

We were okay.

The rain turned to a drizzle, and I carefully watched the twitches and spasms of the undead with each step they took. There was no purposeful direction. They had no purpose. We weren't targets. They weren't weapons. Weapons! We had weapons! It wasn't the same as last time. Preston and I were fully armed. The scenario was completely different. I had to snap out of it. My gaze landed on one of the undead. It was a male or would've been a male. His pale, grey skin was peeled back in places, mostly at the joints, exposing flesh worn down to the bone. His shredded clothing indicated these really were just stragglers. I scanned each of the undead, letting my breathing regulate with each passing observation.

It was okay.

I was okay.

We were okay.

"Stay inside. I'll get rid of them." He flashed

me a smile, but the darkness behind his eyes was impossible to ignore. No matter how much time had gone by, these beings had scarred us all. The outbreak damaged us all.

I shook my head and grinned. "And let you have all the fun? Not on my worst day."

"You're sure you're up to it?"

"I'm okay. I swear. Just a hiccup."

Preston nodded and began rolling down his window to take the first shot. I did the same. The smell of rotting flesh hit me immediately, and I almost regretted my decision to take part until I took aim at the first creature. I never enjoyed taking a life, but during the outbreak I had gotten good at reminding myself that this wasn't a life. These beings were dead in the least alive way of existing. I centered my aim, and the crack of the bullet confirmed the pull of my trigger.

The first shot hit the one in the middle. Blew his head off. My second and third shots took out the ones wandering toward the maples. The fourth shot hit the one closest to our truck.

It wasn't until the last zombie dropped that Preston stopped firing, and I could let myself believe that we were okay.

I opened the door and slid out of the truck, attempting to catch my breath. I gripped my pistol tightly, still warm from use, as I stared at the undead strewn about. It was going to be okay. We were okay. For now.

"Should we move them off the road?" I asked.

"We won't make it to the pit in time if we do. Let's just report them."

"Agreed. I really don't feel like pulling on limbs that fall off in my hands."

I scanned the lifeless bodies and felt my strength return. I wasn't accustomed to setbacks like these. Ever.

These predators weren't hidden shadows lurking, waiting for our weakest moments. The undead that weren't modified were easily dealt with in these numbers. Their movements could be predicted. Their motives understood. And bullets would always be our friends. I didn't have that feeling about the other creations. These weren't the creatures that terrified me. What terrified me were the ones we'd be visiting in less than an hour.

I climbed back into the truck and shut the door as Preston did the same. One thing I really appreciated was that he never turned off the engine.

"That was quite a group of stragglers," I confessed, my pulse finally steadying.

"It was."

"They didn't seem as torn up as I would've thought," I said, glancing at their lifeless bodies.

"But they weren't modifieds."

I nodded. "We need to find the unvaccinated. It has to become a priority or running into these hordes will be never-ending. At some point, it's got to stop, but if the zombies keep finding people to infect—my god!"

"I couldn't agree more." Preston put the truck in reverse and then plopped it into drive as he found the clearest path to get us out of this dead zone and on our way to another one that was far more dangerous and unpredictable

Chapter Six

"What's going on here?" I asked.

The road was completely blocked off, and the field to the right was filled with cars. Up ahead, there was a person directing traffic and pointing toward the direction we'd just come from. The line of cars in front of us inched forward. One by one they were redirected.

"This is where the matches are being held tonight." Preston gave me a quick glance of caution as he rolled down the window to talk to the person in charge of parking.

"Big night?" Preston asked.

"Each event tops the last one," the guy said smiling, as he held the thick wad of cash. "Lot's full here, but I'll take your cash and give you a ticket that'll let you in to the back entrance. Follow the line of cars back the other way and take a right. You can't miss it."

"How much is parking?" Preston asked, taking

out his wallet.

"Fifty." The guy grinned. "It'll probably go up at the next event."

"You'd think it was the *Superbowl* or something."

"It's better. Place this on your dash."

The man handed Preston a purple ticket, and he handed it to me. We turned the truck around and followed the slow-moving line to the other lot.

"This is huge. I can't even believe what I'm seeing," I whispered, staring out the window at all the people walking toward the entrance. "How could it have grown so quickly?"

Preston shook his head as we turned into the new lot, which seemed to be the backyard of a home next to the event.

"I can't believe I'm about to say this, but at least Brenda and Marcus kept it classy or as classy as zombie fighting can be," I laughed, analyzing the new crowd of gamblers.

When I attended my "one and only" zombie fight there were linens, flowers, and cocktails at the venue. It looked like a fall wedding. From what I could see while sitting in the truck, we'd be walking through a field of muck and standing next to livestock to enjoy the show, but I could be wrong.

"No matter how much it pains me, I have to agree," he laughed.

I jumped out of the truck and shut the door, watching the eager gamblers walk toward the large pasture in front of us. Preston walked over and slid his hand along my waist and dipped his head for only me to hear.

"I think we should stay together, appear like a couple," he whispered, with an edge of playfulness. An unexpected shiver ran through me as he straightened up and led me through the rows of cars. There was something intriguing about playing pretend with him.

We reached the patchy lawn that spread between several buildings that appeared like they were meant for cattle, but I didn't hear or smell anything that indicated the buildings were being used for that. The wooden barn closest to us had a line leading to the front entrance, and there were several armed guards stationed at the opening.

I scanned across the pasture to another building, this one metal, and saw a line circling around the side of the building. A small trailer stood in between these two buildings, which looked like a ticket booth from a fair.

As we continued walking toward the center of the activity, I began to smell a faint odor of hotdogs and grilled onions. I glanced up at Preston who apparently smelled the same thing as I did and he just chuckled.

"From cocktail hour to carnival food, things just keep looking up with the new management." I smiled. "Should we place our bets?"

"Might as well. I'm guessing that's what the little trailer's for."

"Thinking so."

The line was short, probably because the first

fight was about to begin. There was a portly man waiting in front of us. Balding slightly and completely nervous, he was dressed in a pair of khakis and a button-down silk shirt. I was guessing this was his first time.

The woman in the trailer motioned for him to move up. We watched him nervously take his cash out of his pocket as the woman explained the rules to him. I was shocked to hear the minimum bet had decreased so drastically. When I attended one of these before, the minimum was hundreds of dollars. Now the buy-in was only fifty-bucks.

We carefully scanned the reader board and agreed on our selections.

The guy waddled off toward the metal building with several tickets in hand. The line to get inside had dwindled, and I was able to spot the guards standing outside the doors. They patted the man down and waved him in.

My heart skipped a beat. They didn't check if people were armed at the last event. In fact, I think it was assumed that everyone was carrying. I shifted slightly from one foot to the other as Preston placed our bets. We both picked the long shots in fights two and three. Hopefully we'd get our answers by then and could leave.

The first fight we bet on was in the large, wooden barn and our second fight was in the other one. We walked over slowly to the large wooden barn, hand-in-hand, not saying a word. What was to be said? We were armed, and we hoped they wouldn't find out.

One of the guards motioned for me and I walked over. He told me to place arms above my head, which I did. He quickly patted the sides of my body, skipping right over my waistband, and barely tapping my legs. He nodded and waved me inside. I didn't dare look back at Preston. Instead, I just slinked into the crowd, knowing he would find me if he got through.

The space held ten times as many as the last one I'd been to, and we were stuffed in here like sardines. If an emergency happened, there'd be very few survivors. Most would be trampled.

I found a spot that allowed me to see the ring and the large entrance that I assumed the fighters would be brought through. In addition to the entrance that we used, there was another small door in the far corner, which I guessed led outside. It was next to a staircase that headed up to a small room that overlooked the floor. I spotted three men sitting with their backs facing the crowd.

I brought my attention back to the empty ring and started to get nervous. Why hadn't Preston found me yet? I was getting anxious, but I couldn't blow my cover. This might be our only chance to see one of these for a very long time.

Glancing around the room, I spotted two snipers who were positioned on a raised, metal platform. Below them was an empty cage, large enough for about thirty people. Not comforting.

I felt a large hand slide slowly along my shoulder, and my body trembled with his touch.

"Glad you finally decided to show up," I said,

glancing behind me.

"Was a little detained. I had to donate my knife to their bin, but they didn't seem to notice the Glock on my ankle." He flashed his adorable grin, and my insides cranked up a notch.

I let out a laugh and felt the energy in the room change. The excitement of the fight ignited the room, and blackout shades rolled down on what few windows there were, and the lights flicked off. The loud pounding of music filtered into the space, but instead of dubstep and electronica, the air was filled with death metal. Before the darkness became anymore unsettling, large spotlights flashed on, dotting and stroking the faces in the crowd.

Preston gently squeezed my shoulder and let go as he found a spot with a clearer vantage point a few people away. I heard the chanting begin and kept my eyes on the large door, which opened slowly. Preston caught my gaze as I glanced up toward the office. The three men now faced the spectacle. I slid my cell phone out of my pocket and angled it toward the small room. Tapping my screen twice to zoom in, I took several shots and slid my phone back in my pocket.

The chants grew louder and clearer as the favorite, Iceberg, was led in first.

Unlike last time, there was no chain-link fence protecting the spectators from the fighters as they were escorted in. Instead, the trainers wheeled the zombie into the arena on a dolly, with only the zombie's ankles and wrists chained to the metal. I shivered at the thought of him getting away and into the crowd. People jetted out their hands in an attempt to touch the creature with the trainers barely shooing the audience away as they made their way to the ring.

One of the trainers opened the gate on the chain-link fence that circled the ring and wheeled the zombie inside to the far corner of the ring. The trainer backed the zombie against the fence. The creature's mouth gaped with hunger as his tongue twitched with its thirst for the living. The chains holding his extremities looked frail in comparison to his strength as the trainer scurried out of the ring.

Chanting from the crowd called in the next fighter, who was clearly the underdog. When his dolly was pushed in, it became apparent why he wasn't favored to win the match. This zombie was half the size, and I couldn't fathom why the organizers paired the two. I watched as they wheeled him in and placed him across from Iceberg. I couldn't decipher his name from the crowd so I leaned over to one of the men next to me and asked.

"Tiny Tim," he responded.

I shook my head. "How clever." It took everything I had to not roll my eyes.

The trainers closed the gate and something glowing red caught my eye on Tiny Tim's wrist. The trainers detached the zombies from the dollies, and a woman's voice came over the speakers announcing the fight was to begin.

I watched Iceberg slowly wander the ring, each step juddering and uncontrolled. He turned toward the crowd and looped his fingers through the links of the fence. He had no interest in Tiny Tim. These fighters were supposed to be interested in their opponent. Something was wrong. As Iceberg squeezed the metal with his fingers, a piece of flesh fell to the ground with oohs from the crowd. The louder the crowd roared, the more Iceberg shook the ring. His raggedy jeans and holey shirt clung to his grey flesh.

Tiny Tim's movements were precise as he carefully cased his victim, snapping and licking the air, tasting his victory with each calculated step toward Iceberg. One of the men upstairs was staring intently into the crowd, while the other two kept their eyes pinned on the fight below. I didn't recognize any of the men.

A loud hiss came from the ring, and I glanced over to see Tiny Tim grab Iceberg's left arm and twist it so suddenly that it fell to the mat with a quick popping sound. Iceberg's good arm swung forward in a dizzying array of lunges and jerks. He swiped his right hand across Tiny Tim's chest, ripping his already tattered shirt, but he was no match for Tiny Tim.

Tiny Tim wrapped his fingers around Iceberg's neck and squeezed. With each snap of the bone, his skin turned into a rubbery mass, the flesh spilling through Tiny Tim's fingers. The sight was nauseating, but the crowd let out another roar of cheers.

Studying the interactions between these two undead made me uneasy. I didn't like what I was witnessing. We weren't dealing with equals in the ring any longer. The men in the office were getting very rich. Maybe this had been Marcus's plan all along, and he just didn't make it long enough to see it unfold. It didn't matter either way. These people managed to wrap their tentacles around the new undead technology while harnessing the old ways of the creatures. It had Marcus written all over it. Merging these two beings had a purpose beyond this ring, and we had to find out what that was.

Gasps echoed through the barn as Tiny Tim swung his other arm toward Iceberg's head. The force behind his punch shattered Iceberg's neck completely. Tiny Tim watched Iceberg crumple to the mat. A roar of boos bounced off the walls as Tiny Tim walked over to Iceberg and stomped on his head. It exploded so quickly I didn't have time to look away. When the audience realized that the fight was over, and most would be in the hole, agitation settled over the barn. There was no point in waiting around for the next two fights. It was getting too heated between these walls, and we didn't need any trouble. We saw what we needed to. The fights had changed. It was no longer modified versus modified.

Preston's fingers gripped my elbow and led me through the crowd to freedom just as the first wave of security marched in to secure the rowdy crowds. It was going to get messy.

Chapter Seven

We walked into the house, and silence sat heavy between the walls. Most everyone had left, taking their coats, shoes, and bags with them, and I had to admit that I liked having the place back to its original state. It was even better now that Emily and Braden were back—more comforting. Preston had been right. Opening myself up to these two had brought solace and a sense of family that I didn't realize I'd missed so deeply. I also found allowing a few in wouldn't be the end of me.

"I bet they're watching news in the family room," Preston said, glancing over his shoulder.

He hadn't brought up the Charlotte incident since the miscommunication, but I could tell he was still riding high. His eyes held a certain mischief that under normal circumstances would drive me insane for him, but the zombie pit colored my mood.

"My kind of night." I grinned and hung my jacket on the hook. "I'll probably want a shower before I settle in to get my nightly news fix. I just feel so dirty after visiting that place, but I'll go say hi."

"Same."

I followed Preston down the hall, through the kitchen, and saw Braden and Emily in the family room glued to the screen in front of them. I didn't pay attention to what was on the television until I heard the newscaster.

How many of these attacks have taken place, we don't know. More reports of violence have been rolling in across the country, but these latest reports have not been verified. Again, police are asking that you stay away from the downtown corridor. We'll bring you the latest updates as soon as we get them.

"What the hell is going on?" I asked, taking a seat next to Emily.

"It's not looking good. Not good at all." She shook her head.

"What happened?" I asked again.

Braden changed from our local news to a national news channel. Images of the undead wandering vacant streets flooded four different quadrants on the screen. The sight chilled me to the bone.

"Looks like Chicago and Austin?" I asked, unable to remove my eyes from the horrifying images. "Not sure about the other two..."

"Atlanta," Braden replied "Looks like Atlanta."

"Yep. And Oklahoma City's the other one, but

it started here," Emily muttered. She looked away quickly and stood up. "Would you like some coffee? I need to get something to drink. I can't handle this right now."

"That'd be great. Thanks Emily." Our eyes barely connected before she turned and walked into the kitchen.

"Pockets of undead are springing up everywhere," Braden said.

The ticker at the bottom of the screen caught my eye.

Seattle Mayor pronounced dead at the scene. His wife is in critical condition.

"You said this started here?" I asked.

Braden nodded. "From what I can piece together."

"Shit." I pushed myself into the back of the couch cushion and tried to understand. There had to be a connection between what we saw tonight and this.

"The zombies on television..." my voice trailed off, and my eyes locked on Preston's. "They're not modified. They're roaming the streets senselessly."

A chill came over me, and I glanced around the room. I'd made this home since I'd left mine, but I was getting an overwhelming urge to go back. The only members of TRAC who were after us were dead. My guess was the ones who were in charge now had risen through the ranks pretty quickly and were just executing the original plans. Preston and I were Marcus's pet project, no one else's. That had to explain how we got in and out of the pit tonight so easily. My home was closer to civilization, easier to investigate from the center. It was time to return there.

TRAC was too busy implementing their plan to worry about us, and we had to use that to our advantage for as long as possible.

"Why are you so quiet over there? What are you thinking?" Something about Preston's deep voice cracked open a longing that I'd been trying to ignore since Gavin's death.

"What did we see today at the pit?" I asked smiling, turning my attention outward. No more of this unreasonable yearning for someone that I wouldn't or couldn't or… who knows what.

A familiar flicker ran through his gaze. There was always a charge that ran between us when we were on the hunt, solving a puzzle, or about to catch a break. It was this shared enthusiasm that drove us closer but also pulled us apart.

"Two very different types of zombies were asked to do a dance." He grinned, understanding where I was headed.

"Exactly."

"What are you talking about?" Braden asked, just as Emily returned. She set my cup of coffee on the unusual piece of furniture sitting in front of us. It was one of Braden's inventions, a coffee table built out of old motherboards that housed some very important equipment.

"The zombie pit we saw wasn't the same. The minimum bets are lower, the crowds are huge, and they aren't only using modified zombies. The pair at the fight tonight was one of each. You can guess which one came out the winner," I said.

Braden's brow winged up. "Really?"

I nodded and kicked my heels under me, settling deeper into the sectional.

"There was a red, blinking device used to control the modified zombie, exactly like before, but the other undead had no such device inserted, at least that we could see."

"He wasn't being controlled," Preston agreed. "He was tattered and rummy, an easy target for a modified."

"I used to think the red device that TRAC implanted not only controlled the modifieds, but acted like a magnet to each other. I assumed each creature had to have one in order for it to work, but I don't think that's the case any longer. I think their technology has advanced."

I turned my attention back to the television and continued to read the ticker at the bottom.

Governor of Oklahoma dead. His assistant is missing. The Deputy Commissioner of the Georgia State Police has been killed in the line of duty.

I felt Preston's gaze on me.

"This is no coincidence. These other zombies that the press gladly captures on video..." I took a sip of coffee as my thoughts began to twist into a cohesive guess. This was a huge break. "They're decoys. They didn't kill any of these victims. Whoever is behind this is using modifieds and regular undead; the stragglers they've collected."

Preston nodded slowly, "Makes complete sense."

"Save the modified zombies for the specific kills and turn loose a group of these stragglers right beforehand to distract. That'll throw everyone off guard and whoever's a target will be downed in a flash. TRAC can round up their modifieds before anyone notices."

The pieces of the puzzle continued to click together, and I wasn't sure I liked where it was headed.

"That's right. The stragglers are completely expendable. In fact, they expect them to be, want them to be." Preston's eyes landed on mine, and a shudder ran through my body.

TRAC didn't have free pickings from the MHA facilities any longer. They'd gotten more creative. My sense was that Marcus had already started preparing before I'd killed him. But why? What was I missing?

"Ron's father," I whispered, as the realization settled over me. "TRAC's going after the unvaccinated across the country, creating new stragglers to distract from the modifieds' attacks. The public expects to see unaware, dazed zombies, and of course, the media is picking right up on it. The news is sensationalizing these undead attacks, while missing the bigger picture."

"You think the community that vanished was rounded up by TRAC?" Emily asked.

I nodded. "I think so. It makes complete sense."

"It does," Preston agreed. "TRAC needs unvaccinated individuals and most of the ones they'll find will have been written off, listed on the burn lists or presumed dead."

My stomach knotted. "Remember that place we were held captive at across the mountains? The ranch?"

Preston nodded. "Hard to forget. I've got the scars to remind me."

I pressed my lips together. "We found evidence of humans corralled there. We found that thumb drive, fabric, blood within those enclosures…"

Preston's expression fell. "That's the perfect place to house the others, isn't it? It's in the middle of nowhere. There's a ton of buildings to house both turned and unturned. Find the poor unsuspecting souls that are unvaccinated and turn them into the disposable stragglers. Shit. I don't know why we didn't think of it sooner."

"Why are they targeting these officials?" Emily asked, as another picture filled the screen. This time it was a woman with honey-colored hair and crisp blue eyes. A strand of pearls set off her peach suit. She was the State Attorney General for Texas and now she was dead.

"I don't know, but it's gotta mean something."

"A vendetta?" Preston asked.

"Possibly. Maybe the Commissioner locked away someone that TRAC wanted, or maybe a policy cut into something TRAC needed."

"My guess is they're just getting started," Braden said, glancing back at the television.

"I'm sure you're right." I sighed, stretching my legs out in front of me.

The screen was filled with a reporter standing in front of a café. It was the scene where the State Attorney General was dining with her aides right before the attack. An eyewitness began describing the horde of stragglers who came out of nowhere. The woman described a chaotic turn of events: people running everywhere, tables being knocked over, undead chasing victims. The eyewitness never mentioned seeing the attack on the Attorney General. I'd be surprised if anyone saw any of the actual attacks. It was probably as calculated and invisible as a team could make it.

"What a great cover." I sighed. "It makes me think differently about the horde we saw on the way to the pit today."

Preston was rubbing his neck. "I was thinking the same thing."

"What do you mean a horde?" Braden asked. "You didn't mention anything."

"There's been a bit of overload since we got in the doors," I laughed, taking another swallow of coffee as Preston began to describe the horde that descended on us earlier, no modifieds, only stragglers.

"Why would they have dumped some off in the middle of nowhere?" Emily asked.

"We can't assume they're part of it," Braden said.

"True, but it's definitely something to be mindful of," I said.

My phone buzzed, and I pulled it out of my pocket. It was a text from Abby.

Have you seen the news? It's crazy. I thought we were done with this crap. Anyway, just thinking of you. Maybe coffee soon?

Shoot! I'd never texted her back. At least she wasn't angry or if she was, she hid it well, which I appreciated. It was tough to think about having to meet with her when I was so deep into this other life now. I looked up at Preston, who was watching me intently.

"Everything okay?" he asked.

"It is. I think. It's Abby. I forgot to text her back. She asked if I saw the news."

I still felt like I was only one misstep away from being turned into the MHA by my friends. It was a fine line to walk and another one of many reasons why I didn't have many friends.

"I've been thinking that maybe I should go check on my house. If all appears okay, maybe even stay there for a few nights. It's closer to everything that's going on..." I kept my eyes fastened on the mug of coffee in front of me. I already knew Preston would think it was a ridiculous idea. He sought the safety of isolation, and I didn't blame him. But I wanted to find answers, and I didn't want to be driving most of the day to get them.

"It doesn't matter what I say, does it?" I felt Preston's smile across the room and glanced up, grinning.

"It matters," I protested. "But I'm gonna text Abby to see if she'd like coffee with me. Should I tell her you're coming too or..."

"Please. Go," Emily chuckled. "It might be nice to have a night or two alone. Ever since Idaho, we've been surrounded by people. No offense."

"None taken. So it's set. When's Charlotte supposed to be back? Did you hear from her?" I asked.

"She completed the task and decided to head back to her house in Idaho," Braden answered.

"Something about her doesn't sit right with me. I don't know what it is." I shook my head.

"Could it be that she had the hots for Preston?" Emily grinned.

I rolled my eyes. "Whatever. It'd be nothing new. Besides he's single. He can do what he wants. I don't care if he dates. I expect him to. There was just something weird about her."

Braden laughed and threw up his hands. "Take it easy."

I stood up too quickly and a head rush threw me off balance. I hadn't eaten anything since this morning, and it finally caught up with me. I rubbed my temple and glanced at the television once again while I got my bearings. A man in Oklahoma died from injuries sustained in a zombie attack. So they weren't all officials.

I pointed at the screen and let out a deep breath. "I'm gonna go take a shower, and I'll come back down."

Preston stood up and followed me out of the family room. He was only a step behind me, and I felt that familiar charge, the one that would happen when we were close to something big.

"What are you thinking?" I asked, clutching

my phone. Abby had texted back that coffee tomorrow afternoon would be perfect, and now I wished I'd never texted her back. Such was the story of my life.

"I'm thinking that you're really sexy," his voice low for only me to hear.

A ping of excitement raced down my bones as his words settled over me.

"You're just using me for my brains."

"Is there something wrong with that?" he asked innocently.

I reached the stairs and turned around on my heels, surprising Preston. The distance between us was less than an arm's length away.

Preston's mussed up hair was a good look for him, and quite frankly, the attraction I felt was disarming.

I forced myself to meet his eyes. I wanted to stay in control, keep my guard up.

"You doing okay?" he asked, his index finger gently tilting my head up.

"I'm not sure."

"I like your honesty," he said, taking a step closer.

The look in his eyes was pure sex, and the pulse between us was almost palpable as my thirst for him grew. The more I kept denying the attraction, the worse my desire for him became. Imagining being held in his arms, being touched, caressed, kissed by this man cultivated an entirely too complicated set of problems.

But it was too soon. I felt that whatever this was or could be would be far worse than a typical rebound relationship. I'd fall fast and hard, and my own sanity was at stake. I couldn't let myself fall for a man who might not make it, and we lived in a world where that was a real possibility.

I cleared my throat and looked away. "Sorry. Listen, you're trouble. I think I'm going to try to find you a Charlotte or something. Well, not something, I mean someone. You're...This..." I pointed at the gap between us. "Is too complicated. Too much risk involved. You know it as well as I do."

He dipped his head and whispered, "You'll come around soon. And when you do, I'll be here waiting."

Chapter Eight

My home looked as I'd left it. A wave of guilt ran through me as images of Gavin flooded my mind, but the sensation was quickly replaced by anger. The man I thought I knew wasn't who he appeared to be, and it still hadn't gotten any easier for me to reconcile. I shouldn't let Gavin bog me down, but it wasn't that easy to control.

"You okay?" Preston asked.

"Yeah. Sorry." I opened the truck door and slid off the seat. "All seems quiet on the home front."

"That'd be a nice change of pace." Preston smiled, slamming the truck door shut.

We walked to the front door, and all my booby traps were still securely in place. Nice.

"Thanks for agreeing to come down here." I opened the door and scanned my house quickly. Everything was where I'd left it.

"Like I had a choice," he laughed. "But with this morning's news, I think your hunch is right.

The closer we are to the action, the better."

I nodded and shut the front door. It was freezing outside, but the house was filled with stale air, which needed to be exchanged for fresh. I walked to the living room and opened the window.

"Mind opening the ones in the kitchen and family room? We need some air movement. It'll get chilly fast, but at least it won't be musty."

"Sure." Preston dropped his bag onto the floor and wandered off toward the kitchen while I went upstairs and opened the windows in the bedrooms. Hopefully that would help the stuffiness.

I stood in my bedroom and glanced at myself in the reflection of the long mirror. On first glance, I appeared smaller, but I was stronger. My body had changed, muscles more defined, fewer curves to confuse my clothes. But all I cared about was the strength, and I could see it, especially in my eyes.

"Which room should I take?" Preston asked, poking his head into my bedroom.

"Whichever one you'd like is fine."

He walked into the room and came up behind me, our eyes connecting in the mirror.

"With the attacks continuing, do you think we should tell the authorities?" I asked.

His jaw tensed, and he let out a deep breath. I turned around to face him. For some reason, seeing him through the mirror felt too intimate, too revealing, which made no sense. Maybe I didn't like seeing myself respond to him.

After several seconds of silence, he answered. "I doubt they'd believe us, but maybe we should try."

"It's such a tricky situation. I don't want to wind up locked up by MHA because they think we're crazy."

"Josh and Ron are certainly good reminders of the agency's powers, aren't they?"

I nodded.

"It's a tough call." Preston put his hands on my shoulders, moving a few strands of hair. "We don't have to decide this second."

"True," I agreed. "But if we could somehow stop more senseless deaths…"

"I know…" his voice trailed off.

This morning's news had brought seven more deaths. The majority were government officials, but there was a kindergarten teacher and her husband thrown into the mix. My hunch was that it was a deliberate ploy to throw the authorities off track.

I glanced at the clock and groaned. "I better change so we're on time to meet Abby."

Preston dropped his hands and nodded, before walking out of my room. The moment he left, I wished he hadn't. He provided comfort and a feeling of safety. No matter how fleeting those sensations were, I didn't want them to vanish so quickly.

I went to my closet and chose a pair of jeans and a fitted sweater. Quickly swapping outfits, I glanced in the mirror one last time and decided this was a good choice. It didn't scream anything one way or another. I looked normal and that would be the perfect cover since I felt anything but.

Hopping down the stairs quickly, I heard Preston in the kitchen. "Whoo. Think we should get rid of some of these items."

I turned the corner to see him holding a clear bag that held a clump of green dust—a little something I would call moldy bread—and a bag of potatoes that had rooted into a massive ball.

"What? You don't trust my pantry?" I laughed.

"Not if this is what I have to look forward to behind the doors." He grinned. "Let's do pizza tonight on the way home."

"Point taken." I smiled, snatching the bread bag out of his hand. I glanced at it, rather amazed, before I tossed it in the trashcan under the sink. He threw the potatoes away, and I closed the cabinet. "You know, we're really lucky the potatoes just tried to grow, rather than liquefy on the shelf."

"What... you've had that happen?" he asked.

"Yep, and that's way worse." I smiled. "It stinks."

"Yeah. Definitely pizza tonight," he laughed. "Should we get going?"

I nodded and pulled my wallet out of my bag, along with my pistol, and glanced over at Preston. "There's a spare key to the house under the lamp over there." I pointed at the blue lamp that was on the end table and pushed out the memory of Gavin and I purchasing it together.

Preston tilted the base of the lamp and took

the key, sliding into his pocket. "Thanks."

I grinned. "It's the least I can do."

We locked up the house, and I texted Abby that I was on my way. As Preston turned onto the main street toward the city, I got a distinct feeling that I was being watched. I flipped down the visor and glanced in the mirror. There wasn't another car on the street or person on the sidewalk. It had to be in my head. No surprise there.

"With these attacks, I was thinking we should reach out to Jeffrey. See if we can get him to use some of his manpower to find more of the unvaccinated encampments across the country. Seems like we've got the perfect cause for concern." I looked over at Preston and he nodded.

"I think that's an interesting idea. We could try. The worse that happens is that he says no, and if he does help, at least we could diminish the number of potential victims."

I nodded and turned on the radio.

"Maybe the news has gotten better," I sighed.

Rather than choose a channel that played music, I found the local news and parked the dial as the commentator continued speaking.

Regardless of what they're telling us, I don't believe these are all coincidences. Come on. How can anyone think that these things aren't tied together? Caller, you're on.

I looked over at Preston as a woman introducing herself came across the airwaves.

I think you are part of the problem. Enough

with the conspiracies. You're exactly what's impairing our society. People like you are the reason our country can't move on. It's despicable that you'd start these kinds of rumors for ratings.

And then she hung up with a click.

The radio commentator didn't let her outburst ruin his program. Instead, it only seemed to bolster his stance as he continued.

This, ladies and gentlemen, is the problem. We are a world bent on closing our eyes to what's happening around us, hoping bad things will just disappear. Go poof before we have to deal with anything. Mark my words. The Afterworld isn't any safer. We aren't any safer in this domain than the one we left behind. If anything, we're less safe because we're weak. We don't stand for anything any longer. We're a bunch of moochers, waiting for our next handout.

I shivered at this man's commentary and glanced at Preston who didn't take his eyes off the road in front of us.

"That's a little harsh," I said, reaching for the channel.

"Let's keep it on a little longer."

I nodded and skimmed my phone as a text from Abby came over. She was running late, had run into some traffic.

"That's weird."

"What's weird?" Preston asked.

"Abby's late because of traffic. When was the last time we had traffic?"

"Must be an accident or something."

I nodded as the radio host welcomed his next

victim.

Tell me like it is. What's on your mind?

The next man began his rant.

That lady's nuts. An idiot. I've seen with my own eyes things that no one would believe.

My skin prickled at this man's voice.

Things that would make your flesh crawl. We aren't going to survive the next one and there will be a next one.

The host hung up on the man and started up again.

Listen people, I'm not saying we are on the verge of another outbreak. That, my dear friends, is a conspiracy theory that I won't have anything to do with. We've been vaccinated. But I will say that I think we can't ignore these latest deaths. Where have these zombies been hiding? Why are they now descending on the streets? There is no such thing as coincidence in the Afterworld. Unlike the last caller, I can see clearly between fact and fiction. We don't have to worry about another outbreak. That wasn't my point. What I'm asking you to do isn't brain surgery. Just open your eyes and—

The radio went dead. I glanced at Preston. "That's odd."

"Do you think that's what we'd sound like if we tried to tell someone what we've seen?" I asked, changing the channel. I found another news channel—this one in the middle of delivering local weather—and rested the dial.

"I'd like to think we'd be more calm and deliberate in our delivery," Preston laughed. "But unfortunately, the content doesn't seem too far off."

"I wonder if his producers got tired of the host's rant?" I asked.

"He's paid to rant."

"Maybe only about certain topics," I mused.

"Censorship in the Afterworld?" Preston's brow arched. "Go figure."

I rolled my eyes and laughed. "Yeah. Can't imagine that."

A female broadcaster began running through the day's top stories. Unfortunately the latest incident wasn't one of her stories, which only highlighted how quickly the media was willing to drop one story for the next shiny object.

"What are your thoughts after hearing all that? Think there's any point in trying to reach out to any local officials?" I asked.

"And up my chance to be admitted to an MHA facility? No, thanks."

"They wouldn't believe us anyway."

"It's going to take a lot more than a few politicians or government officials being caught in the wrong place at the wrong time for anyone to take notice."

I knew exactly what he was saying. The media was handling these occurrences as little blips on the radar. Just another one of those things that happens in the Afterworld, and our government wasn't even bothering to comment. The government's reaction was dictating to the citizens how to respond, which was essentially— don't.

"What do you think it's going to take for people to start to question?" I asked.

Preston let out a deep breath and glanced over at me. "I honestly don't know. It's disappointing how quickly the camaraderie slipped away after the outbreak ended. Didn't it feel like as a community we could accomplish anything?"

I nodded and glanced out the window. "It did. I felt like we were all united as one. At least we got a few good months out of it."

"Did we really?"

I laughed. "Point taken."

It was true. The moment Gavin was killed that feeling of unity vanished. I was able to take a step back. I saw what I didn't want to see when I thought things were perfect. I took the goggles off and haven't been able to slip them back on. We were dealing with a society full of goggle-wearing people, and frankly, I didn't blame them for wanting to keep their rose-colored shades on. It was a lot more pleasant. People had already quickly divided themselves back up into their groups, associating only with those who they felt most comfortable with. Nobody wanted their bubble to burst.

"It makes me sad to think that the only thing that will trigger that there's an issue here is if something happens to them personally. Right now, it's all a distant news story. It doesn't touch home with anyone. I mean I certainly don't wish this pain on a single soul, but I hope something else will wake these people up before it's too late."

"Whoa," Preston muttered under his breath.

I brought my attention to the street ahead and gasped.

A human wall of heavily armed men dressed in urban camouflage flanked the street. Several military vehicles were parked along the sidewalk, and two armored utility trucks were stationed in front of the men.

Preston slowed our truck down as we took in the sight. I glanced out the side window, my eyes scanning along the roofline of the buildings as I exhaled slowly. The streets were still vacant as if all of the inhabitants had been rounded up.

"What do you think?" I asked, analyzing their attire.

"I'm thinking National Guardsmen."

"Wow. With all the private security around, I lost faith that we even had any left, but I agree. It certainly doesn't look like private security. So someone is taking notice of the attacks. Maybe the government found one of the modifieds."

"Maybe. Or it could be something unrelated," Preston replied.

A prickle of unease ran through my bones as I continued to canvas the buildings. A twitch of a movement caught my attention in the shadows, and my eyes narrowed on the roof corner of the building next to us. My heart was pounding, and we continued driving toward the mass of men.

I looked over at Preston, and my breath drew in as a red laser sat directly on his forehead. My pulse hammered heavily at the realization that we were driving into something very bad.

"Preston." I slowly reached for the small mirror in the glove compartment and angled it up slightly to view my reflection.

"What's up?"

"Don't make any quick movements. We've both got laser sights pointed squarely on our foreheads, and I don't want to give them any reason to pull the trigger."

Chapter Nine

"Sorry, sir. We can't let you through unless you're a local resident."

"The road's closed?" Preston asked.

"It's restricted, sir," the man answered. He was still gripping his automatic rifle tightly and staring straight ahead, avoiding eye contact.

"What's going on?" I asked, ducking my head slightly, hoping to play the female card.

"We aren't at liberty to say. Unless you have proof of residence, we can't let you through."

"Is this about the attacks?" I asked.

The man's jaw twitched, and I got my answer.

"Is there a reason why we have two rifles pointed at us?" I waited for a reply and the soldier gave none.

"Is thirty-fourth open if we go around the city?" Preston inquired.

"Yes, sir. If you follow along Oak Street and hop over to thirty-second, you should be able to navigate from there."

"Thanks." Preston nodded and turned the vehicle around. The red laser was no longer centered on him.

"What the hell is that all about?" I glanced in the mirror to confirm I was no longer a target as well.

"We'll probably find out soon enough."

"Don't you find it bizarre that there's nothing on the radio about this? Not even a heads up about a road closure?"

After turning down Oak Street, Preston pressed on the accelerator and our truck sped up. The engine's deep roar added to the sense of urgency as my mind raced in several directions. The streets were quiet and calm, offering no clue to why a large stretch going into the city was militarized. In fact, this part of town was deathly quiet as if it had been evacuated, but that didn't make sense.

My phone buzzed, making me jump and I glanced at the text.

Weird! Had to go through a checkpoint to get into city. Anyway, at the coffee shop now. Saved us a table.

"Abby had to go through a checkpoint to get into the downtown corridor."

"That's not what I wanted to hear." Preston tapped his finger lightly on the wheel.

"Question for you."

"Yeah?" Preston's brow arched.

"Maybe I could feel out Abby and see if—"

Preston smiled and shook his head. "See if she'd be into believing that you've been captured, tied up, and escaped from members of a former government contractor. Not to mention that you've discovered incubators full of undead. Plus an entire community that you visited this week vanished overnight, and two of the men you rescued are now being held against their will at an MHA facility."

I couldn't help but laugh. "Well, when you put it that way, I guess I'll keep it to myself."

I craned my neck to catch a glimpse of a group that had gathered in front of a bank. Some were holding signs that read, "Stop our government" while others seemed to be in heated discussions over goodness knows what.

As we drove closer to the heart of the city, life began to emerge. We were no longer the only vehicle on the road, and there were people walking along the city's sidewalks, which made me slightly calmer.

"There's a checkpoint up ahead," Preston said, giving a slight nod toward the barricaded street in front of us.

"We're only like a block away from where we're meeting her. Let's just park and walk through the checkpoint. Since I have no idea what's going on, I'd rather have our only way out of here on the right side of the barricade for an easy escape."

"Such faith you have in the Afterworld." Preston's devilish grin reinforced the attraction I had for him, and I rolled my eyes, more at myself than him.

"There's a spot up there. It's back-in parking only." I pointed toward a brick building that had an alley next to it.

"Looks good to me."

Preston reversed the truck and angled into the stall before turning off the engine.

"Are you ready?" he asked.

"I honestly have no idea. I have nothing in common with Abby any longer. We're in such different places…"

"You have a past together and that's important, especially in the Afterworld," Preston offered. He slid his hand to mine and held it. "Remember, you're supposed to be into me as well." Preston winked.

"Don't get your hopes up." I grinned and slipped my hand from his.

"Never do with you." He climbed out of the vehicle, and I did the same, meeting him around the front of the truck.

A woman holding a bouquet of flowers caught my eye and she smiled at me. "Insane, isn't it? Here I thought we were on the right track with our country, and now our military is in our own streets." She walked toward the barricade, shaking her head as she went.

"Sounds like some people are getting disgruntled," I whispered.

"Only because their lives are disrupted. Don't let it fool you into thinking they'll be of any help."

We crossed the street, and I looked behind

me, memorizing where we parked. I spotted a florist shop on the corner, the one the woman must have gone to, and made a mental note in case we needed to escape.

"Let's hope for the best," I whispered.

"And what would that be?" Preston mused, sliding his arm around my waist.

"Maybe the government has everything handled, figured all out..."

"That certainly would be nice, wouldn't it?" Preston smiled, and the skin around his eyes crinkled slightly. "We can always dream."

A line of people stood in front of a barricade as they waited impatiently to be let into the city. I glanced at the uniformed men holding their rifles, their expressions like stone, as people peppered them with questions. No one was given answers. One person after another would hold up their arms, spin, be patted down and then ushered through the maze of barriers. It was civilized and quiet. I expected to see news crews. I didn't.

The blank expression on the National Guardsmen chilled me to the core. They were sent here for one thing, to keep things calm. Slowly moving through the line, I listened to the comments around me. Some connected the zombie attacks with the National Guard's presence while others took it one step further by placing the blame on the government in the first place. Many seemed to feel if the government had spent more time attempting to capture the rogue zombies—the stragglers—none of this would've happened. What no one guessed was that these weren't stragglers from the outbreak. As I listened to the chatter, it became apparent that proving our theories might be the easy part compared to getting the general public to believe us.

"Next," the National Guardsman called.

I gave Preston a soft nudge forward, and he walked over to the open station where he complied with the orders, lifting his arms up, spinning, and enduring a quick pat down.

The guardsman ushered him through and motioned for me to come forward.

A woman dressed in uniform stepped out and quickly directed me to raise my arms and spin, which I did. Her hands ran along my arms, down my sides, hips, and legs.

"You're fine," she muttered, and ushered me through the barrier.

Preston was leaning against a light pole, waiting for me. His eyes flickered with amusement as he caught my gaze running along his body. I stretched my arm out, and he reached for my hand, his fingers entwining with mine. The coffee shop was on the corner, and depending on where Abby was sitting, she might be able to see us.

"They're not looking for weapons," Preston muttered, his chin tilted toward my ear.

"How do you know?"

"Because the guardsman's hand ran right over my Glock and he didn't even flinch. He knew I was carrying and let me through."

"Then what on earth could they be looking for?" I spotted Abby sitting next to the window, nibbling a piece of scone.

Preston shook his head. "I don't know, but it's really got my interest piqued.

We walked down the sidewalk toward the door, and I eyed the tall building that loomed across the block. The metallic siding had dulled from lack of upkeep, but the offices were lit up. There were several soldiers stationed at the entrance and along the side.

"Wonder what's inside that building?" I gave a slight nod in the general direction. A shiver ran through my spine. The city no longer felt familiar. It was cold and unsettled.

"Your gut was right. I'm glad we came back to town, to civilization," Preston whispered close to my ear, as he opened the door for me.

"If you can call it that."

The wood floor underneath me creaked when I stepped inside the coffeehouse. The walls were painted a soft green, and the overall vibe was rustic with a few modern twists like exposed ducts in the ceiling, and gnarly pipes running out of the walls. Generic, unframed artwork hung from wires along the wall.

My eyes landed on Abby, who gave me a quick wave as we walked over. She stood up quickly and dusted her hands off before wrapping her arms around me in a tight hug.

"It's so good to see you," she squealed.

I knew I should be feeling the same level of delight she was apparently experiencing, but I didn't. Preston's hand rested on my shoulder, a slight reminder of the part I needed to play. I was glad to have him by my side.

"I'm so happy you could meet us," I said, in the best perky voice I could muster.

Abby let go and sat back down. "You look amazing."

"Oh, thanks. You do too."

And she did. Her wavy, blond hair hung loose around her shoulders, and her high cheekbones were no longer severe from malnourishment. She seemed happy and healthy.

"I mean it." Her eyes darted to Preston. "Nice to see you again."

"Likewise," he responded, his grin intensifying.

"You wanna go get something to drink?" she asked.

"Sounds good to me. It's freezing outside." I put my phone on the table to wrangle my wallet out of my pocket as Preston took a seat. "What do you want?"

"A coffee's fine."

"That's not very exciting," I teased, tying to get in the spirit of things.

"I've had enough excitement for the day." His brow arched. I nodded and turned around to stand in line.

"Isn't that the truth?" Abby asked Preston. "I don't know what's going on, but it's intense out there."

"That it is. We haven't heard much about what's happening," Preston said.

The cashier called me up, and I placed our orders and paid. I glanced behind me at Preston and saw that the two were deep in discussion. It was killing me not to know what they were saying, but our drinks would be called any second.

The coffeehouse was one of the few places in the city that felt unruffled by what was going on outside. The energy running between the walls was what I'd expect on a typical day. Students were poring over their textbooks, parents were amusing their children while they snuck sips of coffee, and a few lone individuals were staring intently at their laptops. There was a sense of normalcy that existed as long as my gaze didn't wander out the window.

I heard Preston's laugh, and my attention shifted to their table. A twinge of envy shot through me as I watched my friend's lighthearted interaction with Preston. It was as if she had completely forgotten she'd just gone through a checkpoint to enter a city and was unaffected by the armed soldiers wandering our streets.

I wanted those blinders. I really did.

Our drinks were called, and I shook myself out of the ridiculousness. I took a sip of my hot chocolate on the way over and set down Preston's coffee.

"You got a text while you were over there," his voice distant.

"From Emily?" I asked.

"Who's Emily?" Abby asked.

"A friend of mine up north."

"How'd you meet her?"

"Through him." I pointed at Preston, and his eyes held a wariness that I recognized.

"It wasn't from Emily," he responded.

My heart hammered as I picked up my phone and clicked it on, dread filling me with every passing second. I felt Preston's gaze on me, waiting for my reaction as the text filled the screen. It was from Jeffrey.

Found some information on Preston's mom, but that doesn't mean she's still alive. Still waiting to hear back. I'll keep you posted when I find out more. Still looking into the guys.

"Is everything okay?" Abby asked. "Judging by your expression, I'd say no."

My eyes met Preston's, but no words came. I meant to tell him, but so much had gone on.

"Everything's fine," Preston replied, his jaw tensed as he took another sip of coffee. "Just some news about family."

"Your family?" Abby asked, eyeing me.

"No. His. Would you excuse us for just a second?" I asked her.

Preston placed his hand on my knee and squeezed it. "Nah. We can deal with it later. You don't get to see Abby often."

I examined Preston's expression, unable to read him, and nodded slowly.

"I know how these things go. One of my friends in calculus had finally started to come to terms that she was the only one in her family who'd survived, and then she got a notice from the government that an aunt on her dad's side was in an MHA facility. That messed with her more than thinking everyone was gone."

My gaze flicked to Abby's. "When was this?"

"Three days ago," Abby replied. "She's not doing well."

"Is the aunt still in the MHA facility?" I asked.

"As of now the aunt is still being held there. I think that's part of the problem. The letter recommended her release, but it had to be to family." Abby nodded and finished off her scone. "I don't know how I'd react."

I nodded and glanced at Preston who was surveying Abby's reaction.

"I mean if she's crazy…" Abby shrugged.

"Not everyone who's in the MHA facilities should be there," I responded before I could stop myself.

"I doubt they'd just lock up people who don't belong," Abby countered.

Preston slid his foot over to mine and applied gentle pressure with his toes as a friendly reminder to watch myself.

My eyes locked on Abby's. "I think their admittance policy is a tad subjective. I'm sure a lot of people got locked up who were only trying to deal with the aftermath of the outbreak the best they could."

"Possibly," Abby replied, shifting uncomfortably in her chair.

And I knew just how close I'd come to being

turned in by my own friends.

"Anyway, let's talk about school. How's it going for you and Caleb?" I asked.

She shrugged. "You know, when we first went back it was almost euphoric. There was this idyllic sense of community. It felt like we were moving on—moving forward—as a group."

"Not so much now?" Preston furrowed his brows.

Abby shook her head. "Not at all like that anymore. It's sad. People have split off into their own groups. The campus feels really fractured."

"That's too bad. How much longer do you have?" I asked.

She shrugged. "If I go through the summer, I'll be done in the fall. I plan on doing that just to be through with it all."

"I thought you loved it there."

"It's not the same as it was."

Preston's fingers slowly circled his cup. "Are there any clubs you can join to get that sense of camaraderie again?"

"God, no. None that I'd want to join. The ones that have sprung up recently are just depressing. Mostly conspiracy theory based ones. I showed up to one that was supposed to be for the arts, and the entire night was spent discussing some sort of new pit or something for fighting."

My breath caught, and I glanced at Preston. So TRAC's infiltrating colleges to recruit more gamblers.

"Like our world needs more avenues to fight each other." Abby rolled her eyes.

"You said the pits?" I asked.

She nodded. "I can't even imagine. Maybe it's MMA or something. Caleb wanted to go, but when he saw the look in my eyes he quickly changed his mind."

I laughed and nodded. "I can only imagine."

"It's sad. I'm slowly beginning to realize that things may never go back to the way they were, but I'd like to think they're not going to be worse." She looked out the window to a group of soldiers who were marching down the sidewalk. "I mean things can't get worse, can they?"

I let out a sigh and watched Preston, who was lost in his own thoughts.

"I hope not. I'd like to believe we're better than that, but I honestly don't know any longer."

Abby bit her lip and stared at the table. "Do you think it's weird that the White House hasn't responded? I don't know. Maybe it's not. I'm just getting weirded out."

I shook my head. "I don't know. I barely saw any news," I lied, glancing out the window at the empty sidewalk.

She sat forward and lowered her voice. "I just think it's odd that groups of undead are suddenly appearing out of nowhere, and now the city is crawling with soldiers; yet we've heard nothing from the President. Couldn't he assure the nation that everything is being handled; whatever everything is."

"Maybe they don't know what's going on and don't want to mislead the public," Preston replied, draping his arm around my shoulder.

"I've heard that these new zombies are mutated. That our vaccines don't work against them," she whispered.

"I hope that's not the case, but it's impossible to know until the government starts the dialogue. Maybe the government feels they're isolated incidents," I offered, avoiding her eyes.

"With all this action going on? Please." She waved her hands.

Abby's mouth pinched as she thought about what I said.

I wished in that moment that I could trust Abby, let her know what we'd found out so far, assure her that the vaccine still worked. But I couldn't. She was still too much on the fence.

"It's actually kind of comforting to see our military on the streets getting ahead of things, being proactive," I lied.

Abby's smile widened. "That's true. I need to quit being so pessimistic."

Not wanting to squash Abby's suddenly observant nature, I shook my head. "Hey, I think it pays to be on the lookout and mindful of the things that are going on around you. If you feel things are a little off, trust your gut."

Abby nodded, but her expression turned to horror as something caught her eye behind us.

I turned quickly in my chair to see a sight I never imagined would happen in our country.

Chapter Ten

My heart drummed in my chest as I watched the soldiers round up citizens, ordering them to get on their knees. Preston grabbed my hand and hauled me out of the chair.

"There's a back exit," he muttered, motioning for Abby to follow. I reached for Abby's hand, and she clutched mine tightly.

The coffeehouse hushed as the patrons watched the activities outside with alarm. The music that hummed through the air was silenced as we zigzagged through the tables toward the bright green exit sign.

"I don't know what to expect once we open the door, but if I run you run," I told Abby. She nodded, and I squeezed her hand right before Preston pushed on the door, letting the light and chill from the outside in.

The alley was vacant, but we could hear the shouts from the soldiers on the other side of the building. We walked quickly but carefully, not wanting to draw attention to ourselves as we reached the checkpoint.

The entry line was long, and it seemed as if the soldiers had stopped letting anyone through. The exit was clear with only two guardsmen at their posts. Abby let go of my hand as we made our way to the barricade.

Preston gave a slight nod to the soldiers as we passed through the exit, and the air I'd been holding in, finally escaped. We continued walking to our truck at a normal pace, determined not to bring attention to ourselves.

But then the first shot was fired.

Our truck was only fifty feet away, and we bolted as fast as we could. Preston reached the door and unlocked it quickly, opening it wide enough for Abby and me to slide in at almost the same time.

Preston jumped onto the seat and slammed the door as I watched the line of people disperse in fear as more gunshots rang out. Within seconds, he managed to get the truck on the main street and headed for our home.

"What's going on?" Abby was almost in tears.

"I don't know." I turned on the radio, hoping for some piece of news that would explain the confusion that was erupting all around us. Instead, we were met with useless chatter.

"Why isn't the news covering this?" Abby's voice trembled. She was digging in her purse and pulled out her cell phone, dialing Caleb's number.

"He's not in the city, is he?" Preston asked.

She shook her head while the phone rang and rang.

"Where are you?" Caleb's voice came over the speakerphone, his breathing heavy.

"I'm going to Rebekah's house. I'm in their truck."

Caleb's breathing was ragged as he tried to absorb everything.

"What are you seeing on the news?" I asked. "We can't get anything on the radio."

"I'm not seeing much, but I saw the coffeehouse Abby was meeting you at and I panicked. The press hasn't been allowed to film. Some people managed to post film clips of some of the shootings, but the moment the clips went live, the channel went dead. I've only seen glimpses."

"What do you mean they're not allowing the press there?" Abby glanced nervously at me.

"Babe, I've never seen anything like it. Nothing is making it on the news."

Preston turned onto the street leading to my home, and everything appeared as calm as when we'd left. One of the neighbors down the street waved at us as we pulled into the driveway. It was like nothing was happening. These pockets of violence were being contained and made to vanish.

"I'll be there in twenty minutes," Caleb said.

"Whatever you do stay far away from the city," Preston said. "They've got streets closed in many different directions, and it's hard to tell they're closed until it's too late."

"Thanks for the heads up."

"We'll keep her safe," I told Caleb. "Just drive carefully."

"Love you," Abby sniffed into the phone. "See ya soon."

"See ya." Caleb disconnected the phone, and I saw tears in Abby's eyes.

"It's all going to be okay. Let's go inside and see if we can get some news."

Abby nodded and opened the truck door. I slid out after her and studied Preston as I tried to gauge his reaction. We had a lot to discuss, and once again, now didn't seem like the moment, but I needed to apologize for what I'd done.

Abby's hands were shaking as she put the phone back in her bag. We walked up to the front door, and I opened it. I took a deep breath in and noticed the mustiness had already vanished, which was perfect since Abby was now with us. I didn't want her to know that I hadn't been living here for a while. I walked down the hall and through the kitchen with Abby close behind. The remote was on the coffee table in the family room, and I quickly found my favorite news channel, only to be disappointed. I heard Preston in the kitchen and handed Abby the remote.

"Need anything to drink?"

She shook her head and made herself comfortable on the couch while I wandered into the kitchen to talk with Preston. He'd found a bottle of wine in the cupboard and pulled out the cork.

"Would you like a glass?" he asked.

"That'd be wonderful." I took a seat at the table and watched as the red liquid splashed the sides of the glass as Preston poured the wine.

He took the seat next to me, his gaze landing on mine. I didn't know where to begin, but I knew what I wanted to tell him. A mixture of grief and confusion rested behind his eyes, and it killed me because I was the one who'd put it there.

"I'm sorry. I never meant to hurt you, and I'd planned on telling you, and then time just slipped by."

"I'm not hurt." His jaw tensed, and he looked out the window as he swallowed.

"I understand if you're angry at me..."

He shook his head, and his eyes darkened as he drank the entire glass of red wine. Minutes that seemed like hours passed between us without a word. My gaze dipped to the table, and I loathed myself for overstepping the boundaries. I had no right to interfere the way I did, open old wounds for him. Now I faced the possibility of losing a friendship. One of the only ones I had.

I looked around the kitchen and thought back to the first time Preston had ever come over. A straggler had torn through the fence and was repeatedly attempting to get through the sliding glass door. After the appropriate agency came and scooped up the problem, Preston repaired everything instantly. He'd been the one constant in my new life of uncertainty. He gave me fuel to continue going when I had none left, and he believed me when no one else did. He made my life better just by being in it and now that was all threatened.

"I'm not mad at you," he said, finally breaking the silence.

"You're not?" I asked, relief slowly spreading through me.

He shook his head and his eyes locked on mine. "Not at all. You did what you did because you cared...because you do care and that gives me hope."

"Hope for what?"

"For us," he replied flatly, eyeing me closely.

I let out a deep breath and sipped my wine.

"I do care," I whispered, unable to look at him. "I care more about you than anyone since..."

"I know."

"But I can't go there, Preston. I don't want to hurt you or lead you on. I'm not ready. I might never be ready. I just can't go through that again. I won't go through losing someone I love..."

It felt like all the air had been sucked out of the room. I was attracted to Preston in a way that I'd never felt before, not even with Gavin, but that was precisely why I had to stay away from him romantically. Too much was at stake and there were so many unknowns in our lives.

Preston leaned over, resting his elbows on his knees, as he waited patiently for me to look up at him. Feeling his gaze on me continued to do wild things inside me. Unable to handle it any longer, I slowly looked up at him through my lashes. The tension running between us was almost unbearable.

"I'm in no rush. I've told you that before. I'll be here when you're ready," his voice stirred up the very desire I was trying to push down.

I saw the intensity in his eyes as he stood up and leaned over, swiping a kiss along my cheek. The spark that I felt from that slight touch was more than I could handle as my body longed for another kiss. No matter how irrational, I wanted to maintain control over my feelings for him, but instead I was left breathless as he walked out of the room.

My mind was reeling, but I had to pull myself back to reality as I heard Abby and him discussing the lack of information being reported on the news. I braced my arms against the table and closed my eyes. It was unreasonable to think that I could continue to control the feelings I had for Preston and he knew that, but I also realized I had to try for my own survival, my own sanity.

The doorbell rang and I jumped up quickly to answer it, thankful for the distraction.

"I got it covered," I called, my voice cracking.

Sure I did.

I peered out the peephole and saw Caleb standing on the porch. He appeared anxious, and I felt bad for delaying his reunion with Abby even a second longer than necessary. I threw open the door, and he immediately seemed more at ease once he spotted me.

Abby came running up from behind, and I stepped aside so the two could reunite. Preston came down the hall and slid his arm around my waist. Abby and Caleb slowly let go of one another as I glanced anxiously at Preston.

"You must be Caleb," he said.

"I am and you're Preston. The man who helped get Rebekah back out of her shell." He grinned, but Abby playfully swiped his arm.

"She still likes to waddle back into her shell more often than not, but I do my best." Preston smiled, and I couldn't help but grin.

It was true. "Waddle, and not crawl, huh?" I left Preston's embrace and walked down the hall.

"How'd the streets look on your way over?" Preston asked Caleb.

"Pretty bare, and nothing like the few video clips I saw outside of that coffee shop." He shook his head. "I can't believe you guys were only feet away from being in the center of something so awful."

"And the worst part is that we don't even know what it was that caused it," I said, picking up my wine glass off the kitchen table.

I turned to Caleb and Abby and offered a glass of wine. Abby nodded, but Caleb declined. "Any beer?"

"Believe it or not, no." I smiled.

"Caleb and I could run to the store," Preston offered. "We need to pick some stuff up anyway."

The thought of him leaving the house without me spurred a wave of anxiety. With the mess we'd just left, I hated the idea of him being out there, but we were out of the necessities.

"Did you see any National Guard on your way here?" I asked.

"Not at all. It seems like they're focused on the city."

"We've gotta get some food and drink. We're completely out unless you count the can of cream of broccoli soup."

I pressed my lips together, and Abby and I traded glances.

"I'll keep my phone on," Preston assured me.

I nodded and stepped toward Preston, my hand running along his arm. "I'll text you if anything comes up on the news. In case you need to come back."

"You have to promise me that you'll come right back if anything feels weird," Abby said, hugging Caleb.

"Of course. I don't want to get involved with any of this mess," Caleb scoffed. "It's bad enough we've got the loonies predicting doomsday again."

A shudder went through my spine. Would he throw us in that group? Preston's eyes met mine and he grinned. I knew what he was thinking. It was the same thing as me. The new Afterworld motto seemed to be, "Keep your eyes closed tight and the bad stuff won't ever sneak in".

"Okay. I expect to see you guys loaded with lots of junk food and beer when you return," I joked.

We actually did need food and if anything started getting worse, we'd have a very slim chance of getting anything we needed during a crisis. Now was the time to grab what we could at the store while the stores still had something to grab. Granted, I had rations and enough water for nine months downstairs, but I didn't think now was the time to pull out the dehydrated pot roast to serve to the guests.

"Okay. Love ya," Caleb said, planting a kiss on Abby's cheek.

"Love you too."

A pang of guilt ran through me as I glanced at Preston. He smirked and took a step forward, dropping his mouth close to my ear. "See ya soon, babe. Need anything in particular?"

I shook my head and smiled. He certainly didn't promise to make it easy on me. I watched as Caleb and Preston walked down the hall and waited for the door to shut before turning to see Abby who was staring at me with a bewildered expression.

"What?" I feigned innocence.

"There is something really weird going on between you two. I didn't want to say anything, but it's just getting more awkward as time goes on."

"What do you mean?"

"Well, no offense, but it's mostly with you."

"How so?"

"It's plain as day that Preston is beyond into you, but you don't seem to send quite the same signal. It's almost like you're fighting it or something."

Abby was never one to hold her tongue, and I guess I shouldn't have expected her to start now, but I hadn't been ready for it. After all, I thought I'd done a good job of playing up a relationship with Preston. Maybe partial honesty was the best way to divert this conversation.

"It's been complicated," I confessed, taking a seat and pouring us both a glass of wine.

She nodded. "I'm sure it has, but it's been long enough. If you're worried about us or anyone…"

I shook my head "It's not that."

"Then what is it?" she asked.

"I'm afraid of what will happen if I lose him." And that was true.

Abby let out a sigh and shook her head. She swirled the wine in her glass but didn't take a sip. "That's no way to live."

I bit my lip and looked around the kitchen. The news in the other room was barely audible, and it didn't sound like anything more was being reported.

"I know the outbreak's over. I understand that normalcy can exist in the Afterworld, but I don't feel that's the part of the world I see. I can't ignore that in the last twenty-four hours undead have killed innocents. My eyes don't hop, skip, and jump over the fact that we now have military in our own streets." I twisted my lips as I debated whether or not to say what was eating at me. "And I can't pretend that Gavin didn't die by the hands of evil, and that evil still exists in our world."

My heart raced as Abby stared at me in silence. I'd gone too far. I shouldn't have brought up Gavin again or implied that the evil was ongoing. I needed to temper my reaction.

"I know you've been through a lot, and I'll be

the first to admit that seeing what I saw right in front of me and on the news has made me question exactly what's going on..." She stopped herself and took a sip of wine. "But your fear of losing Preston, or anyone for that matter, will stunt you. It will stop you from being who you're truly meant to be. Not because you need a man or you need a best friend, but because you'll be so busy fighting your feelings that you'll miss what the world has to offer. It takes a lot of effort to push away emotions, and it'll distract you from what's really important. Think about it. Since you've given up the whole conspiracy theory thing about Gavin, your life has opened up."

I bit my tongue. There were so many ways I could go with that statement. Instead I nodded and strangely felt better for it.

"So you think rather than waste my time fighting the feelings I have for Preston, I should just roll with it." I laughed.

Easier said than done.

"I do." She smiled.

"There is something about Preston that is so amazing, special. I know if I let myself fall..."

"You'll fall hard."

I nodded. "I don't know if I'd be able to handle losing someone a second time, especially him."

Abby reached for my hand and squeezed. "You're only fooling yourself if you think you haven't already gone there emotionally. You can't reverse those feelings. Your fate is as good as sealed."

"I'll think about it."

Abby shook her head, rolling her eyes. "You do that…" She paused. "You just want to get back to watching the news, don't you?"

My cheeks reddened and I laughed. "Kind of."

"You never really were that great at being girly."

I smacked her playfully and grinned. "I take complete offense to that."

She shrugged and stood up. "It's true. Now let's get you back to your beloved news."

I snatched the bottle of wine and followed her into the family room.

The weatherman was organizing clouds on the screen when a large *Breaking News* logo flashed on the television. We both took a seat and waited impatiently.

"Terror threats have been received in eleven major cities," the newscaster reported.

"What does that mean?" Abby asked. "Like terrorists? I don't believe it."

"I'm not sure either."

"Martial law has been declared in the following cities: Atlanta, Austin, Billings, Detroit, Little Rock, Los Angeles, Raleigh, Seattle, and Tampa. We will continue to revise the list as we receive updates. Authorities are asking that citizens remain inside their homes. Only essential personnel are allowed on the roadways, and checkpoints have been set up in each of the cities and outlying areas."

My cell phone rang, scaring both Abby and me. I clicked it on, and Preston's voice came over the speaker.

"Troops are moving in. Heard what's going on? Is there anything on the news?" he asked.

"Martial Law has just been ordered, but I thought it was only in certain cities. You need to come home now."

"We're on our way. We loaded the groceries and had already hit the main road when we saw the trucks."

"This looks like a knee-jerk reaction based on pure speculation and fear. This isn't going to end well if the government's fighting the wrong people," I said quietly.

"No. It's not."

A bullhorn echoed in the background, demanding people get off the streets.

"I gotta go. We'll be there in a few." And he hung up to the sound of more shouting.

A cold chill climbed my spine with the realization that the Afterworld might be more dangerous than the one before it.

Chapter Eleven

The moment we heard the truck pull into the driveway, Abby and I ran to the door and flung it open. To have the guys safely back was a huge relief. The uncertainty that was bogging down our airwaves and streets around us was beyond unsettling. Caleb crawled out of the truck, looking somewhat shell shocked, but he managed to smile at Abby who was already running across the lawn. Preston's eyes met mine, and a grin touched my lips as I walked over to greet him. The strength behind his eyes was one of the many things that made him so attractive and so hard to resist. To Abby's point, maybe I should stop trying to resist.

"Pretty bad out there?" I asked, peeking behind him to see several grocery bags.

He picked up a few of them and leaned against the truck. "I've seen worse." He flashed a wolfish grin.

"I bet you have." I blinked away my chuckle and reached for two paper bags full of food that had to be way better than the dehydrated goodies I had in the basement.

There weren't many people in the world—if any—who would get our jokes. That, at least, ought to tell me something if nothing else would. Plus, we shared a bond that very few would ever understand.

As they walked into the house, Abby had her arm around Caleb, who appeared more than a little freaked-out. Preston and I lingered outside; neither of us wanting to go into the house to face what might be coming over the news.

We knew that from this moment forward our lives would never be the same. It didn't need to be said. We could feel it, hear it, and most disturbing of all—see it.

"Hey, I was thinking you and I could go to a little spot to escape all this," he said, only half teasing. "It's a place in the woods, underground..."

I laughed, a bit nervous that the walls I'd built around my heart were so easily torn down by Preston. "Is it a place where we can sit back and watch the world go by? Because that sounds really enticing at the moment."

Preston's laugh produced an intense sense of longing—maybe it was belonging—that briefly calmed me before he spoke again. "You know the moment we went there, you'd be itching to get back at it, don't you?"

I sighed and adjusted the grocery bags on my

hips, unable to hide my smile.

"Yeah. I know. But it sounds nice on the surface. How'd Caleb do with seeing the soldiers? Did it change his mind any?"

Preston threw his head back, holding in a chuckle.

"That good, huh?"

We walked toward the house as I heard the faint rumble of military vehicles a few streets away.

"Maybe this is what it'll take to wake them up," I whispered, more to myself than Preston.

"Don't get your hopes up."

I shut the door with my foot and Preston turned the top lock, clicking it in place.

"You've got to check this out," Abby called from the kitchen.

We promptly made our way down the hall to dump off the groceries on the kitchen counter. I passed the walls adorned with pictures that didn't mean much any longer. I brushed aside the guilt for that and kept on walking. Abby was standing in the doorway that led into the family room, her back facing us. Caleb was in front of her, leaning against the wall, watching the television.

I shoved the bags onto the counter, listening intently to the television.

It's complete chaos out here. They are ushering the press out of the downtown corridor, but they haven't given us any answers as to what's going on, and we won't leave until we get some.

Yeah, right. Good luck with that one.

"That's right where we were," Abby muttered, wandering into the family room, mesmerized by the scene of terror unfolding on the screen.

The reporter stood staring at the camera, but the view behind her was chilling. Soldiers kept their guns pointed at a crowd of people who were being forced onto busses—for what reason no one knew.

"This can't be our government," Abby said, shaking her head as she slumped onto the couch.

"I'm sure there's a reason," Caleb replied, sitting down next to her.

Preston brought in a six-pack and placed it on the table, taking one for himself, before sitting in a chair.

"What if there's another outbreak? I don't think I could do it again," Abby said, pushing back tears.

"There's not another outbreak," I assured her, flipping off the cap from a bottle of beer. "But you could do it again."

"How can you be so sure there's not another one?" Caleb asked. "That's a logical explanation. It would explain why they're quarantining everyone."

"We don't know that's what they're doing," I countered.

"That's true," Abby began, staring at Caleb. "That could be me on that bus. The only reason it wasn't was because of them." She pointed at us. "They got me out of there in time."

Caleb watched us with skepticism lining his

expression as he reached for a beer. "Say what you want. I think it's a new bug, a variation. I've been hearing a murmur about that at school. It makes sense."

"Really? And if I'd been treated like cattle with the rest of those people, would you be so sure of that? Do I look sick? What reason do they have to blindly sweep a city block? You're smarter than that." Abby's voice was traced with bitterness.

Preston and I traded nervous glances. This was a far more heated Abby than I'd ever seen before.

"I'm *smarter* than that?" Caleb's tone biting.

The images on the screen caught my attention as I watched two soldiers grab and bind the reporter's hands behind her. The camera fell to the ground, capturing only a scuffle of feet before the live feed went dead.

The television flipped back to the reporters at the station, and rather than miss a beat they began announcing school closures. Never had we experienced censorship like this, not even during the outbreak. Where was the concern over the lack of information? For the press being shut out?

I followed Caleb's stare to my bookshelves that were still lined with all things tactical, ranging from nano-technology and surveillance to weaponry.

Yeah...Nothing going on here.

Preston's phone rang, and he stood up, pulling it out of his pocket.

"Excuse me for a moment," he replied,

walking out of the room.

I was certain it was Braden. Not only would Braden want to make sure we were okay, he'd want to see if we had the inside scoop.

"Listen, I think it's pointless to speculate. It's even worse to let this get to any of us. The best thing to do is stay inside and try to keep a pulse on things," I said, hoping to soften the tension in the room. "From the looks of it, we've got plenty of food and drink to get us through."

Caleb pulled his attention away from my reading selection and focused on me, nodding. "You're right. It's pointless. It just freaked me out and I'm sick of the Afterworld."

Abby rubbed Caleb's knee and leaned her head against his chest. "I know, baby. It sucks."

Finally! These two admitted the obvious.

Preston came into the room. "Everything better?"

I hid a smile and nodded. "All better."

"Can I talk to you for a second?" he asked me.

"I'll be right back. Drink more beer. It works," I teased, hopping up and following Preston out of the room.

He didn't stop in the kitchen. Instead, I followed him up the stairs and down the hall to my bedroom. He closed the door and began pacing.

"You're making me more nervous then the tanks a few streets over," I joked, sitting on the bed. "I've never seen you like this. What's going on?"

"Sorry," Preston replied, slowing his steps.

"I'm assuming you heard from Braden?"

He nodded and ran his fingers over his whiskers. "I did. Our girl Izzy had a bad accident."

"What?" My heart thumped inside my chest at the thought of something happening to her. She went to live with Emily's sister, Isabelle, in Idaho and everything had been going really well. Izzy loved living somewhere with horses and freedom to explore. "Is she okay? What happened?"

"Her horse took off, and she was still on it. It went wild and Izzy couldn't control it. The horse ran straight into the barn, not even slowing down slightly. Izzy's head smacked right into one of the low hanging rafters, and she fell off the horse, completely unconscious."

"Oh, my god," I whispered, shaking my head in disbelief. I noticed a glimmer of something unrecognizable behind Preston's eyes and dread filled me.

"Isabelle and her boyfriend rushed her to the hospital. She was unconscious the entire way there, and she had several broken bones."

"Why are you talking in past tense?" I asked, barely able to swallow. "Please don't tell me..." My voice caught.

"Sorry. I didn't mean to imply that. She's alive, but—" his voice trailed off.

I let out a big exhale and bent forward, my elbows resting on my knees. "But what?"

He bit his lip and sighed. "I think we finally have the answer to what's driving TRAC, what their part in the MHA really was. We need to find Dr. Falino. There is a lot she didn't tell us. There's a lot she needs to tell us."

Preston's jaw clenched, and I watched as anger replaced concern.

"And there's a lot you're not telling me... like everything," I replied. "Would you just spill it?"

"They pulled the car in front of the emergency room, and by the time Isabelle opened the back door to get Izzy into the hospital, she woke up."

"Okay," I said slowly. "That's good, right?"

"Her body had healed itself," he paused. His eyes met mine. "Completely. It was like nothing ever happened."

"Wait a second. You're telling me her broken bones healed themselves? Her head injury disappeared?"

"The cuts and bruises vanished as well." Preston took a seat next to me on the bed.

"TRAC managed to isolate what it was that makes the undead stronger. They somehow zeroed in on the thing that makes them difficult to destroy. The modifieds are just the byproducts of their testing..." I whispered as I shook my head in disbelief. "So whatever they were feeding her, forcing down her while she was being held at the MHA facility, had to have been a compound they developed from their research on the undead."

"Which was why at the first sight of trouble, TRAC always ensured that the patients were evacuated. Those were the guinea pigs."

"They didn't account for leaving a patient

behind who could heal herself and be found by someone." Preston stood up.

"What did Isabelle do?"

"They still took her into the emergency room to be checked, but at that point, they just seemed like overly concerned parents. The doctors did a complete evaluation of Izzy, and it was like nothing ever happened."

"To say Isabelle and her boyfriend were panicked by what they witnessed would be putting it mildly. Isabelle called Emily the moment they got outside of the hospital and explained everything that had happened."

"So we're dealing with a group who thinks they've found the answer to eternal youth...a method to heal the body," I sighed. "They'll stop at nothing to protect that you know. But why the unprovoked attacks?"

Preston shook his head. "Maybe to throw people off while they continue their research and testing?"

I shook my head. "I think there's more to it. Not only have they stumbled upon something that might change the fate of man's future forever, but they've also developed a fighting machine like never before. They're testing it out and so far it's worked flawlessly."

Preston slid his tongue along his lips as he mulled over what I was saying.

"Imagine a world where the wrong people gain control, where purely evil men position themselves in places of authority, where they build an army of undead to protect what they've built, and then they use the substance to keep themselves healthy. They've held enough power to know what that feels like."

"But I was able to destroy the clone of Sophie," Preston muttered.

Something wedged in my mind, and I hated to say it, but it had to be said. "I don't know the science behind it. Maybe the modifieds are only incubators for whatever compound or substance they created. It could be they're like a vessel and don't actually reap the benefits or healing, but who knows."

Preston let out a guttural sound, and he shook his head, as his balled fists hung at his sides.

"If what I'm thinking is right, our world has never seen this kind of evil. They'll stop at nothing to dominate the world, to ensure that they'll stay in control. The Afterworld would become their world. We can't let that happen."

"What about what's going on in our streets now? Do you think TRAC's already infiltrated our government enough to do this?"

I shook my head. "I don't. It feels like our government is operating on fear right now, and fear isn't what fuels TRAC. Besides, why would they let out the undead in swarms and then use the troops against their own? It doesn't seem logical."

"I wonder if the government somehow got their hands on one of the modifieds."

I shrugged my shoulders and stood up. "Not that I don't have faith in our officials, but I'm not sure even if they had noticed they'd understand what it was they had. I mean the modifieds look like the other undead."

"True."

"I think TRAC's testing out the waters right now, and I think the government is trying to figure out what's going on, and the only thing they can think of is that someone is letting hordes of undead loose in the streets. I doubt if they've moved beyond that."

My phone rang and I dug it out of my pocket. "It's Jeffrey."

My insides stilled at the realization that Preston, and I still hadn't really talked about his mother.

"What's up?" I spoke into the speaker.

"Sorry it's taken me so long to get back to you about Ron and Josh," Jeffrey apologized.

"Not to worry. We've had plenty of things to keep us busy. So did you find anything out?"

"I did and I can tell you it makes me uncomfortable enough to bow out of everything."

"What do you mean?" I glanced at Preston.

"They were both admitted into the MHA facility in Southwest Washington, but from what I can tell when all of these horde attacks started, they began looking at those two differently."

"They think they have something to do with it?" Preston asked.

"No, but I think they're willing to listen to their story. I think the government has been able to put two and two together about these hordes, or at least that the hordes aren't all a coincidence. The person I spoke to said that Josh and Ron had been transferred to another facility this afternoon, but it wasn't an MHA facility. My guess is that someone figured out these hordes are being created using the unvaccinated individuals being snatched out of the woods, and the government doesn't want that information leaked to the general public."

"That wouldn't explain the military's action in the street."

"My thought is the government's trying to send a message to whoever is letting the undead loose. That message being that they've got more force and gun power than whoever's letting the hordes out. Listen, I don't want anything to do with where I think this is going. I appreciate what you've done for my business, but I have my family to think about. I'll send you a list of facilities that my men moved those creatures to, and I'm out of it. I'm done. My job in life is running a security company, which you helped to enlarge, but that's all I want. Whatever it is you two think you're onto is none of my business, and I want to keep it that way."

I traded a worried look with Preston, but there was nothing I could do to change Jeffrey's mind. That I was sure of.

"Okay, Jeffrey. I understand."

It felt like my world was getting smaller, like my existence depended on so many factors outside my own control, and I didn't like that one bit.

"One more thing. I found Preston's mom, Tricia Blakely. She's started out in an MHA facility out in Vermont and has since been transferred between several other locations. I don't know her condition other than she's alive."

Chapter Twelve

My eyes stayed on Preston as we both absorbed the news. A chill in the air made me reach for a blue chenille throw. I wrapped it snugly around my shoulders—only it didn't help. After several beats of silence, Preston wiped his brow and leaned against the dresser. His gaze lowered to the floor before meeting mine.

"I guess I should be happy. This is good news, right?" It was less of a question than a statement and all I could do was nod, but I saw a look of anguish settle behind his eyes. "I gave up on her too early. She was my mom and I gave up on her."

I stood up, the throw falling off my shoulders, and walked over to him. I reached for his hands and held them tightly as I stood in front of him, debating what to say.

"You did the best you could."

He released his hands from mine. "I'm not

sure I did. I was told she had died and then I left it at that."

My blood froze. He'd never mentioned he'd heard that his mother wasn't alive any longer. If he had, I certainly wouldn't have gone searching her out.

"Why didn't you say anything to me?"

He straightened his posture and his jaw set in place. His eyes settled on a photograph I hadn't yet removed of Gavin and me on one of our hiking trips. It was right after the vaccinations. We'd gone up to the mountains and the wildflowers were in full bloom. It was such a happy time, a time filled with hope. It was also a time apparently filled with lies and deceit. The man I loved and trusted was involved with something I still couldn't fully grasp. I shook away the memories and looked up at Preston. He was studying me intently, and I took a step back, distancing myself from the sensations that washed over me.

"I don't think I believed it. I didn't want to believe it, but I'd seen so many horror stories about the MHA that it was easy to accept," he admitted, his brows furrowing.

"Well, let's not forget those things did happen and continue to happen at the MHA. There wasn't any reason not to believe what you were told," I reminded him. "When the MHA first opened up, I remember hearing left and right about wrongful deaths, suicides, you name it... The agency didn't earn its bad name by accident."

He let out a sigh and took a step forward, his finger tracing my cheek softly. "Thank you for always managing to ground me, see the light in the darkness."

I shook my head and looked away, letting out a deep breath. "I doubt I do that but thanks for thinking it's me."

He smiled. "It is."

I shrugged. "No matter how much we try to forget our past, sometimes we need to be reminded of it just to center where we are in life. How we got here. It's easy to second-guess ourselves..." my voice trailed off.

"I'm usually pretty good at forging ahead and not looking back." He flashed a faint smile and dropped his hand away, and I longed for his touch again.

"I think most survivors excel in that area." I grinned, noticing the scent of something enticing wafting into the bedroom through the door cracks. "Do you smell that?"

He sniffed the air, and I had to chuckle as his nose crinkled in pursuit. "Garlic."

"Huh," I said, taking a step back. "We'll have to go check that out. Since I think our guests aren't allowed to leave the house, I might as well change and get comfortable before settling in for the evening. I'll meet you downstairs in a few."

Walking toward the door, his expression fell and he nodded slowly. He stopped and turned to watch me. "Thanks for asking the question that I was afraid to ask about my mother."

My stomach knotted, wishing I could take

away his pain, but instead I just nodded. "We'll figure out how to get her out."

Regardless of her condition, a shot on the outside had to be better than being on the inside.

He pressed his lips together, and his eyes locked on mine. "I know."

He walked down the hall, and I closed the door behind him. Opening up my dresser, I snagged a pair of pajamas for Abby since she now had to spend the night. I tossed them on my bed and searched for a pair for me.

Settling on a pair of Tic Tac pajamas, I undressed quickly and slipped the flannel shirt over my head. I stepped into the loose, pajama bottoms and tied the satin strings around my waist. Oddly, stepping into these pajamas brought a sense of comfort I hadn't expected.

I walked over to the photo of Gavin and me and examined it closely one last time before stuffing it into a drawer. Slipping on my fuzzy slippers, I grabbed the pajamas for Abby and left the bedroom. As I walked down the hall, I couldn't help but think about the irony of the situation. Martial law had been declared. We were all holed up in my house, and for the first time in a very long time, I felt almost normal. Or at least what I'd consider my crazy normal to be. I couldn't remember the last time I'd worn a pair of pajamas and had houseguests. Granted, the houseguests were here somewhat involuntarily thanks to the military roaming the streets, but regardless, I was—for once—feeling somewhat decent again.

It reminded me of what we were fighting for, why we were searching for the truth. The survivors deserved a better world; one based on kindness and compassion. We were dealing with people who wanted to create a new world that capitalized on people's weaknesses and exploited their flaws. It would be a world that perpetuated fear and great darkness. The thought created a dull ache in the pit of my stomach, and it only got worse as I continued thinking about what needed to be done.

Human lives were unimportant to TRAC. They were testing the boundaries of the country and of the people. The longer we stayed quiet as citizens, the more power they'd manage to secure. It wasn't only up to the government to thwart TRAC. It was up to the citizens to stand up and fight for what we held dear. We had to expose the dirty deeds of a few in order to stop them. We didn't want an entire generation raised by war. Enough lives had been lost to the undead and the outbreak. The thought of more people dying at the hands of humans using the undead as weapons spurred something inside of me. A message had to be sent to TRAC.

The friendly voices in the kitchen shook me out of my daze as I watched Preston, Caleb and Abby take bowls and dishes to the table.

"Whatever this is, smells amazing," I said, glancing at the table.

"Hot spaghetti with meatballs and don't you look comfortable," Abby said. I waved the other set of pajamas at her before setting them on an empty chair.

"These are for you. I thought we might as well get comfy since none of us seem to be going anywhere for a while. And spaghetti sounds delicious." I picked up a platter filled with garlic bread and carried it to the table as Preston set down the last two glasses of water.

The news from the other room could be faintly heard over the dishes clanking and chatter between Abby and Caleb. It seemed like those two had completely patched things up, which was good.

I took a seat next to Preston and eyed the delicious food. No doubt, this was better than the silver packets waiting in the basement for whoever dared to open them. Preston reached for the large spoon and poked at the pile of meatballs, scooping up two and rolling them onto my plate.

"Thank you," I said, smelling the goodness of basil and garlic.

"So where in the world did you find a pair of Tic Tac pajamas and why?" Abby laughed. "I had no idea you were such a fan of the breath mint."

A clash of emotions settled like a big thunderstorm over my heart. This was what was so difficult about tidying up the spattering of emotions that were tied to Gavin. I'd been in love with him. He'd been a good man.

Abby placed a spoonful of pasta on her plate, and her eyes settled on mine, knowing I was vacillating with something far more complicated than why I liked Tic Tacs, but I couldn't say a word about the Gavin I'd discovered. They knew the side of him I'd known for many years, not the one that got him killed, but maybe that earlier version of him was what I had to concentrate on right now.

"It's a weird story... But a few months into the outbreak, Gavin and I had gotten used to eating next to nothing and life's little luxuries had completely vanished."

"Sounds familiar," Abby chided, taking a fork full of pasta. "I used to fantasize about Rice-A-Roni."

I laughed. "Well, out of the blue, all I wanted was an orange Tic Tac. It was the weirdest craving. I never even liked them that much before the outbreak. During one of our moves, we found this convenience store in the middle of nowhere. It had been completely ransacked except for an entire case of Tic Tacs sitting on the floor near the empty beer cooler."

Preston chuckled.

"It was the coolest thing ever until I picked up the case and saw there were twenty-four boxes of white, peppermint Tic Tacs. There wasn't an orange one to be found. Of course we chewed them right up over the course of a few days, but how I longed for an orange one. At one calorie a Tic Tac it really wasn't that exciting after the tenth box, but it was better than chopped dandelion leaves. Anyway, from that point forward it seemed like wherever we went, we found white Tic Tacs and never orange ones. It became a game and something to focus on besides pure survival. The Tic Tacs would appear in the weirdest places. We'd find a pack on a kitchen table in a vacant house or in the console of an abandoned vehicle. I had no idea how popular Tic Tacs were until then."

"What was the weirdest place you found some?" Preston asked.

I felt warmth rush to my cheeks and smiled. "On a dancer's vanity at a vacant strip club."

"I'm not even going to ask," Abby laughed.

"Needless to say during the entire outbreak, we never found a box of orange Tic Tacs, but he did find these pajamas for me after the outbreak, and they were orange."

Preston leaned over and touched the fabric, examining the material. A thoughtful smile traced his lips. "You know. It looks like your luck continued..."

"What do you mean?" I asked, perplexed.

"It looks like the pajamas were actually the white Tic Tacs, but Gavin must have colored orange inside the center of each of them."

My breath hitched as a pang of guilt dug into me. I hadn't even noticed. I shook my head and forced away the tears. That was the man I wanted to remember, I needed to remember.

I wiped the wetness away from my eyes and smiled at everyone. "He was always caring like that."

Abby reached across the table and touched my hand. "Yes, he was."

"Sorry. Not sure what got into me." I twirled a bite of pasta onto my fork and glanced at

Preston.

"It's okay to mourn the man you loved," he whispered, once Caleb and Abby began talking again. "No one is perfect."

I glanced up at him and nodded. "Thank you."

"That's what I'm here for," he teased. "Somebody's got to be your rock."

"Excuse me? I thought I was your rock," I joked before the sound of the male broadcaster's voice interrupted our banter.

The suspects are considered heavily armed and dangerous. Until these suspects are apprehended, the public is in grave danger. The authorities are asking that if you see them to dial 9-1-1 immediately. We are waiting on more details.

"Wow. I wonder what the hell's going on," I muttered, pushing away from the table along with everyone else.

We quickly found seats in the family room, our eyes glued to the screen. Maybe the government was onto something. Maybe they did find out who's behind everything. Maybe our lives could begin again...

The authorities believe that until they are caught, deaths by undead will continue. The public is not safe until the suspects are apprehended. The FBI and police are asking the public to be vigilant and mindful of any suspicious behavior. They believe that they're not working alone and are asking the public to report any suspicious activity or sightings of the suspects to 9-1-1.

The reporter touched his finger to his earpiece and stopped speaking, nodding as he listened to his headset before continuing.

These suspects are wanted for questioning in connection with a long string of crimes, and it is imperative that the authorities find them. The FBI and local police are requesting the public's help, but they are also asking that no one confront the suspects. The moment we have their names, we'll provide them on the screen, along with recent photographs.

"This is intense," I said, shaking my head. A wave of goose bumps crawled along my skin. "I wonder what happened."

With the news that the government was on the trail of the murderers, the hum of the military vehicles provided a strange sort of comfort. Preston rubbed my back lightly, and I glanced around the family room. Maybe we'd get to stop chasing and get to enjoy life the way it was meant to be lived.

"This is crazy," Caleb whispered, shaking his head.

We're putting up the pictures of the suspects. Remember, they are considered extremely dangerous. Please do not approach or try to subdue them under any circumstance.

We all stared intently at the screen waiting for the images to appear but darkness remained.

They are wanted for questioning in the recent murders of both government officials and civilians. We are waiting to hear from the FBI. Mr. Edward Jamison will be detailing the activities that have led to current developments in a press conference shortly.

A twinge of discomfort shot through my veins, and I didn't understand why. I glanced at Preston before hearing Abby gasp. I flicked my eyes back to the television, and my heart stopped as my eyes focused on the two suspects pictured on the screen.

Preston Blakely is considered armed and dangerous. His partner, Rebekah Taylor, is also considered armed and dangerous. She's known in the MMA community to be a brutal fighter. Do not approach either of them.

What? No, I wasn't. There was no community.

The pictures minimized but stayed in the far left corner of the screen as a person dressed in an FBI-issued jacket stepped up to a microphone.

It has come to our attention that a criminal underworld, led by these two individuals, has infiltrated our society. But we mustn't allow a few to control the fate of humanity. These two individuals cannot be allowed to roam the streets any longer. We will stop them. We will destroy their gangs. It is imperative that you do not approach them. That you dial 9-1-1 immediately if you spot them. Rebekah Taylor is wanted for the murder of her husband, Gavin Taylor. Preston Blakely is wanted in the murder of his sister, Sophie Blakely. They are also wanted in connection with the abduction and kidnapping of Izzy Morgan.

A new picture appeared on the screen, this one of Izzy, and my stomach knotted while I continued staring straight ahead. I couldn't swallow. I couldn't breathe. I felt the air in the room change to a sharp silence built on hatred and fear.

We are asking if you know the whereabouts of Izzy Morgan to please call 9-1-1 or your local sheriff's office. Ms. Taylor and Mr. Blakely are also wanted for the capturing of undead, which has been tied to the illegal fighting of zombies. Ms. Taylor and Mr. Blakely are also tied to a string of arsons, one at a contracted CDC affiliated facility. They are also suspects in a string of kidnappings relating to the unvaccinated survivors. They have done the unthinkable and infected these unsuspecting victims, which led us to the string of undead attacks that our nation has recently witnessed. These individuals are ruthless. The Afterworld will not be safe until Rebekah Taylor and Preston Blakely are apprehended, and it's up to the public to help us catch them, which is why we are offering a bounty to the individual or individuals who aid in the capture of Rebekah Taylor and Preston Blakely. The most recent footage we have of the suspects is video surveillance from one of the illegal matches between the undead that they organized.

I watched as the screen zoomed in on Preston and I standing in the crowd at the zombie pit. Preston's fingers gripped my knee as I slowly turned toward Caleb and Abby. They were both expressionless, and Caleb had his hand wrapped tightly around his cellular phone.

We have evidence placing them at one of the most recent captures of unvaccinated in our state. We also have surveillance of them abducting Izzy Morgan. They are predators.

The screen continued to change from video to video depicting exactly what he was describing, and I knew there was no talking our way out of it. Our only option was to run. Our only way to stop running was to prove our innocence by proving someone else's guilt.

I continued watching the screen as our images ran across the bottom with still snapshots taken from the released videos, but I refused to be beaten.

We will keep the public informed as we have further information. Sweeps of the cities will continue as we pursue our suspects, which is the reason for martial law. We are asking citizens to please stay inside, at home, until this situation is resolved. With your help, we can make that happen quickly.

My mouth was so parched, my tongue felt disconnected. I felt disconnected. It was as if I was watching someone else's nightmare unfold on the big screen, but this was my nightmare. We had been set up.

I stared at Caleb who was ready to dial the three life-changing numbers, but Abby was cupping his hands.

The rumble of the military vehicles silenced, and I knew it was time to run, but we had nowhere to go.

Chapter Thirteen

"What they're saying is not true," I said, standing up slowly with my gaze directed at Abby.

"The sweeps were because they were searching for you," Caleb said, the hostility in his voice stung. "Something could have happened to Abby because she was with you. She thought you saved her, but you put her in danger." His fisted knuckles turned white; his hands shaking as he stared directly at Preston.

"It's not like that," I replied, nervously glancing at Preston.

"Abby was all excited that Rebekah had found someone, but I knew something wasn't right." Caleb's jaw clenched, and he glanced at the bookshelves and then at Preston. I saw the loyalty to Gavin hiding at the surface, waiting to explode.

"It's in your hands," I began. "You can turn us over right now. Someone is about to come through the front door any second, or you can give us a chance to prove our innocence."

My eyes remained fixed on Abby, whose hands trembled as she held onto Caleb.

"You can count me out. I'm not falling for whatever you're trying to imply," Caleb replied, readying to dial the phone.

"The pictures..." Abby's voice trailed off.

"We were set up. There's an explanation for the footage, but we don't have the time to explain."

Abby shook her head and tears filled her eyes. They finally had their chance to turn me in. Only this time it wouldn't be to the MHA. This would be far worse. Preston and I edged toward the slider. We had minutes, if that, to escape.

"Here," Abby said, holding out her trembling arm. "You'll need this."

I looked in her hand and spotted a phone. She nudged Caleb who also held out his phone.

"You realize what you're doing..." Preston confirmed.

"If it goes that way, we'll tell them you stole the phones from us," Caleb replied.

I glanced down at my Tic Tac pajamas, silently cursing myself for getting too comfortable, and glanced at Preston. It was now or never. We took their phones, and I snatched the Maglight flashlight I'd kept by the door while Preston slid the glass open. The cold air hit me like a million daggers, begging me to turn back, but we couldn't afford to.

I glanced over my shoulder one last time and

smiled faintly at Abby who seemed more terrified of me than if a horde of undead stood in front of her, but for some reason she had decided to help us. The newscaster continued reporting in the background and my gut twisted in knots.

The bounty is set at one million dollars per suspect.

A chill ran through me as Preston slid the door shut, and the night's silence sliced into me shattering my hopes of an easy escape. The military vehicles no longer idled down the street. They were probably already preparing for a sweep of the area.

My house backed up to hundreds more like it; many vacant homes awaited in vain for their owner's return. Beyond the neighborhood was a greenbelt, and past that a woodsy area surrounding a lake.

"Don't stop running," Preston whispered.

I nodded and followed him to the back fence. It was only a six-foot wooden fence, which I scaled and dropped to the other side. The dampness of the ground quickly soaked into my slippers.

Preston jumped down beside me and scanned the area. My house had been one of the few with a fence, which I always thought was odd considering the roaming stragglers, but now I was grateful for my neighbors' lackadaisical outlook on life. My hope was that they'd continue to keep the blinders on as we bolted through their yards.

As we ran through the first patch of lawn, I

saw a flash of light from behind us reflect in a window at the same time I heard a bang. They had entered my house. I refused to think of Abby or Caleb. They would be fine because they weren't us.

My heart raced as blood surged through me with new urgency. I ran as fast as I could through the grass and weeds, hopping over shrubbery, attempting to keep up with Preston's pace. We hit drive after drive as we zigzagged through the neighborhood. I tripped over a curb but recovered before hitting the ground. Each breath caused a sharp pain in my abdomen, and my chest burned with each inhalation. I didn't know how long I'd been running, but I saw the clearing ahead. I could make it. We were getting close.

My completely soaked pajama bottoms slapped against my ankles as I ran through the tall, wet grass. The heat rolled off my body as I continued running at a pace I'd never maintained before.

And I regretted each meatball I'd eaten.

Every so often, a porch light would flip on or a back patio light would blaze into a yard that we flew through. There was no stopping until we were out of the direct view of the phantom bounty hunters.

"Hey, you." The voice came from behind and jolted me, but I kept running and Preston didn't even flinch.

Preston climbed up a retaining wall and squatted down, waiting for me to arrive. I dug my foot into the first boulder and scrambled up the wall, my hand meeting Preston's as he hauled me up the rest of the way. I glanced behind me and saw darkness. Whoever had hollered probably went into their home to place the call.

My chest was heaving as I attempted to catch my breath, but there was no time for rest. Preston's fingers stayed intertwined with mine as we started running again. When we reached the clearing, Preston looked behind us and grimaced. "We need to keep going. We can't stop."

I nodded and didn't let my legs slow down one bit. Instead, it was like tasting freedom sped them up, made me run at speeds my body didn't know possible. But as my feet pounded the ground, my knees began to ache. My body was reaching its limits. Sweat no longer trickled, it poured out of me. Every cell was on fire, my vision no longer clear.

A deep, rhythmic beat echoed through my body as my ears pounded with lack of oxygen. Panic arose as my body began to fail my mind.

I wasn't a quitter. Never had been.

I also wasn't a marathoner. Never wanted to be.

"Preston. I don't think—"

Before I had a chance to finish, my knees buckled, but Preston scooped me up prior to me hitting the ground.

"Cover is only a hundred feet away, if that," he said, tossing me over his shoulder like a ragdoll. Under normal circumstances, I'd protest.

But we didn't have time for that, and it wasn't

just me I'd be endangering so I let my body go slack as I was propped over his shoulders. His grip tightened as he continued to run toward the trees that promised shelter.

The first branch hit my behind, and relief trickled through me as we met cover, but Preston didn't stop running. Instead, limb after limb brushed my back and slapped my legs as he ducked underneath trees and beside overgrown bushes. I kept my eyes clenched shut.

When I thought the man would never stop running, and my body continued to clunk against his, a moment of lucidity bolted through me. We were on the run from the government, and the entire nation was on alert for us. We had nowhere to go and no one to turn to, except a certain few. Where were we really running to?

Preston finally stopped, and his breath stilled almost instantly as he slid me off his shoulders onto the ground, which was mostly covered in large, sprawling ferns. The woods were damp with an eerie darkness, the moonlight even fearful to enter through the towering conifers.

"We need to call Emily and Braden," I whispered, thankful to have my breath again.

My eyes hadn't adjusted to this level of darkness, and I could only make out Preston's shadow.

"We can't trust them or anyone," he replied, gruffer than I expected.

"Come on. You can't think that Emily and Braden are in on it or would turn us in. They're fighting for the same thing we are—truth."

"We can't take that chance," he said.

"You were the one who told me I had to learn to trust. Those two hold the key to helping us get our names cleared. They can help us," I insisted.

Preston was no longer only a shadow, and I watched as his expression changed to anger. He leaned against a tree trunk and folded his arms.

"I wouldn't be surprised if the government is already tracking their phones," Preston said.

I nodded. "True, but if we use Abby's to make that first call it might throw the authorities off long enough to get what we need."

Preston let out a deep breath. It was a risky thing to do, but anything was a risky thing to do.

"We can live in fear—hide forever—or we can take a chance, work to clear our name, and try to bring down the people who've started this," I said, walking toward Preston.

Preston nodded, tugged the phone out of his pocket, and dialed Braden's cell. Keeping the cell on speaker, Preston lowered the volume all the way and waited for Braden to pick up.

"We're in the car. Ready to pick you up and take you wherever you need to go. This is sick," Braden's voice was filled with pure hatred. "You were set up, man. It could be Emily and me next. I just can't believe what I saw. It's—"

"I know, man. Listen we have the cells of two of Rebekah's friends. We left ours at the house. We need you to wipe them. Can you do that from the car?"

"Absolutely. I rarely leave home without my laptop."

"Okay. Great. Get that done. We need to go into hiding while we plan our next steps."

"You name the place, and we'll get you there, come hell or—"

"No. We'll get ourselves there. You can turn the car back around and go home. We don't want to bring anyone else down if we can help it," Preston replied, and my heart dropped.

No matter what he said, he still didn't completely trust Braden, and now I wasn't sure how we were going to get out of here and to a safe place.

"Wherever you think we're headed, we need help to get there. Speed isn't on our side when we travel by foot. We have no vehicle and a bounty's been placed on our head," I whispered.

"She's got a point," Braden replied.

"We'll manage just fine. Listen, we'll get to some shelter for the night, and we'll contact you as soon as we have a plan. It may be with this number or it may not." Preston dug his hand into his eye and rubbed it. "If we're lucky, we'll be able to get a couple disposable cell phones."

"In the meantime, I can jumble the signals from this number. It'll make it more difficult for the feds to track it, track you. It should buy you some more time to use the phone if you need, but that's something I have to do back at the house so try not to use it for another thirty minutes or so."

"Perfect. Thanks, man. I'll talk to you soon."

Anger zipped around my body as Preston hung up the phone. "You do realize they could have picked us up within an hour and dropped us off somewhere safe, right?"

"Never rely on others to get you where you want to go in life," Preston said, grinning. "Besides involving too many just complicates things."

"I hope I'm not part of that *too many* you refer to." I arched a brow and his smile widened.

"Even in the middle of nowhere as we're running for our lives, you manage to make me smile."

"At least I've proven my worth. So what's your plan? Getting somewhere far enough away on foot is going to be next to impossible," I said, shifting my weight from one soggy house slipper to the next.

"You're absolutely right," Preston said, a gleam of something in his eye.

"Good, I'm glad we can agree on that."

"There's a campground on the other side of the lake. We get there, borrow a car, maybe some clothes for you, and if that doesn't work, there are some tracks that follow along the edge about a mile away from the campground. Either way, we'll be covered."

"Great. So now we can let the feds add more to our ever-growing rap sheet?"

He chuckled slightly. "At this point, we might as well not worry about it."

"True. I guess grand theft auto and freight hopping sounds pretty harmless compared to murder, kidnapping, and arson."

He shook his head and gestured for me to

follow his lead.

We worked our way through the dense woods. The lake glimmered in the distance as we half-walked and jogged, dodging tree limbs, and thorny blackberry vines on our way to pick a victim.

Since our pace had slowed slightly, the chill began to work its way into my bones. I tried not to think about it, but the slippers were completely saturated, and my wet pajama bottoms clung to my skin. The thought of a car heater intrigued me and increased my pace as we worked our way through the thicket.

"I think the campground is only another ten minutes or so," he whispered. "With the time of year, I'm guessing it'll be filled with mostly RVs and trailers."

I nodded and kept pace with him, watching for a flicker of light up ahead. The snap of a twig made me jump, and we both quickly squatted as we searched the darkness behind. It wasn't until I saw a twitch of a tail that my pulse slowed to a normal pace.

"Just a raccoon," I whispered, my breath still a little shaky from nerves. "Enough of this. Let's hightail it to the campground."

I stood up and Preston followed, nodding. "Alright. You think you can handle a quicker pace again?" he asked.

"Completely. If it means getting in front of a heater."

"Let's do it. You set the pace, and I won't be far behind."

"You better keep up," I teased, already several steps in front of him.

The slippery ground was getting more difficult to navigate the heavier my slippers became, but I knew that soon I'd be able to dump them. I saw a soft glow in between the trees ahead, and a bit of excitement escaped my lips at the thought of getting to hide in a vehicle instead of these woods.

"See. There. Up ahead," Preston whispered, resting his hand on my shoulder as we came to a stop. "A trailer and a truck."

I couldn't help but smile as I thought about getting far away from here.

"How are we going to steal it without being heard?"

"Push it and hotwire it once we're out of earshot."

My heart hammered in my chest as I thought about how very close we were to being found. We were only one mistake away from being captured for crimes we didn't commit.

We slowly made our way into the campground, careful to step over the short concrete blocks that partitioned each campsite from one another. Most of the ground was slick mud, which made it extremely difficult to traverse in my slippers.

Preston motioned toward the rusty, blue truck, and we both walked quickly and quietly over to the hulk of metal that promised our escape. Preston slid his fingers along the door handle, and we were met with a quiet click of luck as the door opened and he slid in. Releasing the emergency brake, he popped the truck into neutral. I couldn't help but feel giddy inside as I watched our plan unfold flawlessly. Preston worked the steering wheel, but it didn't budge. There was no steering this thing. He caught my look and grinned just as he busted the steering column, freeing the wheel.

If my slippers weren't glued into the mud, I probably would've done a little hop in celebration. Preston slipped out of the driver's seat and motioned for me to take his place.

"I'll push. You steer."

I nodded, and he went behind the truck and began pushing the truck forward. The exhilaration ran through my veins at an unstoppable rate. The tires hit the concrete of the campground road, and I could literally taste our freedom. We were minutes away from getting to the highway and getting the hell out of here.

I glanced at Preston in the rearview mirror and smiled as he leaned into the truck, pushing the massive vehicle ahead.

It wasn't until the first shot rang out into the air, and someone racked their shotgun to reload that I realized our luck still hadn't changed. The truck began to slow, and I couldn't spot Preston in the rearview any longer. All I could do was silently pray that Preston wasn't hit.

"Get the hell out of my truck before this lead greets you in the ass," a gruff voice yelled, as the truck rolled to a stop.

Chapter Fourteen

I turned and looked through the back window. I saw Preston with his arms up, my heart steadying as I slid out of the truck. It didn't appear like he'd gotten hit. My eyes focused on the older man who was pointing the shotgun directly at me while I carefully walked over to Preston.

The man's eyes dropped to my pajamas and bewilderment flashed through his eyes before he brought his eyes back up to meet mine.

"What in the hell do you two think you're doing?" the man asked as he lowered his shotgun. "Have you been drinkin'?" His grey eyebrows furrowed as he shook his head; the barrel now pointing at the ground. "Think this type of thing is funny?"

"What's the racket about?" a woman asked, who was walking down the campground's main road in sweat pants, holding a glass of wine.

The man in front of us waved at her and laughed. "Nothing to see here. Just got overly excited about a raccoon."

It was killing me not to see Preston, gauge his thoughts on the matter, because I was beyond confused with the situation.

The woman laughed and turned around. "I should've known, you old coot. You're messing with my shows. Now I'm gonna have to go back and rewind so I can find out the ending."

The man chuckled and shook his head. "Exactly why I don't have television. Give me a good book any day and there's never any rewinding involved. So, you two, what's your story? Better give it to me quickly before I get tired of waiting."

My pulse quickened, and I glanced at Preston who took a step forward and extended his hand.

"My name's Preston and this is my girlfriend, Rebekah."

The older gentleman—I felt he certainly upgraded to gentleman status at this point—shook Preston's hand and my nerves settled slightly.

"The name's Ted."

"Well, we've gotten ourselves into a pickle."

A pickle? Preston could certainly schmooze with the best of them.

"In more ways then one, I imagine," Ted replied, a smirk appearing on his lips as he glanced at my Tic Tac pajamas again.

"We've been wrongly accused in a string of—"

Ted's hand flew up, palm out, and he shook

his head. "Say no more. Tell me you're innocent, and I'm not a man to question. Ever since the outbreak ended, people are getting thrown in institutions left and right for any kind of squeak that doesn't sit well with their neighbors. Not my cup of tea, if you ask me, but no one ever does."

A shiver ran through me, which Ted caught. "Why don't you two come inside and regroup."

I glanced at Preston and noticed the same hesitancy I was feeling.

"How about this. I'll go back inside my trailer, and after you discuss what you think you need to discuss, I'll open the door if I hear a knock."

I slowly nodded and Ted grinned in satisfaction. "Just know, if you try to steal my truck for a second time, I won't miss the shot next time around."

"Yes, sir," Preston said.

I watched Ted walk into the trailer and shut the door before I let out the air I'd been holding inside.

"Is our luck turning for the better?" I whispered.

"I doubt it, but it's nice that we happened to run into the one person on the planet who doesn't own a television."

I nodded at the same time another shiver ran through my system. The cold, wet pajamas were taking a toll, especially now that we weren't moving.

"Or it's a trap. Should we take off for the train?" I asked.

Preston ran his hands along my arms in an

effort to warm me up. "That's the only option we have left, but maybe we can go inside and see if he'd be willing to spare something to wear."

"I'd rather just wear these."

"Don't be ridiculous. You'll freeze to death, especially once we hop on the train. The wind will be a killer, regardless of what you're wearing. Something wet is just asking for trouble."

"How do you suppose we go about asking a perfect stranger for socks and—"

The trailer door opened and Ted dangled some clothes. "These trailer walls are a lot thinner than I'd like them to be..."

I couldn't hide my smile as the decision was made for us. I walked over to the entrance to the trailer and peeled off my sopping wet slippers that were completely caked in mud. I tossed them on the porch and heard a grunt from Ted.

"I wouldn't do that if I were you. If someone is looking for you, leaving something like that behind is a little too helpful, don't you think?" A sparkle in his eye told me this wasn't his first time around the block.

I picked up my soggy slippers and placed them in a plastic bag that Ted handed me so I didn't dirty his trailer. I stepped inside and immediately began to feel the warmth penetrate my skin. I began trembling as my body tried to reconcile the cold, wet clothing with the warm air. Preston closed the door and stepped inside the kitchen where we were standing.

The kitchen was tidy with every plate in its

place. The cupboards were knotty pine and the counters a polished grey stone of some sort. A doily sat atop the dining table, which was in the kitchen. Beyond the kitchen, sat a tweed couch with several crocheted pillows dotting the cushions. The trailer definitely had a woman's touch, but I didn't see any evidence of another person living with Ted beyond the décor.

"My wife did the decorating," Ted said, answering my unasked question. He handed me the clothes, which I'd assumed were his, until I took them from him. There was a woman's flannel shirt and jeans, along with a pair of wool socks. "They were my wife's."

"You can change in the bedroom down that way." Ted pointed over my shoulder down a narrow hall with wood paneling gracing the walls.

"Thanks." I glanced at Preston, who gave a slight nod, and I wandered down the tiny space.

I unfastened the door and slid through the opening where I was immediately confronted with a queen size mattress and not much space to change. The paisley quilt on the bed was frilly and pink, but what caught my eyes was the carpet square next to the bed that was turned slightly, the weave not quite matching.

Not my business.

I quickly traded my pajama bottoms for the jeans and the plaid flannel shirt for my pajama top. The moment I slid the wool socks on I felt immediately warmer, which allowed my mind to get a better grasp on the situation at hand. We

KARICE BOLTON

were holed up in a stranger's trailer, making ourselves an easy target for him or anyone to turn us in or be captured by the authorities.

I opened the door, pajamas in hand, to see Preston sipping from a mug as he listened intently to Ted. Preston gestured for me to join him on the couch as Ted offered me a cup of coffee, which I greedily accepted.

"Ted belongs to a network that keeps tabs on the MHA and other government facilities," Preston began. "He lost his wife to the agency."

"How can he keep tabs if he doesn't even have a television?" I asked, casting a dubious look toward Ted.

"Please." Ted threw his hands at us and laughed. "Television is the government's best tool for deceit, and it's only used when they want the news channels to cover some hot topic. You won't catch me getting my news from those places."

"Then how do you find out what's going on?" I asked, taking a seat on the couch.

"You connect with the right people and eventually a web of truth begins to emerge," he answered. "A network is established. You really ought to think about joining one."

"Was your wife involved in the network?" Preston asked.

"Heavens no." He shook his head and a feeble smile canvased his mouth. "Sheila was strong headed, a person with a mission and a mouth to use as she saw fit."

"Seems logical enough to me." I smiled.

"Well, a few of our neighbors in Montana certainly didn't like what my wife had to say, and they turned her in. I was helpless. There was nothing I could do once the train started rolling. In hindsight, I'm surprised I didn't get thrown in with her. I wish I had." The sadness in his eyes made my heart tear in half. Judging by his age, I'd guess the couple had been together more than half of their lives, maybe more.

I nodded. "That seemed to happen to a lot of people."

"Is that who's after you?" Ted asked, his brow arching.

"No. It's a little more complicated than that," I said, feeling my pulse begin to race again at the thought of staying here too long.

"I'm sure they'd love to get their hands on us too," Preston laughed, and stood up, outstretching his arm. "We sure appreciate your hospitality, but we don't want to press our luck or yours."

"No trouble at all. You two remind me of my wife and me, years ago, of course."

My body tensed, unable to understand where this was all going.

"Tell me this..." Ted paused and took a swallow of his coffee. "You're fighting for something aren't you? You know something that needs to be known."

"How do you figure?" I asked, narrowing my eyes.

"I've heard about a group who discovered information that's said to change the course of our existence. I don't know what that information is, but my hunch is that you two do. Is that the case?"

I nodded. "Yes. That's very much the case."

"By the look in your eyes, I can tell I don't want to know what you know. I don't want that burden. I'm too old..." Ted's voice trailed off and he shook his head. "Hell of a time to exist."

"If we can call it that," Preston laughed, as he wiped his hand along his jeans.

"My thoughts exactly," Ted agreed.

A low steady beat in the distance prompted me to take Preston's hand and squeeze it.

"Do you hear that?" I asked, standing up slowly with Preston.

"It's a chopper. Slow and steady," Ted replied, pressing his lips together. "I think my humble little abode is about to get some visitors."

"I'm so sorry. I, we—"

Ted's eyes glinted with some sort of satisfaction and he smiled. "Anything that's got the feds on your ass like this has got to be something worth saving. Nothing to apologize for."

The sound of blades whooshing through the air rattled the trailer walls as it approached.

Ted opened a drawer and handed us two pistols and a pocketknife, along with a card.

"In my bedroom, there's a floor panel you can remove. It leads to a tunnel and a way out. Call the number on that card and tell them Ted sent you. They'll help you with whatever you need. You can count on it. Some of us remember what it was like before the outbreak, and those that do want to get back to that time. The future of our country is at stake." He reached for his shotgun and smiled with a wily expression sitting behind his eyes.

I didn't know what he was going to do or why he was going to do it, but the beating of the chopper blades overhead seemed to give him the opportunity he'd been waiting for.

"My wife's name is Sheila Benson. When you find her, tell her I'll be waiting."

I was frozen in place as the impact of Ted's statement washed over me. Preston nearly dragged me down the hall and into the bedroom. He glanced around the room, looking for the opening, as I watched Ted pick up a grenade from the drawer and grip it tightly as he stood fearless in the kitchen.

"Over there." I pointed at the section that had caught my attention earlier.

Preston nodded and tugged on the trap door, opening it as wide as it would go. "Get in. Quick," he directed.

"You've got three minutes," Ted said, barely glancing in our direction.

I stayed in a daze, unable to resolve the fight going on in my head about Ted. Preston clutched my upper arm and shoved me down the opening. "Sorry, but we don't have time." His abruptness woke me up to the seriousness of the situation, and I quickly got my wits about me.

My feet found the wooden ladder, which I climbed down, relieved to meet the dirt floor of the tunnel. The little bit of light from above revealed a shelf with several flashlights and other survival equipment that might prove useful. I tied each of the legs of my pajamas together and began dumping matches, lanterns, MREs, rope, and anything else I could fit in. Preston's feet rested on the lower slat as he closed the trap door, and I tied one last big knot using the legs of my pajama bottoms.

I turned on a flashlight and handed it to Preston.

"I made a bag out of my pajamas bottoms and filled it up. See anything else we need?" I asked, as he scanned the shelves with the light.

"Not a thing, but we've got to get out of here."

The whooshing of the chopper blades now sounded like a drumming as it hovered directly above the trailer.

Heaving the pajamas over my shoulders, I took off running down the dirt tunnel, following the glow of Preston's flashlight as we wound deeper underground. Mere seconds went by before we heard the explosion. Ted had pulled the pin.

The sound of dirt crumbling and rocks tumbling behind us made us run faster into the unknown darkness ahead, and neither of us wanted to look back.

Chapter Fifteen

"End of the road," Preston muttered.

Preston climbed the ladder and nudged the top open. He stuck his head out the hole and then ducked back down.

"Looks clear. This opens into the middle of the woods."

"Really? I thought it might pop up in a house or something."

The phone in Preston's pocket buzzed again, and he shook his head. "No such luck, but the important thing is that the tunnel got us away."

Preston climbed out through the hole and reached his hands down to bring up my makeshift bag. I quickly climbed the steps and was relieved the moment I pulled my legs out of the hole.

I attempted to shake off the dismal feeling that settled over me, but it had no intention of leaving as I glanced around the forest. The ladder led to temporary freedom, but it carried a heavy burden. An innocent stranger took his own life because of a cause he'd only vaguely heard about. It made me doubt the importance of the cause. Was it even a cause?

"I'm sure the explosion covered up the entrance to the hole or at least I hope it did," I said, a lump forming in my throat as I thought of Ted.

Preston nodded and placed the lid back over the tunnel and tapped down soil, leaves, and rocks to get it to blend in again with the rest of the forest floor before he looked over at me. Our pursuit to stop the creation of modifieds had turned into something bigger for me. It was impossible to reconcile what Ted just did on our behalf. It made me wonder what kind of rumors were circulating through these other networks and groups of people and if they were even half accurate.

My head was cloudy, and we hadn't even begun to fight for our innocence. The more blood that covered my hands made me forever bound to this new life on the run, and I didn't want to see other lives tangled in the mess.

"I don't want more innocent people to die," I whispered.

We started walking through the brush when his phone buzzed again, but he pressed ignore this time rather than letting it ring to voicemail.

"That's one of the things that separates us from TRAC. They don't care about that. We do," he replied. Preston placed the bag over his shoulder, and we took off at a brisk pace.

I glimpsed a roof through the trees and tapped on Preston.

"Check it out," I said, pointing in the general direction.

My socks were once again drenched and tiny twigs and thorns made their way through the wool, poking and ripping at my skin. The thought of getting to regroup, even if only for a few minutes, energized me.

"Seems promising," Preston replied.

As we approached the cabin, it was clear it hadn't been used in a long time, possibly since the outbreak. The front window was shattered, but the front door looked solid.

"If anyone's inside, my guess is that they have as little desire to be found as we do."

Preston chuckled and nodded. "I don't see many law-abiding citizens wanting to call this place home."

The stain was worn on the siding of the cabin, and the splintered frames barely held the windows in place. I tapped the first step with my foot and the wood crumbled away. Preston kicked the other two steps away and climbed onto the stoop. He leaned over and reached for my hand, hauling me up the rest of the way. I tried the door handle, which was locked. Preston leaned his shoulders into the wood and pushed hard enough to break through.

We both turned on our flashlights and scoped out the room in front of us. The elements had wreaked havoc on the cabin. A couple of grimy animal mounts hung on the wall over what I assumed was once the fireplace. All that remained was a pile of rubble and torn drywall. The level of decay in the home gave me the creeps, or maybe it was the two deer heads staring at me anywhere I moved.

"I bet this was someone's old hunting cabin before that campground even came into existence," Preston said.

"What makes you think that?" I teased.

He laughed and nodded. "What can I say? I'm exhausted, and my usual witty comments just aren't rolling out like they usually do."

The floor creaked with my weight, and a shudder ran through me at the symphony below my feet. A brown couch sat against the far wall, and a coffee table lay smashed in the middle of the floor. As we continued studying the cabin, our flashlight beams captured the dust particles dancing in the air. It had to have been ages since someone actually inhabited this place.

I walked into the kitchen where a metal table had been knocked on its side. A couple of chairs with missing legs were scattered around the space, which led me to believe that at least one zombie attack had happened between these walls.

There was an antique stove, next to a fridge of the same age and caliber. The rust streaks added quite a dramatic flare. I frowned and turned to face Preston. "You know. I don't think we should stay here for the night."

He nodded. "I tend to agree. My guess is the tunnel entrance is long gone but why risk it?"

"My thoughts exactly, but where do you propose we go? My socks are already soaked and I'm freezing. Believe me, I'll do what it takes to stay out of their hands, but it's going to be a miserable go. I'd kind of like to wrap my head around our destination so I can focus on that instead of my frozen toes." I leaned against a wall and tore my left sock off, wringing it out, before sliding it back on and doing the same to the other foot.

Preston flashed his light to the ever-growing puddle of water from my socks and nodded, glancing at his cell phone. "Fourteen missed calls from Braden."

"You might want to answer the next one."

"I will. According to the GPS the tunnel led us near the train tracks. I say we go with the original plan. Take the train up north, which will get us close enough to my underground place. There'll be a hike, but it won't be at a quick pace."

I nodded. "Might as well get a move on. Who knows how long we'll have to wait for a freight train to pass."

I mindlessly opened a drawer, hoping to find a knife, and almost fell over when a mouse scurried out. "Shit."

Preston chuckled and whipped his light over to me. "Not what you were hoping to find?"

A shiver ran through me and I laughed. "Definitely not. No more snooping for me."

I walked past Preston and out the door as his phone buzzed again. "Might as well get that," I told him, jumping down from the stoop.

"Your socks just left a trail out the door. It's like following *Casper the Friendly Ghost*."

I laughed and heard Preston answer the

phone. He didn't seem the least bit tired whereas I was completely exhausted, every muscle fatigued and every nerve on end.

"Braden, what's up?" Preston asked, putting the phone on speaker. He crawled down and stood next to me.

"Thank God. Emily and I didn't want to believe it."

"Believe what?" Preston asked.

I moved closer to Preston, listening intently. Braden's breathing was heavy, and I heard Emily talking softly in the background, but I couldn't make out what she said.

"The news shows a trailer completely engulfed in flames. They're reporting that the two fugitives have been killed... that you two were in that fire," Braden answered. "Were you guys even there? What would make them think that's where you were hiding?"

I shivered from the breeze that picked up, and Preston placed the bag on the ground and wrapped his free arm around me. Feeling the warmth roll off his body made me wish myself into another time and place, away from all the worries.

"We were there..." my voice trailed off. I looked at Preston, waiting for some sort of acknowledgment that he was willing to trust Braden. He gave a slight nod. "Someone helped us escape from the trailer before it went up in flames, but he didn't make it. Ted was his name."

"They're showing how they tracked them down," Emily muttered in the background.

"Looks like they used dogs."

"That's odd. We never heard any," I said.

"They're showing overhead footage of where the trailer was. There's just about nothing left," Emily informed us.

"The chopper belonged to a news crew?" I wondered aloud. "Not the military?"

"Sounds like it," Preston replied. "But who knows."

A shiver ran up my spine, but this time it wasn't because I was cold.

I shook my head and glanced at Preston. "It doesn't make sense. None of this makes sense. If dogs had been on our tail, no pun intended, they would've caught up to us. We would've heard them, and they would have gotten to us while we were futzing around with the truck. The feds knew where we were going."

"That's impossible. We didn't even know where we were going." Preston bit his lip and looked toward where we came from.

I leaned against the cabin, thinking about that missing piece that was eating away at me. It was one of those thoughts that wouldn't fully formulate. Instead, the thought would tease me—come and go—before I had a chance to completely grasp it.

"I hope you're far away from the scene because it's crawling with all kinds of officials," Emily said, obviously still watching everything unfold.

"I bet it is," I sighed.

"Where are you headed for the night?" Braden

asked.

I heard the background noise on the cellphone change and wondered what was going on at the house.

"Planning on going to a hideout that's been in the family," Preston replied.

I clicked my tongue against the roof of my mouth as I analyzed what my mind was trying to weave together. Preston inclined his head slightly and smiled as this newly discovered habit exposed itself.

I rolled my eyes and stopped the clicking, but he continued to smile.

"I figured it out."

"Figured what out?" he asked.

"What's been bothering me. It's not just the location of the trailer," I began.

"Wow. They just arrested a girl…"

My heart stopped and my mind raced. "What does she look like?"

"Really pretty. Blond, wavy hair and it looks like they've got a guy in the back of a black sedan."

The government had been helped out all along.

I heard the sound of a car door slamming over the speakerphone and looked over at Preston.

"Are you guys going somewhere?" I asked.

"We're on our way to pick you up. Wherever that is," Emily replied.

"That's a really bad idea," I said. "Listen, not only did the officials know to find us at the trailer, they knew when both Preston and I were at my house. Before that they knew when we were at the coffee house. They're tracking us. Somehow they're tracking us..."

"How's that possible?" Emily asked. "They think you're dead. I doubt they're tracking you now or they'd find you."

I was quiet as I mulled over exactly how to approach the thoughts that were colliding in my mind.

"The one constant factor in this whole mess has been TRAC. It was never the government, not until today." My heart raced as the clues started connecting. "We all know Preston and I were set up, but that doesn't happen overnight. Think about it. Everywhere we've been, TRAC hasn't been far behind. We went to the woods, stumbled upon that community, and then boom—TRAC was there hours later and scooped it up. On our way to the pit, a horde of undead magically appeared on the road at the exact moment we were driving down it. TRAC has been setting us up, and we've been falling perfectly into their plan."

"But how would they be able to track you?" Emily asked.

"And if they're able to track us, they'd know we're alive right now, not buried in the ashes," Preston countered, not buying my line of reasoning yet.

A shudder passed through my body as the answer slid into place so effortlessly.

"Because it's a game to them, and we've become the pawns," I whispered, upset I hadn't seen it sooner. "TRAC is letting us go tonight because they've had their fun with us for the moment. They've been feeding our whereabouts to the feds just like they handed the list of crimes we allegedly committed to them. It got the heat off them. TRAC's up to something big, and we must be the only ones who are close to figuring out what it is." I took a step back from Preston as his arm dropped away.

I stood reeling as my mind placed things together, and it all started the moment Gavin was stolen from me. That was the day I'd become a player in a game I didn't even know existed.

"But how are they tracking us?" Preston asked, linking his hands behind his head.

"When they captured us, we removed those red, blinking lights that were just under the surface of our skin..." my voice trailed off.

"There was more to the tracker than just that device. We left the important part in our body." Preston's jaw twitched as both our minds rewound to everywhere, everything we'd seen since we'd been tagged.

"They know exactly where we've been and what we've seen." I shook my head.

"Then why not just kill us?" he asked.

"Maybe we have something they want." I crossed my arms and sighed.

"Or it's just a sick game," Braden offered.

"Either way it makes me so angry that I'm actually grateful that they're finished with us for the night," I said, my tone not even half as bitter as I felt. My body didn't even feel like my own as

I stood hugging myself, knowing I had something inside of me.

"Well, that solves it then," Emily said, jarring me out of my downward spiral.

"Solves what?" Preston asked.

"If TRAC has been tracking you this entire time, there's no reason why we can't pick you up and bring you back. No matter where you go, they can find you."

She had a point.

"Thanks for the uplifting thought," I laughed.

"Believe me. That's one of the most uplifting ones I have at the moment," Emily replied. "So, where are you at? Is there a road close to you?"

Preston proceeded to tell them where we'd be waiting. It was close to the tracks that we'd planned on heading toward. I was lost in my world, feeling violated in a way that I'd never imagined, wondering if there was a way to make it stop. I felt a lump form in the back of my throat and pushed it down. I wasn't going to let TRAC weaken me. I refused to fall into their hands.

"See you soon." Preston hung up the phone and picked up the bag. "You think you're ready? They'll probably be there in thirty minutes or so."

I nodded, hoping to shake myself out of a mood.

"I was kind of looking forward to riding the rails with you," he said, smiling.

"The one and only time I tried it things didn't go well," I admitted. "It was toward the end of the outbreak when all the military convoys began delivering the vaccines. We didn't know that was going on, but the train was headed in the right direction so Gavin explained how we should do it. I fell flat on my face while he managed to stick his jump. He hauled me up, but I was pretty beat up."

Preston twisted his mouth and let out some air. "Sounds like a good thing we aren't relying on that form of transportation after all." He opened up his map app and calculated the direction we needed to go.

"I'd like to think I've gained some skills," I laughed.

"No doubt you have." He flashed me a wicked smile, and I had to look away.

"Off we go," I said, pulling the bag away from him. "I want you to have easy access to your pistol. I'm too tired to be accurate."

"All right," Preston said, his pace matching mine.

"You doing okay?" I asked. "It's been pretty nonstop and we haven't gotten to talk about things."

"What *things* in particular?" he asked.

We maneuvered through the trees quickly and quietly. Only the occasional snap of a twig to give our location away.

"Your mom..."

Preston sighed and was silent for a few seconds as we continued our pace. "I'm adjusting to the idea that my mom is alive, but in what capacity? And there's nothing I can do about it now." He stopped walking and turned to look at me. "If ever. What Ted said about his wife hit home and made me realize that regardless of who took over MHA or even if it's overhauled someday, there's a high probability that the damage done is permanent. The patients might never be right. My mom might never be right."

I nodded. "I'm so sorry for going behind your back and asking Jeffrey..."

He tipped my chin up slightly, his eyes steadying on mine. "Don't be sorry. It's something I needed to know. In an odd way it gave me incentive. I just didn't expect to have the shit hit the fan before I completely absorbed it."

His gaze dipped. I wanted to comfort him, and tell him everything would be fine, but I didn't know if it would be.

"Are you tired at all?" Preston asked.

"I think I'm so wired that even if I had three layers of goose down to dive into, I wouldn't be able to sleep. I know I need it, but I think it's going to take days for me to come down from this. Whatever this is. Not to mention I feel extremely squeamish knowing that there's something inside of me transmitting my whereabouts and who knows what else."

I heard a skitter across leaves to my left and flashed my light to catch a possum climbing a maple.

"I know the feeling." Preston glanced at his phone again. "We head east and then we should reach the road."

As we walked along our route, the woods thinned out and the moonlight lit our way.

Graceful ferns had exchanged for tall, bowing grass as we approached the pasture. A tinge of excitement ran through me at the thought of getting far away from where we were, far away from civilization. However, it was met quickly with the realization that no matter how far we ran, we could be found, but in a way it was almost freeing. There was no guesswork involved. They had the upper hand right now, and it motivated me to get that changed.

"Ready for a jog?" Preston asked.

"Sure." The grass felt so much better on my feet than the sticker bushes and twigs as I ran through the field and up a small knoll before coming to the two-lane road.

I followed his gaze and saw the small train crossing to the north. There was a single light but no gate.

"That's where they should be."

I sat down on the crumbling asphalt and moved the flashlight to my socks, which were filled with thorns and twigs. I began picking the blackberry thorns out of my foot and cringed when I'd find another that had embedded deep into my flesh.

"You know what just occurred to me," I began.

"What's that?"

"The fire we escaped..."

"What about it?"

"When we used those towels saturated in that circulated liquid that came from the undead we—"

"Never got burned," Preston finished, shaking

his head in disbelief.

"We should have had some sort of burns, our lungs should've needed some oxygen..."

"And Izzy didn't have a scratch. She had to have faced the flames to even get the hose through there to extinguish the fire."

Preston nodded.

"We were so wrapped up in getting out of the flames, we didn't even stop to notice that a wet towel couldn't have saved us like that."

"But a towel dipped in something that TRAC was willing to kill for certainly might." His eyes stayed on mine.

I nodded and smiled. "We need to find Dr. Falino. She might be our answer for getting Braden to walk again, and that's just the beginning. I don't even think that would've occurred to me if it weren't for these wet socks," I concluded.

"Well, that's certainly a glass half-full way of looking at tonight's events," Preston grinned.

"The other hasn't really worked for me lately so I think I'm going to switch it up a bit," I laughed. "There's got to be something good that will come out of this. I firmly believe we can make that happen."

A set of headlights that matched Emily and Braden's car barreled down the road. I held my arms up, and Preston grabbed my hands and hoisted me up. Our eyes met, and I felt that familiar sensation of excitement run through us as we became one step closer to getting where we needed to go; even though neither of us knew where that was.

Chapter Sixteen

"Do you want to catch some sleep?" Preston asked.

My elbows dug into my knees as I leaned over and cupped a mug full of coffee. I was grateful to be warm again. The television was on, and it was hard to take my eyes away from the reporter broadcasting in front of a burned shell of the trailer. A glimpse of Ted's truck stuck out from behind the reporter, and pictures of Preston and me were in the bottom of the screen showing as deceased.

"I can't." I shook my head. "There's too much to do. Besides, knowing that TRAC could arrive any second isn't what I'd call relaxing. Keeps a person on edge." I looked up at Preston. His gaze was intense, protective.

He nodded and remained standing in front of me; his arms folded on his chest. "I get it. But we're both going to have to sleep at some point.

Besides, apparently they could've crushed us long ago." A sardonic grin spread across his lips, which was irresistible.

"Bugs to be crushed," I said, shaking my head. "We're going to have to change that."

Preston kneeled down, his gaze on mine. "Once and for all."

"I feel so exposed...so violated, actually. It's hard to focus when all I can think about is being watched. It's paralyzing. It's disgusting. I've read about the nano-surveillance technology, but I never imagined I'd had something like it inserted into my body." I placed my mug of coffee down, and Preston laid his hand on my leg, squeezing gently. "I thought we'd gotten it out..."

"Braden's got a guy coming over who'll be able to tell us what we're dealing with. We don't want to jump the gun, let our imaginations get ahead of..." Preston stopped himself and dug his hands through his hair. "Who am I kidding? It's taken all the control I have not to start cutting and digging out my skin where that monitor was inserted." The anger in his voice matched mine, and I nodded, sliding back into the couch.

Preston stood up and slumped onto the couch next to me. "This'll just become one of the many bad memories that we'll be able to forget someday, maybe even laugh about."

I turned to face him, sliding a leg under my body. "The old remember when routine?" I laughed and shook my head. "Do you really believe that someday this will be over?" My eyes dipped to the space between us on the couch, and my body ached to be held, to be touched.

Raising my chin with his fingertips, he nodded. "Not only will it be over, the world will be a better place."

"Do you think we'll be alive to see it?" The question rolled out before I had a chance to stop it, but it was something I'd been asking myself a lot lately.

"I believe we will or I wouldn't bother," he laughed, and his fingers ran along my jaw down to my neck.

A slight tremble moved through me as his fingers continued to slide along my flesh, leaving a wave of goose bumps in its wake.

"So can we trust the guy that Braden has coming over?" I asked, trying to distract myself.

"I don't think we can afford not to," Preston said, his expression darkening as my body responded to his touch.

The gap between us had narrowed, and an overwhelming desire to be held in his arms began to consume me. My gaze ran along the corded muscles of his forearms, and it created an almost intoxicating experience as I imagined my hands running lengthways against his arms to his shoulders and down his chest.

It had been so long since I'd had human touch like that. My cheeks warmed, and I was certain my most private thoughts had become public as he continued to respond.

Preston leaned over, his lips scraping my ear as his mouth parted. A surge of desire ran through me, and I realized how much I desperately wanted Preston. He understood me. He got me like no one ever had, and he never asked me to apologize for being myself.

"You're a beautiful woman, Rebekah. The most beautiful I've ever come across." Hearing him say my name made my body shudder. The partnership we'd built had saved us both countless times, and now we were about to begin the fight of our lives.

But all of our history brought us to this point; this moment in time when all I could think of was his hands caressing my body as I entwined my fingers through his hair. It was true that times of desperation brought heightened awareness and emotions, but I wasn't desperate. For once in my life, I was clearheaded. I knew what I wanted in this world and it was to love again.

Preston moved his lips slowly down my throat, and my body reacted exactly how I'd predicted. I wanted more. My hands ran along his bare arms as he placed gentle kisses along my neck. A low moan escaped my lips, and I felt his mouth curve slightly in appreciation.

I ran my fingers through his hair as my head dipped back, allowing his lips to tease as my body trembled with wanting.

His lips broke free from my throat and a wave of disappointment washed through me. Our eyes connected, but this time a new connection had formed, one that I deeply wanted to explore. Now.

"Sorry," Preston murmured, "but it sounds

like Braden's coming."

I snapped to, not realizing how wrapped up I'd been with Preston's touch. I drew in a shaky breath and nodded, a smile touching his lips as he realized just how wrecked I'd become.

I straightened my shirt and sat back, hiding a private smile as I let myself enjoy what had just happened.

"Paul will be here shortly," Braden announced.

"And he'll be able to get it out, whatever it is?" I asked.

Braden shook his head. "No. Unfortunately, he'll just be able to tell us what type of tracking device you have inside. Once we know that, then we can figure out what we have to do to get it out of you guys."

My stomach knotted at the thought of having to spend even more time with the device inside of me, but it wasn't Braden's fault. He'd done an amazing job of finding the help we needed.

"Thanks for helping. It pays to know a techie," I laughed, allowing myself to feel slightly more at ease. Preston was right. If TRAC really has been able to track our movements for so long, there's a reason they haven't taken us out. Shoot! They could've swooped in at the cabin and taken us down since the government was busy at the trailer site. There was a reason they didn't, and I was very interested in finding out what that reason was.

"No sweat. It's what we do. It's how we'll beat these bastards."

Preston nodded. "We have a good team. You know, we might even have a bigger team if what Ted told us was true."

"Which was what?" Braden asked. He rolled his wheelchair to the end of the coffee table.

Preston snaked his fingers into his pocket and pulled out a card. We'd already filled in Emily and Braden on how we managed to survive the wrong end of Ted's shotgun barrel, but we hadn't said much more.

"Ted Benson and a Jack Snedan. Do you think you can research those two? Ted alluded to another network that he was involved in and gave us this other guy's name if we needed help. He said he'd heard about a cause, our cause. I want to find out what's being said, what the rumors are. It would be interesting to hear what's circulating about what we're investigating."

"We can manage that," Braden responded. "We've been hearing murmurs of other groups popping up as well, but I didn't follow up. Had no reason to until now."

"Ted apparently felt whatever it was he heard was important enough to die for."

"If these other groups are legitimate, we might have a lot of untapped potential on our side," I said. "Or a lot more people to worry about. Either way, we need to know what we're dealing with. I want to find out if they've heard about the modified zombies or if they have learned about the possible healing factor that these modifieds might produce. We didn't have time to find out from Ted."

"Sounds promising. We'll get right on it," Braden replied.

"And how are the rumors getting out?" Preston asked, his hand settling on my knee.

"No kidding. I know I haven't said a word," I said, glancing at Braden who agreed.

"It's not from Emily or me either, and I doubt her sister or sister's boyfriend said a thing. What happened to Izzy freaked them out too much. They're hiding; waiting for an explanation that won't put any of them in harm's way."

"Let's hope we can provide that soon," I replied.

Braden nodded just as Emily poked her head into the family room. "Looks like Paul's already here. I saw his vehicle coming down the drive."

I let out a breath and nodded. "Let's hope for some good news."

Emily smiled and took off toward the front door. Before Paul had a chance to knock on the door, we heard Emily greeting him and offering him beverages. My heart started beating quickly as I heard his footsteps get closer. I was placing so much hope on this guy. I wanted an easy fix— a quick fix—to get whatever this was in my body, out.

Emily led him into the family room, and Preston and I both stood up and greeted him. Paul was in his fifties, and he appeared rather professorially dressed. He held onto his briefcase tightly and studied the room. Round, wire-framed glasses sat high on his nose, and he wore a black trench coat that was buttoned one off. I liked him already.

"Glad to meet you," Paul said, shaking my hand. "I've heard a lot about you."

I laughed. "I didn't think there was that much to be said."

He arched a brow and glanced at Braden who grinned. "Told ya."

Paul looked amused while he searched for a place to set down his briefcase, settling on the coffee table. "I've always liked this little invention of yours, Braden. Very creative."

I smiled as Paul unclicked his briefcase and opened it up. There were all kinds of gadgets that I didn't recognize sitting inside.

"My hunch is that they didn't use an X1 tracer on you, but since that's the easiest one to detect and remove, we might as well check for it," he said, removing a small unit, the size of a breath mint box, and attached two wires to it. He placed two rectangular pads to the ends of the wires and glanced at Preston and then me. "Who'd like to lend me their entry point?"

I had to laugh at the technicality of it and nodded. "Fine with me."

"I got this," Preston said, waving my hand away from my sleeve.

"No. No. I've got it," I laughed, knowing full well the idea of seeing him work the waist of his pants down wouldn't be a good idea.

I turned over my arm and Paul stuck the two rectangular pads onto my skin and pressed a button on the unit. The sensation of needle pricks radiated under the pads. It wasn't painful, but it wasn't comfortable either. Paul stared at the unit he held in his hand until it beeped about a minute later.

"Like I thought. It's not an X1. Too bad, though. That's an easy one to get rid of." He removed the pads from my skin and tucked the equipment back in his briefcase.

The next piece of equipment he removed was larger and looked far more invasive. I glanced nervously at Preston and smiled. "Maybe it's your turn," I laughed.

His hands moved toward his jeans' button and I shook my head. "Never mind."

"This isn't bad. It looks worse than it is. The first detection system was used to see if there was anything that had attached itself to your nervous system. This piece of equipment will tell us if there's an electromagnetic tracking device in you. Basically, this is a big magnet, and it will respond to similar material if it's inside you."

I let out a deep breath and nodded.

He flipped on the device, and as it powered up, he watched Preston. "I hope it's not this one. It can be hard to remove. The devices often imbed themselves deep within the muscle tissue."

My pulse raced with the revelation.

"The problem with the technology now, is that these devices can grow and multiply as if they're living organisms. There's no such thing as inanimate objects any more in the spy game." He stopped himself. "Well, that's not entirely true, but quite often it's the case."

Preston let out a deep breath and reached for my hand. I intertwined my fingers with his and watched as Paul began to move the block along my arm up and down. I didn't feel anything, and my gut told me I would if it had been inside, but I couldn't know for sure. Paul continued to run the heavy block up and down my arm before finally shaking his head.

"Not this either," he sighed, sitting with the block in his hands.

"So what does that mean?" I asked.

"It means there are a few more we can test for," he set the piece of equipment back in his briefcase and mulled something over as he glanced at some other items in his briefcase. Paul grabbed a pair of rubber gloves, and I looked over at Preston as I tapped down the fear that was rising pretty quickly. Paul picked up a small white pouch, about the size and shape of a syringe, and ripped off the top. He reached for a small testing square and set it on the table.

"This will be a quick prick," Paul assured, working the syringe out of the pack.

"You think it could be a blood—"

"Need to check all the options," Paul interrupted as he grabbed my index finger and pricked it quickly. He then dispensed the drop of blood onto the square. I was mesmerized as I watched the red liquid spread into the fibers.

We stared at the piece of fabric not knowing what to look for. After a few minutes Paul let out a deep breath and looked over at Braden. "We found the culprit, and it's tricky."

Not what I wanted to hear.

"It's a hemotracker," Paul said, pressing his lips together.

"Is there a way to get it out? To make it stop?" I asked, the pounding of my heart echoing through my ears. I felt lightheaded as I sat there, Preston's hand in mine. I had something pumping through my veins, through my heart. I no longer felt only human. I'd been manipulated, modified. I glanced at Preston and noticed his jaw twitch as he glanced at Braden.

"There is," Paul said. "But it's not without risk."

"I would gladly face any risk to get it out of me," I muttered, as the anger ripped through my soul.

"We both would," Preston confirmed, squeezing my hand.

"Do you have the technology to do it?" I asked.

Paul shook his head. "No, but it won't be hard to get our hands on it. The technology was developed long before the outbreak. Portable devices were even manufactured."

"What kind of machine can do this?" Preston asked.

"They developed a portable machine that's a cross between hemodialysis and an ECMO. They produced them in the thousands when the swine flu pandemic occurred."

"I'm sorry. What's an ECMO?" I interrupted.

"It stands for Extracorporeal Membrane Oxygenation. It was invented to take over the work of the lungs and, in some cases, the heart for babies and children who are very, very ill. Doctors also realized the machine offered benefits to adults who were sick as well. It was used during the swine flu pandemic first. Then they tried it in the early stages of the outbreak before they realized that the patients would turn into zombies."

"And the hemodialysis is what... like a dialysis machine?" Preston asked.

Paul nodded. "In its initial use, yes. But researchers realized that by possibly combining two treatments, a new machine could be far more versatile. Scientists wanted a way to capture foreign bodies in the blood and essentially filter the blood like a hemodialysis machine while offering the oxygen benefits of the ECMO. Rather than take over the functions of a kidney, this machine filters for foreign bodies that aren't recognizable based on what is programmed into the machine beforehand. There are different filters that can be used to capture the different foreign bodies. Whether it's a virus, bacteria, fungus, or something else, the filter catches it and clean blood is pushed back into the body."

"Sounds dangerous," Braden said.

"It's not without its risks," Paul confirmed. "Think about the DRBs back in the day. The Designer Red Blood Cells that researchers engineered in order to deliver targeted cancer treatments kicked off this idea. It's like taking the idea of DRBs and reversing it. Essentially these machines are able to capture the blood cells that carry the foreign bodies and strip them away before delivering clean blood back to the patient. In this case, you." Paul's eyes darted between us both. "Anytime we ask the body to operate with the help of outside machines, things can go wrong."

"But what else can we do? If these tracking devices are part of the very blood we pump through our system, I'd rather..." I didn't finish my sentence.

"Because this is so taxing on the body and most often the patient has already been quite ill, the doctors realized that adding the benefits of an ECMO machine would buy the patient time by pushing oxygen back into the blood, while the hemodialysis machine filtered the blood. This combining of machines saved millions of lives."

"I feel like there's a catch," I said, my eyes falling to Preston's.

Paul nodded. "No doubt. There's a catch."

"Since we don't exactly know which protein is being used to carry the tracker, there's a high chance that one of you will have to endure the process multiple times with different filters. The risk can be death."

"I'll be the guinea pig," Preston said, before even a second passed.

I turned to him, my brows furrowed, as I shook my head quickly. "That's ridiculous. I'm doing it."

Preston's forehead wrinkled as he glanced at Braden. "Sorry. Not going to happen," Preston said, bringing his gaze back to mine. "How fast can we get the machine here?"

My body cranked out a mixture of anger and fear as I stared at Preston. I hated being overruled and wasn't about to let it go down like this. I turned to Paul. "Yes, how long will it take before I can plug into it?"

Paul bit his lip. "I've never seen two people more—"

"Determined," Emily said, laughing, as she brought in a tray with some more coffee and a few cookies. "We just like to call it determined."

"We should be able to get the machine here by tomorrow. I can probably arrange to pick one up tomorrow morning," Paul replied. "But the one thing you need to do is get some rest... whichever one of you decides to do it. If your body is worn down, it increases the risk of infection and all kinds of things. This is serious."

I nodded, feeling Preston watching me. "We'll be sure to sleep. Thank you for your help." I stood up and shook Paul's hand.

"No. Thank you for what you're about to do. We can't let these creatures be used as weapons. Our world will never be the same if we don't stop TRAC, if we don't stop their modifieds," Paul said, now shaking Preston's hand. "I'll see you tomorrow. I can let myself out."

I watched Paul leave, briefcase in hand, and wondered how in the world I was going to convince Preston that it was going to be me hooked up to that machine tomorrow.

Chapter Seventeen

I woke up to Preston shaking my leg. "Get up."

I groggily studied the clock. Five hours of sleep. I guess that would have to do. It was more rest than I'd gotten in a while. I sat up, trying to focus my eyes when I saw the panic etched on Preston's face.

I threw the comforter off my body and shot out of bed. "What's going on?"

Preston was dressed in jeans and a Henley. A knit cap was pulled down around his ears, and he was holding a rifle.

"TRAC's screwing with us again." He walked over to my bedroom window and shoved the curtains aside. "Emily picked up their movements around the edge of the property."

"TRAC members?" I asked, slipping my feet into a pair of Converse. I tied them quickly and walked over to the window.

He shook his head. "Undead. And for sure

some are modifieds. Too deliberate with their movements not to be."

My heart hammered in my chest as my eyes landed on the first group of slow, stumbling creatures walking across the pasture toward the house. I spotted another group coming from the woods that edged the property. It was barely dawn, but enough light allowed us to see what we were dealing with.

"Please let it not be..." I whispered. "How many are there?"

"Emily's been able to spot upwards of fifty. Maybe more. We don't know."

"We can't let them into the house. I'm almost positive they're after us, not Braden and Emily. Those creatures won't stop until they've ripped us to shreds."

"Regardless of what kind of undead they are, we've got to treat all of the zombies the same. Kill 'em dead in the head," Preston said.

Emily appeared at the door. "Braden's stationed in our bedroom. The open window gives him a clear shot at the ones headed toward the front of the house."

I nodded, remembering back to the horrors of that fateful day with Gavin. There was no stopping their groping hands as they punctured Gavin's torso, as they ripped him apart...

"Every shot counts. Aim for the head. These zombies are stronger than any you've ever encountered. If they get a hold of you, they won't let go unless you slice off a limb, and I doubt that guarantees it," I said, taking the shotgun from

Emily as she held onto a rifle.

"I'm going out there with you," Emily said. "They're not after me. I'll be able to do more damage as they line up for you."

Preston eyed the floor as he mulled it over, but I didn't need to.

"No," I replied, shaking my head. "You need to make sure no one gets into the house."

"As long as you're not in the house, they shouldn't have any reason to come inside," Emily objected. "The more fingers out there pulling triggers, the better."

"You're assuming they're only modifieds," I said. "And we're the only targets."

"True, but if we kill them before they kill us, it doesn't matter what kind they are," she said.

She certainly had changed since I'd first met her.

"You're right. The more of us out there the better our odds. We'll start on the side of the house and attempt to lead them away from the building. We'll be able to coax them from both the front and back of the house," I said, glancing at Preston. "Do you think that's a good plan?"

"I think that'll be a good start as long as there are only fifty or so," he acknowledged.

"One thing at a time. We don't want numbers to distract us." I walked back over to the window and glanced down at the ground where the zombies were creeping closer. "Let's exit out the front and run to the side yard. Our goal is not to fire until we reach our destination. We don't want them swarming around us even quicker.

We'll form a tight triangle formation, back-to-back, where each of us can fire at the zombies. If needed, we can rotate as we reload. Sound good?"

"Perfection," Preston replied, the corners of his lip tipping up slightly.

Emily nodded and tossed us each a two-way radio and clicked on. "We're headed downstairs and out the front door. We'll be drawing them away from the house. Don't fire until you hear our first shot," Emily relayed.

"Ten-four," Braden replied, and a smile spread across Emily's lips.

"Ready?" I asked, the adrenaline pumping wildly through my veins. It had been far too long since I'd kicked some undead ass. I set the shotgun down and emptied several boxes of shells into a leather pouch that I looped across my shoulder.

"Ready." Emily already had a backpack filled with ammo clips on her back.

I reached for my holster and belt off the table and cinched it around my waist, securing more clips to the belt. If I ran out of shotgun shells, my Glock might be the difference between surviving and well... not.

Preston glanced out the window and nodded. "They're about a hundred-fifty yards out." He shoved the two-way into his pocket; his gaze settling on mine.

I nodded and we took off. Descending the stairs quickly, we landed in the foyer and Emily peeked out the window. This new vantage point provided the same information. The undead were still a ways out, and there weren't any close enough to cause real problems, yet. That would change soon enough.

"If TRAC thinks this is a game, it's about time we show them we're serious players," I whispered and Emily nodded. I loaded my semi-automatic shotgun and looked over at Preston.

"Good luck and don't do anything foolish. We work as a team and only a team," Preston said.

I nodded at Preston, and he opened the front door. We all slipped outside slowly, escaping the attention of the undead. Preston quickly secured the lock before we took off running along the front of the house toward the side yard. The clearing allowed us to see the undead as they came for us from all directions. It was an ideal zombie-slaughtering location.

Our quick movement caught some of the undead's attention, and they began turning their focus from the house to the direction we were running. The moment my feet traveled from the gravel to the grass, another bolt of fury raged through my system. TRAC wanted us to understand the power they held, the damage that they could do. We needed to send them a message as well. We wouldn't give up.

We reached the center of the lawn and got in our formation as the undead changed their direction and staggered toward us with new determination. Preston and I were living and breathing homing beacons that beckoned the living dead. Now we just had to figure out what advancement led TRAC to be able to do this.

Footsteps crunched all around us, and the grunts of the undead signaled the nightmare that was about to begin.

"Let's get this over with," I muttered.

I faced the driveway, Preston toward the back of the house, and Emily pointed herself toward the woods. I steadied my breathing and pressed my cheek against the stock as I aimed the barrel at the closest undead programmed to kill me. Her silk blouse and pencil skirt indicated the freshness of her existence, newly infected by the monsters behind the new wave of undead. Her eyes wide and jaw clicking as bone-met-bone, beckoning the first shot as my finger curled around the trigger and pulled. The head exploded like a piñata spreading candy, and I quickly found my next target as I heard Emily's rifle go off behind me, and Preston's next to me.

Several undead quickened their pace, tottering in a jerky upsurge of movement toward us as I took aim and blew the head right off another one, but I missed on the second. Instead the shot blew a hole through the undead's chest, leaving him fully capable of clopping toward me. I tried again. This time I didn't miss, but unfortunately all the noise accelerated the others pace.

A head exploded from the back of the pack, and I realized Braden had begun picking them off one by one as well.

"We've got more than fifty," Preston said. "I have that many coming toward me."

I shoved my panic down and reloaded. "Me too. We need to keep them back far enough while we clip each one off."

"One by one," Emily breathed. "One by one. We've got this."

Load the shells.

Pull the trigger.

Repeat.

"Don't think about anything but what's directly in front of you. I have two males and a female." I pulled the trigger once, twice, my pulse racing. "Now I have one male still standing."

"Brunette, floral dress, and great legs," Preston laughed, as he pulled the trigger. "Down."

I took aim at my next victim.

"Middle-aged, male accountant. He's seen better days," I called, pulling the trigger, and down he went.

Load the shells.

Pull the trigger.

Repeat.

The stench of the undead began wafting over to us, which meant one thing. They were getting too close, but the smell of gunpowder was closer. The groans came from every direction as the reanimated creatures rocked their bodies toward us. For every modified that went down, it felt like another regenerated in its place, but I knew that wasn't possible.

"We're going to run out of ammo at this rate," Emily yelled, in between shots.

I didn't respond. I just kept firing, my ears

ringing.

The pile of collapsed undead grew, but the pile wasn't big enough. Too many just kept coming. I glanced in Preston's direction and disappointment spread when I saw he had as many as I did.

Load the shells.

Pull the trigger.

Repeat.

I shoved the last shells into my shotgun and made bull's eyes out of the two closest foreheads, dropping the undead instantly. I was out. I tossed the shotgun down and removed my pistol from the holster. I noticed Emily had already resorted to her backup weapon as had Preston.

"We need to spread out. Confuse them," Preston said.

I nodded as he walked slowly away from us— aiming as he went—when part of the horde split away from the main group and followed him. My heart pounded at the thought of him being outnumbered, but I knew I was facing the same issue. It would be ideal if I could turn the horde around somehow so Braden could take more shots. But that was risky. I could get torn apart, or Braden could miss and hit me.

An undead dressed in a long jean skirt lunged at me, and I shot her square in the head and watched her fall as another undead trampled her. I took aim and dropped him immediately for being so disrespectful. I couldn't accept these creatures as humans. They were machines. I changed clips and kept shooting. My heart rate sped ahead of my nerves as I clicked in the last magazine.

I heard a grunt and turned around quickly as a zombie swiped at me, its lips smacking in the air.

One had gotten through Emily's area. I knelt down and aimed my pistol up, pulling the trigger just as a hand came toward the short barrel. The zombie dropped, but I spun around quickly to face the ones that had now gotten a head start toward me.

Almost mindlessly, I shot again and again, dropping one zombie after the other until the dreaded click of an empty chamber echoed through the air.

"Out of ammo," I hollered. "I've got eight undead left."

"I've got seven," Emily yelled.

"Five," Preston called.

"I'll run inside and grab some more ammo," Emily shouted.

I stared at the beasts in front of me. If Emily left to get ammo that would put us at twenty modifieds between the two of us, but with each twitch and lurch forward, the answer became obvious. We needed ammo. There was no fighting these by hand.

"It's the only solution. Go now," I called.

An undead's hand reached for me—frail skin barely covering each of her fingers—as I sprang out of the way. I rolled onto the ground and landed next to a misshapen arm that had been detached and dropped, missing the pile. I turned around and scooted quickly as the zombie's pale eyes turned toward me—not focusing—just blankly staring as he lunged forward.

I picked my shotgun up off the ground and cracked the butt of it into the undead's skull. It stunned him, but he didn't drop, so I rammed the butt of the shotgun into his forehead, this time making an impression. His body slumped to the ground with only a few spasms before he stilled.

Filth had splattered onto my sweatpants, and a wave of nausea hit me as I watched the remaining undead—their bodies rocking, heads tilting—as they made their way for me.

My heart pounded as I ran toward Preston, but my foot caught on a corpse of one of the undead and I fell. Scrambling to get up, I tripped and fell again as a hand suddenly wrapped around my ankle.

"Get up," Emily hollered from the door.

Like I was doing this on purpose.

At least her appearance meant she'd gotten more ammo. I shook my leg free and bashed the head of the clingy undead with my shotgun before I took off again, but it was too late. Another modified caught me. His pale eyes stared me down as his fingers wrapped around my throat. I swung my arm at his head repeatedly, as he began lifting me off the ground. My feet kicked in every direction as I struggled for a breath.

The whistle of a bullet sent a shockwave through my system as rotten flesh exploded onto me, the hand of the undead loosening. I collapsed to the ground on top of the undead as I attempted to catch my breath.

When I saw the unthinkable walking toward me, I attempted to scream, but my voice didn't work. It was too painful from the undead's earlier death grip. I tried sliding backward off the body as my eyes adjusted to what I was seeing. Shots continued to ring through the air. We had to be getting closer to an end.

"Holy shit," Preston said, and all I could do was nod as I saw into the eyes of Ron's father, Jay. They'd turned him and saved him special for us. Another gentle reminder of TRAC's powers, their evil willingness to deliberately use innocents as pawns.

"Look away, babe," Preston said, as he pulled the trigger.

But I couldn't look away from the horror of it all.

It had become part of me once again.

We'd managed to purge the area of undead, but the scars it left behind were countless. I felt Preston help me up, but everything else was a blur as I tried to comprehend the evil that we faced, the deliberate calculations to taunt and tease terror out of someone bit by bit. I was strong mentally and physically, but I knew we all had a breaking point. When would I reach mine? Had I already?

The most damaging nightmare wasn't necessarily the one that woke up a person in the middle of the night. It was the one that lingered and haunted the soul while it hid in the shadows of memory. The mind was a powerful weapon against itself.

I felt a cold compress against my forehead and looked around the kitchen. Braden was sitting at the end of the dining table and Preston was standing next to me. His eyes focused on mine. I didn't know how I got here, or when Braden came downstairs, but here I was. Here we all were, and we were alive. For now, we were alive.

"It's one big game to them," Emily whispered, dabbing a washcloth on her wounds.

"It is," Preston agreed, wiping the grime off his face with what was once a pure white towel.

"Psychological warfare," I said, shaking my head as the grogginess traded for anger. "If this is a game, I raise them by ten. And I promise you, we'll gain the winning hand."

Chapter Eighteen

"We've got a new location," Braden told us. "Got confirmation that it was available before everything happened this morning."

"New location?" I glanced at Preston and he nodded.

I scooted the chair up to the table so I could prop my elbows up while I rubbed my temples. Since I'd become a zombie's ragdoll outside, a dull ache had centered squarely in my forehead.

"When he removes the tracers from your blood, they'll still be active for several days. My thought is that we leave the filtered material here, and it'll buy us some time. We've had a location in mind for a little bit. One of our members in Utah offered it up."

"We're going to Utah?" I asked.

"No. That's just where he lives. He's in the oil business, and as we all know, after the outbreak there was a lot less need for oil so he's got several inactive refineries across the country. One of them is on the coast of Washington. If we're going to make the move there, today's the day."

"True. Once we get the trackers removed, it's our best shot at hiding." Preston ran his fingers across the stubble along his jaw. "Makes sense to regroup."

"And we have to do it quickly while TRAC thinks we're still licking our wounds."

I nodded in agreement, but I wasn't sure about the location.

"There are several benefits to moving to this place," Braden said, as Emily placed various photographs and satellite images on the table.

I stood up and leaned over the pictures. The aerial snapshots showed a large, sprawling complex with several buildings stationed throughout. Extensive pipe networks wound through the compound making entry rather cumbersome for those not familiar with clear routes. Huge processing units could be seen at each end of the compound and the double security fence that wrapped around the property would be a tremendous obstacle for anyone attempting to gain access.

"Those buildings are huge," I said, counting how many there were—looked like six.

"And they're pretty much empty," Braden said.

"Interesting." I took a step back, folding my arms in front of me as I thought about something that I didn't actually want to accept.

"I can get a semitruck here in under five hours to start the move," Braden said.

"Seems like it's a little large for just us four," I said, narrowing my eyes at Preston and he smiled.

"Judging by this morning's wake-up call, I'd say it's time to bring some of the group together," Preston replied.

I let out a deep breath and eyed Emily. She was watching us intently, not saying much. "What are your thoughts?"

"I think that this is just the beginning and strength in numbers never hurts," she answered, placing her hand on Braden's shoulder.

I nodded, tending to agree.

"Those images on television scared people," Braden replied. "It reminded them of the power the government has over us."

"But also reminds them how little the government can actually do to prevent the attacks," Emily chimed in.

"Especially if they're focusing on the wrong suspects," I added.

Preston chuckled and locked his hands behind his head, raising his shirt just enough to be distracting. He caught my look, which only caused his smile to widen.

"When we were back at our house, Jeffrey called. It was right before everything went awry. He's completely stepping out of things. He wants nothing to do with anything we've found out. He doesn't want to hold the modifieds any longer, either," I told Braden.

"Coward," Braden mumbled.

"He's got a family and doesn't want to be affiliated with anything that will put them in jeopardy," I explained.

"Isn't it a little too late for that? How does he think he'll unsee what he's seen. He won't be able to. That shit's going to haunt him," Braden mocked, wiggling his fingers.

"I don't disagree, but I don't blame him either," Preston said.

"Are we getting any closer to Dr. Falino's whereabouts?" I asked.

"Quite a few dead ends," Emily answered. "But we've still got our feelers out."

"Good, because I think we're going to need her now more than ever."

"Why's that?" Braden's brow arched.

"Because we need to get the modifieds from Jeffrey, and it looks like you just found a place to store them," I said, smiling.

"Whoa," Braden said, shaking his head. "I don't want to be anywhere near those things. It's one thing to fight a surge of them, but quite another to share a home with them."

"There are at least six large buildings on that property. We can ensure that the buildings we move them to are secure. But if Jeffrey wants out, we can't be positive what he'll do with them and right now that's all we've got to even the playingfield," I responded.

Preston nodded "She's got a point."

"The moment TRAC began attacking members of the public, I knew the playfield had changed. It wasn't until this morning that I realized how we needed to match it. We can't let fear dictate how this will end. We can't handicap ourselves in this fight. So far, TRAC has been several steps ahead. That has to change."

"But we're missing the most crucial piece of information," Braden said. "We don't know how they're controlling the modifieds or directing the attacks."

"I know, which is why we need Dr. Falino. Something tells me she knows that and more," I said.

A sharp beep sounded from the surveillance room. "I'll go check it out. It's probably Paul coming down the driveway," Emily said, patting Braden's shoulder.

My nerves had just begun to settle from the early morning escapade and now they erupted into a fried mess of emotion. I was still determined to be the guinea pig, but I was certain Preston felt that was his calling as well.

"Yep. It's Paul," she said, returning to the kitchen.

I glanced at Preston and smiled.

"Why are you looking at me like that?" he asked.

"Because you're supposed to be sleeping right now, but TRAC messed with my entire plan."

"Plan?" His brows furrowed.

"I was going to slip some Nyquil into your coffee," I laughed.

"You wouldn't do that," he said, his eyes narrowing on mine.

I smiled and glanced at Emily.

"Would you?" he asked, his head tilted slightly.

I playfully smacked him and laughed as he let out a relieved breath.

"I would never stoop to something so low. Besides, it's already settled. I'm the guinea pig."

"How do you figure?" Preston asked, following me down the hall.

"Because I always get my way." I glanced over my shoulder and smiled just as the doorbell rang.

I opened the door where Paul stood tightly gripping a box, an expression of horror stretched across his face. I glanced toward one of the piles of undead and shook my head. It had become far too easy to slide the gruesome into a tidy little compartment. It took reminders like Paul to remember that not everyone's existence in the Afterworld was so grisly.

"Sorry. We had unexpected visitors this morning, but it's all taken care of," I assured him.

He gave a slight nod and stepped inside the foyer. Preston took the box from Paul, and Emily offered Paul a cup of coffee, which he eagerly accepted.

"Thank you so much for doing all of this for us," I said, as we walked into the kitchen.

"It's the least I can do." He took a mug of coffee from Emily, and I'd be lying if I didn't admit that I wished he hadn't decided to take a morning break. I just wanted this done and over with.

Preston appeared in the kitchen, and his eyes

landed on the mug, and a flash of annoyance ran through his eyes. I hid a chuckle and dropped my gaze. At least we were both on the same page.

"I've been thinking a lot about which filter to start with first. My hope is that we're lucky and pick the correct one right away, but my experience has shown me that well-researched luck works out the best." He took a sip of the coffee and observed Preston. "Have you made your choice as to which one of you will be the test subject?"

A shiver ran through me at the clinical blandness of his terminology. It stripped away all remnants of the person behind the procedure. It made me wonder if that was how Dr. Falino had managed to accomplish so much. Rather than look at humans as humans, they were test subjects. But what changed that viewpoint? Was it her sister? Did it take her own flesh and blood for her to see the coldness, the ramifications of her studies?

"We've made the choice," Preston began. "And it's—"

"Going to be me," I interrupted.

Preston's jaw clenched, and he looked away.

Paul took another sip of coffee and nodded. "Well, the sooner we get started, the better. You'll need plenty of time to rest."

I glanced at Braden, knowing our timeline for the move obviously clashed with Paul's advice of staying in bed while our bodies recovered.

"How much time do you recommend?" I asked.

"Forty-eight to seventy-two hours at the least. I doubt either of you will feel much like moving after the procedure." His eyes steadied on mine. "Since you're the test subject, you'll need your rest, especially."

I gave a slight nod and followed him into the family room. Regardless of doctor's orders, I knew we didn't have time for either of us to be down. If needed, we could sleep on the way to wherever it was we were headed next.

Much to my surprise Emily had prepared the long couch with a pile of blankets and pillows. It was a nice gesture but did little to calm my fears. Paul began removing items from the box, beginning with the tubing. He set a small, plastic machine on the coffee table and plugged it into the wall. He grabbed a clear, glass box and set it next to the machine. It looked like a rainbow of crystals inside.

"What are those?" I asked.

"Each glass piece is a different type of filter. We'll only concentrate on this quadrant." He pointed at the blue glass in various shades. He opened up the machine. "The glass filter goes right there." I followed his finger to an empty square in the corner.

Paul began unwinding the tubing, and my pulse quickened at the sight. He pushed one end of the tube into the machine and reached for another section of tubing, which he unwound and plugged into the other side of the machine.

"Make yourself comfortable," Paul said, motioning toward the couch.

I nodded and did as he instructed. Preston strode into the family room and knelt by the couch. He reached for my hand, and I let him take mine in his. The comfort was nice, and I hoped I could offer him the same for his procedure.

"You're sure you won't let me go first?" he whispered.

"Positive."

"You make it so difficult at times," he grumbled, but without even looking, I sensed a smile.

"We'll be able to test whether or not we have the correct filter pretty quickly. I've set up a method to be able to capture the cleansed blood in this vial. Unfortunately, no matter how quickly we determine the status of the blood, we still have to allow the machine to finish its cycle. That's also where the most danger resides."

I let out a sigh and nodded while Paul snapped a glove on one hand and then the other. He opened a sterile container, and my breath hitched at the size of what he removed.

Not missing my reaction he feigned a smile and glanced at Preston. "It works like a PICC. I'll insert the tip into a large vein near the crook of your elbow, and I'll turn on the machine, allowing the blood to be pumped out of your body and channeled through the filter."

I really didn't want any more specifics. I waved a hand at him and shook my head. "I've got all the details I want right now."

"Ready?" Paul asked.

I nodded, and Paul straightened out my left

arm. He swabbed the skin with alcohol where he planned to insert the tip of the needle. Preston squeezed my hand, and I focused on the fact that soon TRAC would no longer be able to trace me. They'd no longer be able to alter the course of my life without my permission. The surge of pleasure that sprang to life in my veins allowed me to ignore the prick of the needle as Paul inserted it into my vein. He placed a strip of tape to secure the PICC and quickly moved on to a new part of my body, my leg. He scooted the pant leg up and wiped my ankle with more alcohol and opened the sterile package. I hadn't counted on another point of entry or exit, but it made sense we'd need two. He clicked on the machine, and I watched as crimson slowly filled the clear tubes to the steady hum of the machine. Paul wrapped a blood pressure cuff around my other arm and stepped away.

"How are you feeling so far?" Preston whispered.

"So far so good," I responded.

"She won't start to feel any of the negative effects until her blood has had a chance to recirculate," Paul responded.

I bit my tongue. God. Bless. Him. Paul just didn't understand the idea of calming a patient down. He was all business all the time. Preston smiled and studied Paul.

"So what type of doctor were you?" Preston asked.

"I was a researcher. I am a researcher. I never warmed up to patients enough or so I was told.

Truthfully, I didn't enjoy that part anyway so it was a win-win."

I stifled a laugh and tried to even my breathing as I watched the crimson flow through the machine and out the other end. It was about to reenter my body. Other than the psychological effects, I didn't feel any different. I wasn't in pain and didn't have any discomfort.

Closing my eyes, I felt Preston begin to stroke my head softly in a soothing rhythm as the blood reentered my veins.

"We've got our first look, and I'm sorry to say that's not the correct filter."

My heart fell at the news. I wanted to open my eyes and let Paul know that maybe the next one would provide better results, but I couldn't. The amount of exhaustion that suddenly hit me was unlike any sort of illness or injury I'd ever had. My lungs felt heavy, and my extremities were useless.

"We'll get it the next time," Preston assured me.

I attempted to open my eyelids, but nothing other than a quick flutter of lids happened, making Preston panic.

"What's going on?" he asked. "Why's she not responding?"

"It's part of the process. Her blood oxygen level is beginning to decrease, but we have to trust the machine to do its part. Her body's reacting to the change, ensuring her brain is fed the oxygen first."

My feet began to tingle, but I couldn't move

them to adjust the angle. Instead, the sensation began to crawl up my ankles, to my calves, and slowly surrounded my knees. It felt like from my knees down, everything had fallen to sleep, but I couldn't shake it out. I couldn't move my body. What I could do was focus on my breathing, focus on the future.

"Changing filters," Paul said. "She's been through one full cycle. Each one will weaken her body's ability to—"

"I think it's better if we don't discuss it while she's here," Preston interrupted. "But thank you."

Paul received Preston's message loud and clear and remained silent as he changed filters.

The tingling sensation began to creep past my knees to my thighs, and it felt like an elephant decided to take a rest on my chest.

"Her breathing sounds labored," Preston said.

"It will be."

Preston's finger traced along my hairline, and I felt the first bead of sweat roll down my neck.

"Her blood pressure has decreased slightly," Paul said.

I continued to focus on Preston's touch, but the tingling sensation that stretched along my lower body started to morph into sharp, painful jabs. Every time my heart pumped, a new wave of pain would wash over me.

"Her blood pressure is continuing to lower," Paul confirmed.

Forget the blood pressure. With every passing second, it was more difficult to take a breath, and the pain was searing.

"This filter wasn't it, either," Paul murmured.

I tried to turn my head just as a shooting pain spiked up my spine. My entire body felt as if it were on fire.

"Let's hope the third one's the charm," Preston said, as the source of pain spread. My hair was completely damp from sweat, the pain almost unbearable as I heard Paul click the next filter in place.

My body seized and a ripple effect of pain swept through my core, followed by a numbing sensation that I could compare to nothing less than a gift.

"Her body's not accepting the returned blood," Paul said flatly. "But the good news is we've found the correct filter."

Chapter Nineteen

The room was silent and cold, but I felt fingers laced with mine. Every part of my body felt bruised and my lungs ached. My eyes fluttered open to reveal darkness and shadows of a strange place. My free hand ran across crisp, cotton sheets—not a couch. I was no longer in the family room. I'd been placed in a small bed that wasn't mine. I rolled my head to the left and saw Preston with dark shadows beneath his closed lids. He was sleeping in a recliner scooted next to my bed. His hand remained locked with mine as I attempted to slide my body up the mattress with one hand.

I scanned the room, my pulse quickening as it dawned on me that I had no clue where I was, where we were. There was a soft glow coming from a lamp in the far corner, but the overhead lights were off. The walls were blank, and a large window with metal trim surrounding the glass overlooked more darkness. A steady drip caught my attention, and I tried to focus on the origination of the even beat. The metal door that led out to the hall was also trimmed in metal, very industrial. Had we been moved to the refinery? How did I sleep through it? I turned my attention back to Preston, noticing the fine lines near his eyes and mouth. Even with his body exposing his level of exhaustion, he was a handsome guy. Okay, I wasn't really being honest. He was sexy as hell, and I should be struck down for caring at this particular moment.

His wide shoulders, appearing even more so in the chair, drilled in that sense of awe as my eyes traced along his body. Even in a weakened state, he managed to look stronger than most men I'd ever encountered, and his ability to make me feel just as strong was something I knew was special. His black tee tugged up slightly at the hem, exposing his flat stomach and I sighed.

Preston chuckled, and my eyes flashed up to meet his, completely mortified that I'd been caught.

"I imagine that's a good sign," he mused, his brow arching.

"I was just making sure you were doing okay," I confirmed, smiling.

He shook his head, grinning, and leaned forward. He touched my forehead with his fingertips, and his gaze slowly ran along my face, stopping briefly at my mouth before moving on.

"How are you feeling?" he asked, his voice a little hoarse.

"Sore, tired, and confused." I scanned the room and shoved myself up in the bed. "I expected to wake up at the house. I don't understand how I got here." Lightheadedness zinged through me, and I leaned back on my arms, trying to center myself.

He shook his head. "Don't rush things. You've been out for quite a while. You can't expect to just hop up like that." The softness in his voice grounded me in my new surroundings.

"What's outside?" I asked. "Can I see anything?"

Preston couldn't help but grin once he realized I had no intention of listening to lectures about how I should stay anchored in bed. He inhaled a deliberate breath and rubbed his chin. "If I don't help you to the window, you're going to try to make it by yourself."

"Why wouldn't I?"

"You might feel a little—"

"I'm just fine," I said, sitting up and nudging my legs over the edge of the bed. Another bout of dizziness consumed me. I glanced at Preston who was watching me carefully, gauging my every move. My body swayed slightly before I even had a chance to get up.

"Careful," he whispered, standing up quickly. "Let me help you."

I felt like I was on ship battling high seas with every movement. It'd be foolish not to let him help me. I had nothing to prove, not with him, never with him. I sighed and let my body settle into its new position.

"I guess I'm not as strong as I'd like to believe I am right now."

"You will be," he murmured, as I stared up at him. His fingers slid along my hair, and I reveled in Preston's confidence in me. "Your body went through a lot." He studied the room and centered his gaze back on mine. "It went through a lot more than mine did."

"You seem to have sprung back pretty well," I teased, realizing even the smile took a bit too much energy.

"I didn't face the same recovery as you," he paused and looked away, shoving his fingers into his hair. "I really wish you had let me be the one..."

I eyed the linoleum floor, and I nodded as I rubbed the tension out of my neck. "I do too."

That got a laugh out of Preston, and I immediately felt better. "So about everything I've missed—"

Preston held out his hand, and I grabbed it, feeling his strength run through me as his eyes focused on mine. "I'd turn on the lights, but it would ruin the view."

"View?" I asked, as he helped me up.

The room began to spin, and my breathing changed to short breaths as I regained my balance with Preston's help.

"I'm not going to let you fall," he whispered, his arm snaking along my waist. I leaned against him and nodded.

"I know and I thank you for that," I said, biting my lip, wishing I could say more.

"That's what I'm here for."

"You're here for a lot more than that," I replied, seeing our reflection in the window.

Preston's strong build bounced back in the glass. He seemed larger than life, while I suddenly felt like a shrinking violet next to him. He held me tightly, and I appreciated him more than ever as he guided me to the window.

Taking breaks as needed, he held me tightly and helped me along. I hadn't let the uncertainty of the Afterworld deter me from doing what was right, but with every step forward I began to doubt my capabilities and my limits. Would there come a point when I had no more fight left in me? Right now, it felt like that reality might be closer than I ever expected.

"Are you ready to see everything?" he asked.

I let out a deep breath and took my final step, reaching the window. Pressing my hands against the glass, my gaze fell to the sight below. My breath caught as I saw the scene unfolding beneath me.

"Amazing, isn't it?" Preston asked, his arm still around me.

I was speechless. It was like an entire town was functioning below. I pressed my forehead to the glass and watched quietly as hundreds of people worked toward the same goal, building our new compound. There was a man operating a forklift, moving crates toward one of the large metal buildings, and several lines of people waiting to haul items off of one of the many idling semitrucks. Men and women walked in every direction either taking or giving orders, and a steady stream of people pushed carts into another large, metal building. I spotted several groups of men, wearing construction hats, wandering around with all sorts of equipment.

"What are in those crates?" I asked, watching the forklift operator drive into one of the buildings.

"I think those are ammo crates."

I snapped my head and locked eyes on him. "We never had that much ammo. Where'd we get it?"

"A lot has happened while you were recovering." A wry smile spread across his lips. "The name Ted gave us led to another group, and another, and another..."

"You're kidding."

He shook his head. "We have numbers that will rival TRAC."

"I don't understand. How do they know what they're fighting for?" I asked. "We barely know."

He let out a deep breath. "They know what they are fighting against and that's something, but it wasn't hard. More riots broke out. The streets are a mess. Hundreds of people across the country have been killed in less than forty-eight hours, and it seems like it's only going to get worse."

"You're kidding," I whispered. A chill spiked through my blood. "Since we're supposed to be dead, who is the government blaming this time?"

Preston's hand slid along my waist, slowly guiding me to look at him. "That's the problem. From the looks of it..." A flicker of disgust ran through his gaze. "It is the government."

"What?" I asked, my mouth parched.

Preston let out a deep breath. "It's not looking good. They're definitely trying to hide something. The channels have gone black. The only first-hand accounts we can get are vague and often pieced together. For all we know, the death toll is in the thousands."

"I don't understand how this could be."

"None of us do."

"What kind of attacks? Military or..." I couldn't bring myself to say it. I didn't want to think our own government would use the undead as weapons against its own people. That had been my fear all along.

Preston's expression darkened. "Undead attacks. We can't tell if they're strictly modifieds or a mixture. Anyway, we had nothing to lose by telling our story to whoever would listen."

I nodded. "I can see that."

"It was a calculated risk. We could've remained secretive, or we could share what we know. Either way we'd lose some people and gain others."

I slowly turned back toward the window, studying down below. His grip lessened slightly as I watched the next semitruck pull into place. A swarm of people began unloading the contents. A shiver ran through me at the sight of the incubators that were being rolled down the ramp.

"How'd we get them so quickly?" I asked.

"Jeffrey had a change of heart, of sorts," Preston replied, his hand resting on my shoulder.

"That's one way of putting it," Emily said from behind. "I'm so happy to see you up."

I glanced over my shoulder and smiled. "I wish I could say I was happy to be up, but with the way I feel…"

She laughed and walked over to us. "A pretty incredible view, though, isn't it?"

I nodded and looked back down. "It really is."

"More people are on their way," she said, glancing at Preston. "And judging by the sounds of things, we're going to need all the help we can get. Did you tell her about who we found?"

Preston shook his head. "Why don't you do the honors?"

She smiled and nodded. "We found Dr. Falino and her daughter."

"Seriously?"

Emily nodded. "Should be here in the next couple of hours or so."

"Under her own—"

"As if we'd kidnap someone…" she interrupted, and my brow rose immediately as I watched her. "Okay. Well, maybe we would've, but she's coming on her own."

I chuckled and turned my attention back to the long line of incubators waiting to be pushed into their new home. A sick realization settled over me as I observed the monsters that were now my responsibility. There were moments in my new life when I wondered if we were taking on too much—a few trying to carry a burden for many—and this was one of those times.

"I've got to go help Braden with something. I'll see you in a little bit. It's nice to have you up."

"See ya." I watched Emily as she nearly bounded out of the room, giving me one last quick wave.

I turned my attention back to Preston and leaned against the glass.

"Would you think I was weird if I told you I thought the scene below was eerily beautiful?" I asked.

The lights from the buildings and trucks let off a glow, but it held the optimism I needed to see. It represented a possible future filled with productivity and hope to set things right once and for all.

He flashed a wicked grin and laughed. "To the right people, it's beautiful."

"I think I'd like a glass of water and a shower," I said, as my energy level fed off the people below. A community was being built, and I certainly wasn't going to sit on the sidelines, regardless of what my body wanted to do. "Do you think the government has discovered it wasn't our bones in the ashes?"

"It's doubtful the forensic tests came back already, but you never know."

"I just find it hard to believe that our military would start attacking civilians unless they were being helped along again by our wonderful friends."

"I'm sure TRAC's behind getting the government riled up, but why and over what, I have no idea. What's happening in the streets is unthinkable."

"Well, if we can believe it. Who's to say what's actually going on if the television and radio have been blacked out? It could be propaganda spun from TRAC somehow."

"They sure were willing to jump on the evidence TRAC gave them about us," Preston replied.

"True." I nodded and really couldn't disagree. There hadn't been a great record established so far. "Do you mind helping me to wherever a shower is and then taking me for a tour of the place?"

He smiled and nodded, his hand sliding around my waist as I leaned into him. Standing so long had taken a toll on my strength, but I felt absolutely filthy, and I wanted to see everything as it was happening.

I glanced out the window and was struck as I watched one of the modifieds slosh around in an incubator. The man rolling it off the ramp was having some difficulty steering.

"The moment Dr. Falino gets here, I want to talk to her about how TRAC controls the modifieds. No matter who we're facing, if they're using the living dead then that only leaves us one option. We've got to build our own army of ghouls. Fight evil with evil. It's the only way."

Preston slowly led me through the room and picked up a pile of folded clothes on our way out.

He opened the door to the brightly lit hallway, and I shielded my eyes as they adjusted to the blazing light as we slowly made our way to the shower.

"It's just a couple doors down. It's nothing fancy. I'm guessing they were used for the refinery workers," Preston said.

"Anything is better than nothing."

He pushed the door open, and I saw a large room tiled in small, white squares with three showerheads on the back wall and a row of lockers on the left.

"Wow. Well, I guess modesty is out of the question."

His laugh was wicked, and I couldn't help but smile inside and out. "Only if others want a shower at the same time as you."

I smiled and shook my head. "Would you mind stationing yourself at the door so no one gets in."

He let go of me and reached for a towel. "Inside or outside?"

I rolled my eyes and chuckled.

"Emily thought of everything to make the place feel like a home," he said, handing me a towel. "Do you want me to get her in case anything goes wrong while you're in the shower?"

I shook my head and took the towel from him. "I got it. Thanks though. I'll be fine."

He threw the pile of clothes on a bench and turned around, but I reached for him, snagging his wrist to turn him back toward me.

"I have a lot to thank you for."

He narrowed his eyes at me, his head tilted slightly. "How so?"

"I can always count on you, and that's seems to be a rare quality."

Preston shook his head. "You make friendship easy."

I smiled, feeling stronger by the minute, and peeked at the shower. "I've always heard relationships that start as friendships are more successful."

"Interesting piece of information." He stroked his chin and smiled as his gaze rode down my body, burning me in place. "I'll have to keep that in mind."

I nodded. "You do that."

The glimmer of amusement in Preston's eyes couldn't be missed as he spun around, but he didn't try a thing. "Make it quick. I've got a lot to show you, and it seems you're feeling a lot better."

"You have no idea," I muttered, turning on the water.

I heard the door click and I shivered. Just like that, I was alone, which made me want to make this the quickest shower ever. I didn't want to be left alone with my thoughts. I wasn't up to the task of my mind whittling away every possibility that led us to this moment. I knew I'd have to face those questions, but truth be told, I was too exhausted.

Stripping out of my clothes, I stepped into the steaming water and felt it run over my tired, aching body. If I'd been at home, I would've braced myself against the tile wall, but there was no way I'd do that here. Who knew what these tiles had been through? Instead, I lathered, scrubbed, rinsed, and turned off the water and dried myself off. Reaching for my clothes, I misjudged and tumbled to the ground, taking the bench with me.

Preston immediately swung the door open, but I'd already managed to cover myself with the clothes. More embarrassed than anything, I continued clutching my clothes to the front of me as Preston turned the bench upright.

"Sorry," I muttered.

"Don't ever apologize," Preston said, offering his hand.

I reached for his hand and clasped my clothes to my chest with the other as he pulled me to my feet.

"Thanks."

"I'll just turn around, and you can finish dressing. Use me if you need to balance yourself, but I suggest not using that bench."

Laughing, I placed my hand on his shoulder, yanking one leg through my jeans and then the other. "Looks like we're both full of invaluable tips tonight."

I let go of his shoulder and hooked my bra in place and quickly slipped the shirt over my head.

"All set and still in one piece. Thanks to you."

Preston turned around, his gaze connecting with mine. I stepped a little closer than I'd anticipated, and my breath caught as his eyes fell to my mouth. "I don't want you rushing things."

I nodded slowly as his eyes locked on mine.

"How are you feeling after the shower?" his voice lowered, and his lip curled ever so slightly.

"If I admitted that, I know you wouldn't give me a tour so let's just say I'm perfectly fine."

Preston sucked on his lip and nodded. "Off we go then."

I wrapped my arm around his waist, using his body for support as we walked through the building.

"We're calling this building base one. Right now, we're on the top level and there are three more below. The first floor is the grub hall and all the other floors are residence floors."

"How many on each floor?" I asked.

"There are about fifty cots on each floor, but there's plenty more room in this building. We've also got two empty buildings that would allow for even more sleeping quarters."

We waited at the elevator, and I skimmed the open space. I was obviously lucky to have one of the private rooms. The dark tightly-woven carpeting stretched wall to wall, meeting rubber baseboards and grey walls. An exit sign leading to the stairs hung in the far corner of the room, and I saw the opportunity to bunk even more willing individuals if needed.

The elevator chimed and we stepped inside. My head was pounding, but I refused to let my body dictate my abilities. Leaning into Preston a little more, prompted him to hold me a little tighter, which I appreciated. He glanced down at me as the elevator stopped on the floor below.

The doors opened to reveal more of the same on the following two floors and then the doors opened on the main floor. The cafeteria wasn't necessarily up and running yet, but it at least had plentiful amounts of sandwiches and chips piled in the far corner.

I snatched a bag of chips and a bottle of soda before Preston led me outside. The excitement in the air was palpable and provided the energy I so desperately needed to tap into.

"We're on the ocean," Preston said, pointing in the opposite direction. "Port Hollow."

"Never heard of it."

Scanning the property, I was amazed at the beauty of it all in an industrial sort of way. The large network of piping almost sparkled with the enormous amount of light sprayed in every direction. Towers reached toward the heavens and silos mushroomed the soil. Inactive furnaces dotted the landscape and catwalks bridged the many structures together. I could only imagine what the place must've looked like when smoke and steam used to roll out of the towers.

The enormous amounts of metal caging, containers, and piping caught the light, which cast a beautiful, blue glow against the silver backdrop. I actually felt at home here.

"It continues on past those buildings," Preston said, waving his hand in the direction of the largest silo. "We're concentrating on getting everything set up in the center of the action first, and then we'll work out, utilizing more space, as needed."

I nodded, keeping my eyes focused on my surroundings. Any quick movements, and the dizziness threatened to take me down, but I was determined to see at least some of our new home. I took a few sips of the soda, hoping the sugar would do something for my energy level, and opened the bag of chips as I looked around.

The semitrucks were no longer in view. It seemed as if they'd managed to push all of the modifieds into the building. Curiosity created a strong pull to that building. It wasn't that I hadn't seen these beasts before, but I'd never had them under my control.

"Do you mind if we go over there?" I asked, pointing in the general direction.

"Not at all. I figured that would be one of the first stops."

"Since we don't know what to do with them or how to get them started, I suppose that makes it safer for us for the time being."

"They're definitely in a deep hibernation," Preston agreed. "I'd like to keep them that way forever."

I laughed. "If only."

The crunch of our feet against the gravel gave me something to concentrate on as we walked over to the building. As we stood outside of the double doors, my heart rate began to increase rapidly.

"Ready?" he asked. "I haven't seen it since they finished loading it up."

Nodding, I took a deep breath in, trying to steady my racing heart, and Preston opened the doors. The room in front of me sent a shiver down my spine as my eyes fell on the very creatures created to destroy us.

Chapter Twenty

A scene of true horror stood in front of me, and I didn't know which smelled worse, the rot or the chemicals that hung thick in the air. It was hard to reconcile the horror and hope that existed within these walls. As I scanned the room, I began pinning hope on each and every incubator that sat in front of me. Large metal cylinders hung from the rafters, and exposed piping wrapped around posts and along the walls.

"What's that smell from?" I asked, covering my nose with my sleeve.

"One of the early arrivals had a cracked incubator," Preston explained. "They took care of it as best they could."

I nodded as I surveyed the seemingly endless rows of incubators. Each glass cylinder was filled with a clear solution that surrounded the body of a modified. Tiny bubbles circulated through the clear ampules. Bright lights in the building reflected off the steel walls, which provided a sterile quality, conflicting with the smells that my mind had to ignore.

"Jeffrey's people came up with a way to safely mobilize these incubators when they first moved them. We aren't really sure if it matters whether or not the tubing is connected twenty-four-seven, but we decided to proceed as if it was a crucial element."

A man walked over, dressed in a white lab coat, and shook Preston's hand and then mine.

"We were able to tap right into the pipework that's already here," he began, nodding. "Couldn't have planned it better if we had years to analyze it. All we had to do was clean it out and run our tubing inside."

"Nicely done," I replied, smiling.

"Name's Stanley Whinson."

"Great to meet you," I said.

"Honor's mine. If you're interested in seeing one of these up close, I've got one out."

A chill ran through me at the thought of seeing one of the creatures out of their vessel. Granted, I knew firsthand the strength each of them contained within their body, but somehow that glass meant the world to me. Having the creature on the wrong side of it worried me.

I looked into the man's eyes and nodded. "I'd like to see what we're dealing with," I acknowledged.

"I've gotta go check on our latest row of occupants," he grinned. "Then I'll meet you through those doors."

I glanced in the direction he pointed, unsure of my desire to see one of these things up close. What if it awoke from hibernation?

"I'd say he just might qualify as our resident mad scientist," Preston said, laughing.

He wandered away, and I slowly turned to face Preston. "Is it really a good idea to have one of these things out?"

"It's the one that came from the cracked incubator. There wasn't any other place to store it, and Stanley didn't want us to burn it. He thought it might prove useful."

I sucked on my lip as I mulled the idea over. It should only take a quick bullet to the head if it were to awake, theoretically.

Stanley finished up with the latest arrivals and made his way into the room he instructed us to meet him in. Might as well get it over with.

The odor became stronger as we approached the double doors. Stanley reappeared and greeted us with a couple masks. I snatched one quickly and worked it around my nose and mouth.

"It doesn't help much, but it does tone it down slightly," he replied. "I tell you, when we first removed the corpse, it was enough to make a person's eyes water."

He ushered us into the room, which must've served as a chemical laboratory when the refinery was operating. It functioned well for our purposes now, even though I wasn't completely positive what those were. I spotted a few stainless steel gurneys rolled against the wall and several large microscopes sitting on the back table.

I saw a sheet draped over a large form, which I assumed was the subject, and my stomach churned at the possible unveiling.

"I've uncovered some interesting findings," Stanley began.

We followed him over to the gurney with the sheet, and I slid my hand into Preston's. It wasn't like I expected the modified to pop straight up from under the sheet, but seeing this type of gore didn't sit well in my current condition.

"I honestly don't know what's keeping these modifieds in their state of hibernation. I've poked, prodded, and sliced and there hasn't even been a twitch.

He slowly worked the sheet down, and I remained still, breath suspended, as the creature's head was revealed. This subject was a female. Her golden hair matted close to her scalp. The only decay that was evident was from the body being exposed to air. This had been one of the newly created. Stanley continued to slide down the sheet, stopping at an incision near its abdomen.

"I was under the impression this subject might have been a clone, but it doesn't appear to be the case," he said.

"What makes you think that?" I asked.

The moment the words left my lips, I regretted it as Stanley rolled a cart over to me. Tweezers in various sizes, scissors, and a probe lined the tray that sat next to an unrecognizable mass, which oozed on the table.

"That was in her stomach," he said.

And that was the main source of the putrid aroma—a meal from the day before she was turned.

I took a step back and wished I had about forty of these masks.

A breeze from behind startled me, and I quickly spun around to see Emily, covering her nose with the crook of her elbow as she eyed the sight in front of her. She turned instantly green, and I prayed she didn't lose it because if she did, I certainly would.

"I wanted to let you know that Dr. Falino has arrived." She didn't even wait for a response. She just spun around and let the doors hit her on the way out.

"I'll be interested to hear what she has to say about this," I said, motioning toward *Sleeping Beauty*.

Stanley nodded, covering the modified up, as we said our goodbyes.

I ripped my mask off the moment I hit the outdoor air and gasped. "That was horrible."

"But it made you walk a hell of a lot faster, and on your own," Preston said, removing his mask.

"Adrenaline is a marvelous thing," I said, smiling. "Is Dr. Falino going to be staying in Base One?"

Preston nodded, and we made our way back to the building I'd be calling home. We walked inside, and my eyes immediately fell to Dr. Falino who was sitting alone at a table, eating a sandwich. There was no sign of her daughter.

"Nice to see you again," I said, walking toward her.

Dr. Falino's dark hair was smoothed back and securely fastened in a clip. Her lips formed a straight, narrow line and her eyes appeared centuries old. She wore jeans and a bulky, cotton sweater in a light shade of blue.

She nodded, took a bite of her sandwich and swallowed before responding. "You look like you've seen better days."

"Appreciate the honesty," I said, laughing. "And I have."

"Is your daughter with you?" Preston asked.

"I decided to leave her with some friends. I didn't really know what I was coming to, and my trust level hasn't fully been restored with the human race." Her stare would've cut us like razors had we not felt the same way.

"Fair enough. We don't really know what to expect either," I said.

Preston stood up, and walked over to the counter. He grabbed some drinks and chips and sat down with us. I opened another soda and took a drink, enjoying the bubbles that made their way down my throat. I had never been a fan of soda, but it seemed to be doing the trick now.

"When I saw the bounty on your heads, I knew we were all in trouble, the cause was in trouble," she said, sliding her unfinished sandwich to the side. "I want to help you clear your names."

I nodded and looked at Preston. "Thank you. We appreciate that, but I think the only thing that will do that is bringing down TRAC and exposing their plans, whatever those may be."

"No doubt one will lead to the other," she agreed.

"In the pits, I assumed modifieds were controlled by lights and responded to a device inserted under the skin." I shook my head. "But there's more to it, and I don't know what it is. I don't understand the science behind what's controlling them. How are they able to create targets without the targets suspecting anything? It wasn't like that before."

"When I left, they were on the verge of a breakthrough that I didn't want to believe could happen," she began. "I honestly didn't think any of them were smart enough to figure it out, but I guessed wrong."

"A few days ago a horde of modifieds was dropped off to take us down, and they would've succeeded if we hadn't had the firepower to fight back. I feel like we're back at square one. I don't understand how they targeted Gavin...How they have targeted officials and civilians? It's like a big game to TRAC, and we somehow don't have the same set of instructions," I responded, circling a loose chip with my finger.

Anger flickered through Dr. Falino's eyes and she nodded. "It's a game and the modifieds are the playing pieces. Ever since I left, I've been trying to figure out if they'd be able to accomplish what they wanted and by the looks of it they have." She stopped for a few seconds before continuing. She sat up straighter, and her eyes connected with mine. I suddenly felt like I wanted to run. Like she had information that would change the course of my history, and I wasn't sure I was ready for whatever it was.

"Things have evolved much quicker than I'd anticipated. Your assumption was spot on about controlling the modifieds in the pits. That was the test ground for TRAC. They inserted devices into the modifieds that communicated with each other, but TRAC knew for their purposes that would be far too limiting." She exhaled and her stare dropped to the table.

"What aren't you telling us?" I asked.

Her eyes met mine once more. "They learned that there were way too many weaknesses associated with the system they were trying to perfect. They inserted the device into some test cases that were human, which only emphasized the downfalls."

I thought back to the devices that had been inserted into Preston and me, fully understanding the problems. If the target could dig out the device, the modified would be cut off at its knees, unable to complete its mission. Not to mention that in order to insert the device, TRAC would have to get up close and personal with the intended victim.

"Your husband, Gavin, was the first human to have been targeted using the device. We talked him and others in the university system to allow us to insert the devices. It's one of the many burdens I carry around with me daily. It wasn't until after Gavin's death that I realized what they'd done."

It felt as if someone had stabbed me in my stomach over and over again. The pain radiated through my body as if I was living his death once more. It became difficult to breathe as I focused on the woman who helped to murder my husband.

"I didn't realize at the time what they were doing. I was under the impression the devices were to help locate the individuals if any trouble came. I didn't know it was to eliminate people who were deemed dangerous or a flight risk."

Preston began rubbing my back softly trying to calm me down.

"Why was Gavin considered either one of those? He was just a researcher," I barely muttered.

"He was the researcher who held the key to what TRAC wanted. Your husband figured out the scientific solution to virtual immortality," she replied.

"So why did they go after him?" my voice almost hoarse. "If he had what they wanted, why did they kill him?"

"Because he wouldn't turn it over to them. He realized what TRAC was really after, but it was too late. He'd already told them what he'd discovered, and they wanted it. They still want it. That's why you are still alive. They believe you hold the key."

My world came crashing down on me as I continued to stare at Dr. Falino. I was unable to say anything, do anything. My mind was on fire.

Guilt flooded through me. How could I ever have blamed Gavin? I had come to believe that he was part of the problem when, in fact, he put his life in jeopardy to keep his findings away from TRAC.

The one person who should have believed him—should have believed *in* him—stopped trying to understand what drove his actions. My stomach churned with the realization that I'd turned my back on the memory of the man I loved and chose to believe an inaccurate truth.

"It's like they put him down like an animal," I whispered to no one in particular. "And I doubted him. I never should've doubted him."

Preston gently rubbed my shoulders, not saying anything, as I let the information slowly absorb.

"I'm sorry I didn't tell you sooner," she said. "To be honest, I thought you knew. I thought that was what propelled you forward."

I shook my head and fought the urge to scream. I'd spent the last several months demonizing a man who thought it was important enough to sacrifice himself in order to keep information out of the hands of the wrong people. I took a deep breath in and looked at Preston, his kind eyes full of understanding. After all, his sister worked with Gavin. Neither of them were the monsters our minds made them into. The world was no longer tinted in the different shades of deception I'd come to expect.

"So what is it that TRAC wants to do?" I asked, bringing my gaze to meet Dr. Falino's. "What is their ultimate goal?"

"Not to sound trite, but they want to rule the world or at least what's left of it," she replied, leaning back in her chair. "Their goal is to crumple the government in the U.S. first. They want to disintegrate what little trust the people have in the military and government officials and then swoop in like they're the people's solution to a man-made problem. Marcus thrived on power, and the people who followed in his footsteps are just as hungry for it. Maybe even more so."

I nodded, shifting my emotions away from Gavin and back to reality. "So the devices that TRAC initially used were like first generation. They had to feed off of each other. Obviously what they're using to control the modifieds is advancing. What are they using now to target and kill?"

"My guess is that they've figured out how to connect to satellite imagery to pinpoint the targets. At least that's what they were working on when I left."

"So you think they're able to sight someone in using a satellite and send the modifieds to attack that way?" I asked, swallowing down the fear of defeat.

"Satellites and drones," she confirmed. Her gaze shifted away from mine.

"Do you think we can replicate it?" I asked.

She sat up straighter in her chair and nodded. "I know we can."

A commotion behind us jolted my attention away as Preston stood up quickly. Two men were brought in by three others, one appeared to be seriously injured, the other possibly just in shock. Dr. Falino shot over to the men, and Paul strode off the elevator. I glanced at Preston who leaned down and whispered, "Paul's our resident physician."

"These are the only two survivors," a man panted as he helped lay the injured man on the floor. "The rest of the team was wiped out."

My heart raced as I scanned the building. "Are we being attacked?"

Preston shook his head. "We sent a group out to the city to see what was actually going on since we can't get any information."

I nodded. "I guess we got our answer. How many guys did you send?"

"We sent seven. Two females and five males."

I shook my head. "Contrary to previous reports, I think we can safely say the number of deaths aren't only in the hundreds."

We walked over to the injured man. He was sitting upright on the floor with a large gash on his cheek and his left calf soaking blood through his jeans. The other man, still dazed, looked uninjured. Paul and Dr. Falino were tending to the injured man while Preston ushered the dazed one to a table.

Stanley appeared at the door with an empty gurney. I hoped they had set up somewhere else for a medical station because I doubted the man wanted to be wheeled in next to the modifieds. They quickly moved him onto the gurney and wheeled him toward the elevator.

Preston watched my gaze. "We've got medical quarters set up on floor two."

I nodded and took a seat in front of the man who was staring blankly at the table.

"Is there anything we can get you?" I asked.

The man slowly shook his head.

"You're Jack. Correct?" Preston asked, and I wondered how he knew that.

The man eyed Preston and nodded.

"Who did this to your team?" I asked. "Can you tell us what happened? Was it the military?"

Jack nodded and then shook his head. "I don't know. They were dressed in fatigues, but I don't know. Nothing makes sense. What I saw doesn't make sense. National Guard possibly. Maybe not."

"What exactly did you see?" I asked.

"The streets are filled with military and undead, but they aren't fighting each other. The military isn't destroying the undead. They're killing anyone who gets in their way…"

"You're telling me that you saw both undead and military roaming the streets?" I asked.

"They weren't roaming. They were marching."

A shiver ran down my spine. "And you're sure they were in the National Guard uniforms?"

"Yes. No. I think so." He shook his head and covered his face with his hands. "They were killing innocent people. Our government wouldn't do that…would they?"

"I don't know," I replied simply.

Preston stood up and paced behind me. "How were the others on the team killed?"

"They were shot," Jack answered.

"How were they seen?" Preston asked.

"I told them not to, but they didn't listen…" Jack's voice trailed off.

"Tell us exactly what you saw," I whispered, placing my hand on his.

"There were three elderly women who were being ordered onto their knees, and two of them were unable to do so. One of the soldiers raised the butt of his rifle to one of them. Our guys took off toward the soldiers to stop them from hurting the women, and that's when they were shot." He went deathly quiet, and he stared at a crumb on the table.

"What happened to the women?" I asked.

"They were killed. We ran as fast as we could, and Tom tripped, falling down a small embankment. Somehow the soldiers didn't reach us in time and we got to our car."

I nodded and steadied my gaze on Preston as I tried to comprehend what Jack was telling us.

"If you think of anything else, please let us know," I said, knowing Jack needed some time alone.

"I will," he said, tapping the table with his knuckles before he stood up. "What is going on out there is pure evil, and I'm honestly not sure we'll be able to stop it."

I pressed my lips together and nodded. I was no longer sure either, but I wouldn't stop trying until I met my end. The world didn't conquer the outbreak to fall into the hands of an elite and evil few.

Chapter Twenty-One

We were wandering the property, not saying much as the latest revelations about our world sank in. The sun had just come up, but the fog lingered thick in the air. I stopped and closed my eyes. Ghosted by memories of Gavin, I listened to the waves lapping against the rocks. If I'd stopped to give Gavin the benefit of doubt would that have changed my actions? I doubted it, but at least the hatred wouldn't have eaten away at my soul. My lids held back the tears I so desperately wanted to shed in honor of Gavin. The aversion I'd conjured up for the man I once loved was now being replaced with regret and relief, but the damage might already be done. I'd walled off my heart and distanced myself from being human, but I no longer wanted to be damaged. I wanted to be loved. I wanted to love again.

Preston's arms glided around my waist, and

he pulled me into him. I rested my head against his chest, hearing the pounding of his steady heartbeat as I let my body relax into his. I felt his lips press against the top of my head. My breathing quickened in response and his hands moved up my spine.

I opened my eyes, looking up at him through my wet lashes. His finger slid along my cheek, eliminating my escaped tears, and then he placed a kiss on my forehead.

"It's okay to cry," he whispered.

I shook my head and sniffed. "I've spent so much energy telling myself that my life with Gavin had been a lie. I sectioned off my heart because of what I thought he was involved in. Told myself that I didn't need love in my life... That it wasn't worth the risk...I refused to open myself up because I thought it was too dangerous."

"I know," Preston murmured. His gaze only hinted at what he really wanted to say, to do, and it suddenly made me feel truly alive.

I looked away focusing on the beach pebbles as I attempted to piece everything together from the life that constantly threatened to fall apart around me. Dr. Falino thought she held the answer to controlling the modifieds that were in our possession, but there were still so many unanswered questions. Between Izzy's body healing itself and Gavin's findings my mind raced with uncertainty. Would this allow Braden to walk again or were we stretching the boundaries of what it means to be mortal? Would it be playing God, even if only used for the greater good—not evil—as TRAC intended? We didn't want to destroy civilization; we wanted to save it.

The only constant I had in my life was Preston. He was strong, beautiful, and loyal. He understood me better than I understood myself. I felt Preston watching me, and an ache for him spread through my body. My emotions were running at such a high, it was impossible to even know what I wanted, let alone felt in this moment. But rather than think, I just acted.

I reached up with my hand, running my fingers through his hair, and brought his head down as I pressed myself against him. His body responded, and I felt my emotions run wild at the thought of his lips pressed against mine. His finger slid along my jaw, sending a shudder through my body as he tilted my head toward his.

"Please," I whispered, as he moved his mouth lower but then away. He kissed the spot just behind my ear, and my body trembled in response just as his lips broke free. My breathing hitched as Preston cradled my face in his hands. His gaze darkened with every passing moment, and I silently begged to feel his lips against mine.

He was only inches from me as my eyes pleaded with his. I knew what I wanted and it was Preston, all of him. I watched as his eyes fell to my mouth. His lips touched mine, sending a shockwave through my world. His mouth was soft and demanding as my lips broke apart, his tongue sliding, exploring in an unforgiving moment of pleasure that we both desperately longed for.

His fingers ran through my hair, down my back, as my body responded to his touch. He kissed me deeply—passionately—with a possessiveness that I craved, and I knew there was no turning back. I had fallen for Preston, and I was no longer fearful to give him my heart. My breath caught, and my body trembled as he broke his lips from mine.

"Everything okay?" he asked, breathless.

I nodded, still in a dreamy fog as my eyes connected with his. "More than okay." My body continued to tremble, and he wrapped his arms around me. I placed my head against his chest in an attempt to steady myself.

"Apparently my body can't handle what my heart still wants," I laughed.

I knew he was smiling even though I couldn't see him, and he hugged me.

"We might have done too much too soon considering everything your body's been through," he laughed.

I stepped back and nodded, unable to wipe the smile from my lips. He cocked his head, watching me intently, while my lips still throbbed from our kiss. I licked my lips and lowered my gaze, unsettled by my reaction toward him. I didn't want the kiss to have ended, but my body was on the verge of collapse, which he quickly picked up on.

"Next time, rather than sacrifice yourself to

science to show you care, you could just—"

"Just what?" I interrupted, grinning, still euphoric from his touch.

"Kiss me," he said, wrapping his arm around my waist.

"I think I like that idea."

We took our time getting back to the building, and I readied myself for another session of Q and A with Dr. Falino.

"The worst was supposed to be over," I said, as he opened the door to the building.

"It feels like it just might be beginning," he muttered.

The cafeteria was empty so we walked to the elevator and stepped right on. My hand was locked with his, and I leaned my head against his shoulder as the carriage climbed up the building to our floor.

"I'll see if I can find Dr. Falino, and I'll bring her to your room so you can at least get a little bit of rest," Preston said, as we stepped off the elevator.

"Thanks," I said. "I really hope the recovery speeds up."

Preston nodded, and we continued to walk toward my room. Emily and Braden's door was shut, and I hoped they were getting some much-deserved sleep.

"I think Dr. Falino's room is on the floor below us," he said, helping me onto the bed.

My hands were shaking by the time I reclined against the pillows. I'd definitely overdone it, but at least I got to see more of the property.

"I'll be back," he said.

"Thanks."

He left the room, and I stared at the ceiling trying to understand what just happened. Maybe I really was beginning to be human again. I let out a sigh and felt the tears resurface as my mind went to Gavin. I whispered a silent apology to him and wiped away my tears, hoping I could make things right again. I needed to keep the findings out of TRAC's hands that he'd fought so hard to do.

Dr. Falino and Preston were talking quietly as they approached my room, and I quickly wiped away any evidence of tears.

"I had no idea you went through the process to remove the trackers," Dr. Falino said, shaking her head. "Believe it or not, with as many times as he ran your blood, you're doing beyond fantastic."

I nodded, sitting up in bed, as I propped a whole bunch of pillows behind me. "Thanks. I still feel like I've been hit with a semitruck, maybe two."

Preston and Dr. Falino each pulled a chair next to the bed and took a seat. I didn't want to waste any time. I wasn't sure how much longer I'd be able to stay awake.

"The girl we allegedly kidnapped, Izzy, had something happen to her that I was hoping you might be able to shed some light on."

"I saw her on the news," Dr. Falino said, avoiding my gaze.

"You treated her, correct?" I asked, glancing at

Preston. "At an MHA facility."

"I've told you already that I didn't oversee every single patient that was at the facilities. That would be impossible..."

"I know. I know. You just signed off on their charts, blah...blah." I didn't take my eyes off of her until she looked at me, which took several minutes. "You treated Izzy." I tried again, waiting for a response. I had to hear it from Dr. Falino.

"Yes, I treated her," she confessed.

I fought the anger down as I studied Dr. Falino. She had a daughter; yet she was willing to drug a young girl and use her for experiments. Preston cleared his throat as a gentle reminder that we needed Dr. Falino, faults and all.

"She had an accident. Fell off a horse," I told her. "The people she's staying with rushed her to the emergency room, but by the time they arrived her body had already healed itself. Is that the treatment you're talking about? The healing?"

Dr. Falino's brows shot up in shock. There was no hiding her surprise. "Her body healed itself?" she repeated.

I nodded.

"How bad were her injuries?" she asked, her eyes focused on mine.

"Abrasions, cuts, concussion, broken bones," I answered. "She looked as good as new by the time they got her to the hospital."

Dr. Falino shook her head slowly. "It's hard to believe. That holds so much possibility."

"It does." I didn't say anything else while I

waited for what I told her to truly sink in. I felt Preston's gaze on me and glanced at him quickly.

"What were the drugs you gave her? What results were you expecting if it wasn't the healing?"

She let out a deep breath and slid her hands across her lap. "Those were the results we'd hoped for. Apparently we miscalculated the length of time before we could expect them to take effect. It's not a drug. It's a biologic."

"Sorry. You're going to have to explain the difference," I said, crossing my arms.

"A biologic is created in a living system. Depending on the expected outcome, it can be created in a plant or animal cell or microorganisms. This biologic was produced using recombinant DNA technology."

"From the undead," Preston sighed, rubbing his face.

"Correct. We realized that there was something that the virus did to the DNA to make those living dead creatures."

I stared at her, my patience running thin. "Meaning?"

"Regardless of what the virus did to the human body, the body still somewhat functioned. The cells refused to totally die. I started analyzing the cells, trying to replicate the response without an attack from the virus. As I manipulated the molecules, I began to understand that the virus had created a very complex chain reaction within the human body. I knew if I could somehow strip away the disease,

I might be left with something that would allow us to eradicate disease from the human race. In the beginning, I didn't see the ramifications of my research. My vision for the future didn't match Marcus's."

"Not hard to believe."

"One of the most difficult things about biologics is creating the exact same manufacturing process time and again. Well, when undead are the vessels for the production of the biologic, it became obvious that there was too much variance from undead to undead since they all started as a different human being."

"The cloning," I muttered.

"I used the cloning as a way to ensure that our manufacturing process was identical from batch to batch during our research. I didn't realize that Marcus saw it as an opportunity to create a new army."

"And Gavin?"

"At the same time I was analyzing healing compounds in the cell structure, Gavin took it one step further. He was able to narrow in on the DNA breaks that the virus created, and, because of that, he found out a way to regenerate cells so instantaneously that it was equal to virtual immortality."

"Deuterium oxide," I whispered. "What the zombies are floating in..."

"Yes. That's right. Heavy water. Somehow Gavin's genius mind zeroed in on the one thing that can disrupt the circadian oscillations. I never saw the final mixture of molecules that he came up with to disrupt the body's ability to—"

"To die," I finished for her. "He knew what his discovery meant for the Afterworld, and he didn't want anyone to find it."

Our world's population had been decimated from the outbreak, and in some ways, this was one way for Mother Nature to recover from the once over-populated planet's tendencies to destroy her. If Gavin introduced his findings to the world, the earth would never get a chance to recover. Populations would spike and resources would deplete to a devastating low. No one would ever die.

Our eyes met, and I knew Preston was thinking the same thing as me. The information we had couldn't get in the wrong hands.

"Since you never saw the final formula, what Izzy had wasn't Gavin's mixture?" I asked.

"Izzy had my formula. It has the healing components, but at a much slower rate, but I would like to see Gavin's notes someday just for curiosity's sake."

I bristled at the notion and gave her no clue that I still had them.

"Would you be able to recreate your biologic here?" I asked.

She nodded. "I suppose I could."

"Good. Would you be able to start on it right away? Braden needs to walk again, and who knows what injuries we're facing ahead."

"Mine's a much slower process," Dr. Falino countered. "If I knew Gavin's formula, I could speed things along. Make—"

"We know what you've done works," I cut her off. "There's no telling if Gavin's will."

By the expression in Dr. Falino's eyes, I knew that she knew his not only worked, but his was the key to the Afterworld's version of immortality. I hid a shiver that threatened to give away my discomfort at having access to this kind of knowledge.

"Stanley's a good resource and so is Paul," I continued. "You can divide up what you need done, and prepare to show us how we can get these modifieds on their feet and ready to fight. We're going to need every advantage we can get."

"If we're going to war with this country, we're going to need a lot more than a warehouse full of modifieds, my dear. We're going to need what your husband discovered."

Ignoring her implications, I swung my legs over the bed. The sun was shining brightly into my room, and I was no longer tired. My body had rested enough and there was no quieting my mind.

"I'm more concerned with getting our modifieds ready. How long will it take to prepare them and how long will it take to train us to use them?" I asked.

She let out a deep breath, realizing her pleas fell on deaf ears. "It won't take long. I'll have one of the others work on readying the modifieds. I'm guessing days at the most. We'd be able to clone more weapons faster with that information, too, you know."

I didn't know, but I nodded and followed her out of my room. Preston rested his hand on my shoulder as the idea of going to war with our own government settled over us both. I couldn't comprehend what went wrong in the Afterworld.

"I don't understand how the hate formed in this new world," I whispered, leaning my head against his shoulder as we watched her get on the elevator. "Everyone was just so happy to be alive after the outbreak ended, and the government did such a fine job of orchestrating some semblance of order out of chaos. Money was distributed, jobs created, education granted…I just don't understand how we now have rioting in the streets. Our own military shooting at civilians?"

"They have their own citizens' blood on their hands," Preston sighed. "And for what? Why?"

"TRAC had to have told them something, promised them something."

"Or threatened them," he said.

"I think we need to see for ourselves what's going on in the streets," I said, after several minutes of silence.

He took a step back from me, and I spotted a slight curl of his lip. "I knew it was only a matter of time before that came to you."

"What can I say? I don't trust people to tell me what I need to see for myself." I smiled and scanned the building that held the modifieds.

We needed more, and I knew the decisions we'd be facing soon would change the course of history. In some ways, it didn't even matter if we survived as long as TRAC was stopped. As long as the evil that threatened our very existence came to an end. People were being killed like animals. Games were being played with peoples' lives but for what reasons? I'd never felt that need for power, that overwhelming desire to control a population based on fear, but we were dealing with people who had that need thrumming through their veins. The modifieds weren't the things to be feared, it was the ones who controlled them.

Chapter Twenty-Two

We had decided against a group mission. Preston and I wanted to get in and out without being weighed down. We didn't need someone deciding they wanted to play hero. Now wasn't the time. It got most of the last batch killed.

Several armed guards had been stationed at the entrance of our facility, and I'd spotted more along the double fence lines as they paced along the property. The refinery was hidden behind a dense forest, providing the perfect hidden compound for all of our activities.

Things back at our home base felt secure, and I wasn't worried about our day trip. Preston and I were fully armed and ready, with several backup plans if we got separated. I pulled my hair back in a tight braid and pulled a knit cap down to my ears. I hoped with as little makeup as I'd put on that I'd be unrecognizable to anyone who might've seen the news recently. Preston wore a tight knit cap and aviator shades. My hope was that we were yesterday's news and had long dropped from everyone's memories.

The refinery was located on the southern coast in Washington so it took several hours to drive to the city. The freeways looked clear, no real signs of a military presence, as we headed north in our self-driver.

There was one thing that caught our attention on the way toward Seattle. The Army base that usually bustled with activity was eerily still. No military vehicles hummed along the road on the other side of the chain-link fence. No soldiers ran their drills, and no children played outside the military housing. If our military had been turned against its own citizens wouldn't that be an exceptionally busy time for the men and women serving?

Preston turned off on the exit that would eventually lead us to the south end of Seattle. We had no intention of hitting the downtown corridor unless we were unable to find any information on the outskirts. This route ought to provide us with enough insight to see what we might actually be dealing with when the time came.

The area looked exactly as I remembered it: tattered billboards dotting the industrial sections of the city, brick buildings that didn't look like they'd survive the next earthquake or outbreak, and tiny sidewalks leading to pockets of housing.

"Not one soldier, military vehicle, or—"

Preston stopped himself, and I followed his line of sight.

"Spoke too soon, did we?"

I stared through the windshield and spotted three men dressed in fatigues standing on the porch of a home. As we drove by the rickety house, one of the soldiers turned around and glared at us as we passed while the other two men barked orders to the homeowner.

"I wonder what that's about?" I asked.

"The uniforms didn't resemble the National Guard. It looked like Army."

"Are you certain?" I asked.

"Pretty sure," he replied, turning left away from the residential area, toward the city.

"There's a car," I said, almost giddy with the idea that we weren't the only ones on the road. The electric car hummed by silently and was filled with men who appeared to be in a deep discussion. No attention was paid to us.

"I feel like we're in between worlds right now," I muttered, staring out the window.

"It's like a ghost town," he agreed.

We drove a few more blocks until we hit an area that appeared slightly more active. By active, I mean a few people wandered down the sidewalks. Preston parked along the road, and we both climbed out of the car and made our way toward the activity.

Colorful graffiti splashed accents along most of the buildings we walked past, and several large, cardboard boxes lined the sidewalk. Blankets spilled out of the makeshift shelters, and my stomach knotted at the thought of homeless in the Afterworld. The survivors were all given large amounts of money, and yet, we still dealt with the same human issues that plagued us before the outbreak. There were always predators waiting in the shadows to take advantage of people at their weakest moments.

A deli's front door was wide open with workers behind the counter, but there wasn't a customer in sight. The pharmacy next to it was closed.

I spotted a woman walking up to the crosswalk taking a drag off her cigarette, eyeing us suspiciously as we waited for the light to change. She wore a pair of blue sweat pants, a tight fitting halter and an open hoodie.

"Where is everyone?" I asked her, finding it funny that with no cars on the road, we still abided by the laws.

Her brows furrowed, and she took another puff of her cigarette. "Have you been living under a rock or something?" she asked, her voice gravelly from years of smoking.

"Something like that," I muttered. "We're from out of town."

"Why in the world wouldn't you keep it like that?" she asked, flicking ash off the end of her smoke. "There's nothing to see here unless you count this as something." She pointed around the block and laughed to herself.

"They'll be doing another roundup tonight," she continued, as the light changed, and we piled into the crosswalk. "I'd make yourself scarce or go back to where you came from."

"Where will you go?" I asked.

Her eyes dulled by the realities surrounding her, and she answered, "To a place far, far away from here." She flashed a dubious grin as she shoved her sleeve up her arm to reveal her plans for the night. The tiny dots and bruises scattered across her pale arm pained me. The people they left behind were the individuals struggling, not seen as a threat.

I pressed my lips together and nodded.

"Hey. Don't give me that look of pity. I choose to live this way. I lost everything to the outbreak. The Afterworld is my hell. This is my escape."

Her words jolted me and I nodded. Her eyes stayed on mine.

"And another thing. You two obviously aren't dead and stick out like a sore thumb. If I can spot you, I guarantee others will too." She flashed a grin and dropped her cigarette to the ground before she took off, whistling.

My eyes fell to the newspaper bin, and I let out a sigh as I saw both of our faces on the front page. Preston looked over and shook his head.

"Let's speed things along."

"Agreed. So they're rounding people up."

"Where in the world would they be putting people?" Preston asked.

"Jails, hospitals, office buildings...There are certainly plenty of empty spaces to keep people."

"Internment camps for the citizens of the Afterworld." Preston pulled his knit cap tighter.

"But why?" I asked. "Why would the

government want to exterminate the population?"

We glanced down an alley where a man held a cardboard sign reading, *Welcome to the Afterworld. Both Heaven and Hell Rejected Us.*

Maybe he was onto something.

His clothes were dirty and ragged, and his well-rehearsed speech chortled down the empty alley. Spittle accumulated at the side of his mouth as he ranted to the non-existent crowd. I slipped my hand into Preston's.

As we continued walking, we caught his attention and he lunged forward as if he were about to give chase but quickly slid down the cement wall behind him and collapsed.

"I expected to be depressed when we came here but not for these reasons."

"I know."

A low hum echoed from up the road, but I couldn't quite place it.

"Hear that?" I asked. "Think it's trucks or something?"

Preston shrugged, and we both stopped walking to listen.

"I think it's coming from that way." He motioned toward the block of buildings to the right.

We jogged to the corner and peered down the empty road, but the noise had gotten louder. It sounded like chanting. My heart began beating quickly, and I grabbed Preston's hand as I watched a mob of people begin to filter onto the empty street holding signs, and weapons.

"We need to be ready to run," Preston whispered.

I nodded as I watched the group swell into numbers I hadn't expected. No wonder the government didn't want its citizens seeing any news coverage. The footage would show unrest, protests, and disobedience, which would definitely thrust this movement forward.

Only seconds passed before the sound of a male's voice over a bullhorn commanded the citizens to step down and return back to their homes. I looked all over trying to find the source of the voice. I didn't see anyone on the street or in the buildings giving the commands.

"You're in direct violation of the curfew and will be dealt with accordingly," the man's voice continued. It was like Oz.

"This is going to get messy and quick," I whispered.

Preston squeezed my hand. "We've seen enough. We need to get out of here."

I felt the rumble before I heard it. My heart hammered as I spotted the tanks rolling in. The turret guns pointed directly at the crowd. Soldiers marched behind the row of tanks, scanning the side streets for stragglers like us.

I examined the crowd, which had no intention of stopping. Instead, they held their signs higher: *Where is the President? Who watches over you if it's not us? We won't be hostages in our own homes!*

I finally spotted the man speaking to the crowd. He was on the tank farthest from us, giving them one last chance to stand down.

They did not.

The crowd surged toward the soldiers and the first of many shots rang into the air. There was no tear gas, only lead bullets, as the soldiers shot countless rounds into the crowd. Preston and I spun around, running as fast as we could along the buildings. The few people we'd seen on the way here were long gone. Our car was only a few more blocks away when a soldier stepped out from a building about ten feet away, his weapon raised.

"Where are you two headed?" he asked, taking slow steps toward us.

I peeked at the alley across the street and held in my horror as an entire swarm of modifieds filled the space. As I directed my attention back to the man in front of us, I spotted a tiny drone hovering overhead.

Bingo! We found what's controlling them.

"We don't want any trouble. We aren't part of that group," I said, my pulse pounding in my ears.

"If you're on the streets, you're asking for trouble," he replied.

"So what do you plan on doing with us?" I asked.

"What we do with all troublemakers. Get on the ground," he ordered.

I began lowering to one knee when it happened. Preston lunged toward the man dressed in camouflage and plowed him into the concrete building. The soldier's rifle dropped to the ground. Preston kneed him in the groin and smashed his head against the wall, rendering him unconscious. Preston stepped back, and the man's body crumpled to the ground as we took off. There was no stopping until we reached the car.

A woman's laugh rattled me as we approached our vehicle. I threw open the door and slid inside with Preston right behind. I spotted the woman from the crosswalk, sitting next to a wooden fence, her head lolling from side to side. She housed the shrill laughter of insanity as the drugs took effect.

Preston took the car off auto-drive and turned our vehicle around in a quick U-turn. My breathing was still ragged from everything we just experienced. Soldiers were meant to protect. How was he protecting? How were they protecting? What were they protecting? It couldn't be the citizens or could it?

We got to the entrance of the freeway in record time, Preston shaking his head as we hit the open space.

"That guy wasn't a soldier," he said, his jaw clenching.

"Who says?" I asked. "Maybe you just don't want to think he could be."

He rubbed his temple and put the car back on auto-drive. "You're right. I don't want to think it could be our military fighting our own people."

"The equipment, vehicles, uniforms..." my voice trailed off as I thought about the number of casualties that yet again wouldn't be added to the invisible list.

"That wasn't how I'd planned on things going. I hadn't expected to come face-to-face with one of them. That'll only bring more attention to us."

"You had no choice. No one is bulletproof," I replied.

"Not yet, anyway," he sighed.

"True. Not yet."

In the midst of the chaos, I hadn't even noticed it.

"What happened?" I asked. My eyes stuck on the crimson that had soaked his shirt.

"With what?"

"You're bleeding through your shirt."

Preston looked down at his stomach and spotted the blood. "I didn't feel anything."

I lifted the shirt and gasped. "How can you not feel that?"

The wound was deep, like a puncture wound.

"I don't know. Maybe adrenaline."

"That's some adrenaline," I muttered. "I don't like the looks of that."

"I'm sure it's fine. It's probably just when I cornered him against the wall. He must've stuck me with something." Preston did the unthinkable and squeezed the wound. "See. It just looks worse than it is. It's just a step beyond a flesh wound. It's even stopped bleeding." He flashed a half-smile, and I couldn't help but return one.

"You really need to quit getting hurt."

"Thanks. I'll try to remember that," he laughed.

"You do that."

We were only an hour or so away from the compound, and it didn't seem that Preston was that worried about his injury so I tried not to be as well.

"I don't want to think that our government is involved with TRAC to that degree," I said, after a few minutes of silence. "I didn't want to believe that this was really going on in the streets."

Preston nodded. "If the government is willing to do this, what has TRAC offered them? How have they manipulated the situation like this? It makes no sense."

"Yet we've seen it with our own eyes."

"We must be going about this whole thing wrong," Preston laughed. "Maybe we should forget about doing what's right."

"I'm beginning to think it's overrated." I smiled, leaning my head against the headrest.

"It's starting to feel like that."

I watched as the last of the city traded for country, empty fields filling in for buildings when something occurred to me.

"Our government only functions if the people believe in it. TRAC is trying to topple the citizens' trust in our government. Once they can dislodge trust from the minds of many, it's only a matter of time before the government falls and TRAC steps in." I glanced at Preston.

"Well, I'd say the trust in the government is certainly not at an all time high. The question becomes is this our government or has our government been infiltrated?" he asked.

"But how could it be done across the country

so easily?"

"I don't know. That's what we keep circling back to time and again," he said.

"I have to be honest. I'm worried that we don't have the time we need to fully understand what we're dealing with."

"It's only a matter of time before civil war erupts and the government topples right into TRAC's hands," he agreed.

"Not a happy thought."

"What's concerning is why our government can't see it unfolding."

Preston let out a deep sigh and turned to face me. "I think we might want to consider exploring Gavin's discovery. If TRAC keeps at this, there won't be anyone left worth saving."

"We'll know if the time is right."

"Will we?" His brow arched.

"We have to believe that we will. Utilizing that as a tool and not a last resort will alter humanity forever, what it means to be human."

"Don't you think TRAC is already doing that?" Preston argued. "Maybe we need a way to stop them. This is the only thing that gives us the upper hand."

"True," I agreed, looking to change the subject. "I was pleased to see that they're keeping the modifieds together. It will be easier when ours are ready to fight."

"Yeah, it will." He rested his head against the headrest as the auto-driver continued to our destination. Silence sat thick between us as I watched the first raindrop hit the windshield.

KARICE BOLTON

"Do you think fighting their modifieds with ours will work?" I asked.

"To some extent. I don't think they're expecting it so that should work to our advantage. But do I think it will solve the problem? No, but I think it will throw them off enough that we might have a shot."

"Have a shot. That's comforting," I sighed. "We're acting as if rational thought will work with these people and it won't."

"Oh, no," I said, spotting what appeared to be a line of military vehicles parked on an exit up ahead.

"What's that all about?" Preston said, leaning to catch a better glimpse.

A town that we'd spotted on the way into the city was now a completely different species. It seemed like it had been invaded by our own military, like something out of a movie. These things didn't happen in our country.

The exit of the small town was lined with military vehicles and the town itself completely barricaded. I saw lines of people ushered into large tents that hadn't been there hours before.

"They destroyed the post office. It's still smoking," I whispered, turning my body in the seat as our car zoomed by the mess.

When I could no longer see anything besides a blur of chaos, I shut my eyes begging my mind for a rest, a break from the wreckage I couldn't stop discovering. Begging for a momentary recall of a better life, I felt Preston's hand slide onto mine as I attempted to slow my breathing.

"How could they hit someone when they least expect it, when they are most vulnerable, and destroy their entire existence for nothing?" I whispered.

"It's not for nothing. It's very much for something, and we just need to find out what that something is."

I kept my eyes closed suspending the reality that faced us both. I refused to give in to the fear and isolation I felt slowly overtaking my mind and body. I focused on Preston's touch—his voice, but not his words—as I allowed myself to create a vivid existence of my own making. My mind needed to work with me—not against me—if I planned on surviving.

"They are removing the remnants of what our civilization used to be," I muttered, eyes still closed.

"Remnants?" Preston asked.

"In this case the remnants are people."

Chapter Twenty-Three

We'd spent days learning the systems to communicate with the modifieds. I came to understand that these machines would only be a small part of what was needed to destroy TRAC's capabilities. With each jab of a button and tap on the touchpad, I knew we were one step closer to readying ourselves for battles unlike any the world had ever seen. I also knew that these were small steps toward stopping TRAC. They'd tasted the power— manipulated a system that the world thought was untouchable—and now we had to use what small resources we had to disrupt them enough to end them.

I stared at the screen, steadying my thumb as I zoomed in on my targets; too fast and I zoomed in on a shoe, too slow and they escaped my lens. Over the last few days, I'd been alternating between practicing on the drone system and the target system that Dr. Falino developed. The system allowed us to spot the enemy with the satellite equipment and pinpoint their whereabouts so our modifieds could attack. Right now I was stationed on a satellite simulation. I found my mark and slowly twisted my thumb as the target came into focus. Learning to control my breathing and my heart rate were essential for perfect aim. I had a long way to go and a short time to do it in.

The lens focused in on the image, zooming in at a steady pace, when Emily's face finally came into view. I pushed the button and locked on the target.

Success!

Clapping from behind jarred my concentration, and I spun around in the chair to see Preston slowly walking toward me. He looked sensational.

"Nice work." He flashed me a crooked grin, and I felt a flutter deep in my abdomen. It was nice to be valued, appreciated, especially on something like this.

I stood up and took a bow. "Thank you. Not bad with only an average of three hours of sleep a night."

He stood in front of me and slid his arms around my waist, his hair still wet from a morning shower, as he pulled me in.

"You smell delicious," I murmured.

"Soap usually works well," he laughed.

I grinned and took a step back, studying the command station that Braden had built for this stage of the mission. He used the refinery's old IT room and tapped into some of their existing systems. He and his crew also managed to hack into the satellite systems that several broadcasting stations used. If all went well with our trial runs, we would be able to roll this out across the country. Seven of us could train at a time at this location. Right now we were in between shifts. I'd stayed through three of them.

I stared at the wall of security screens that monitored our property, a dozen or more screens with small images always in view to alleviate our worries about being found. The person who was assigned to watch the wall during the night was a nice guy, probably in his late teens. His name was Trek and even though the name might conjure up images of a young guy who liked hiking and the outdoors, he clearly enjoyed the techie side of life and was paler than *Casper*.

All that being said, it was nice having him in the room when questions arose. He was always quick to give me pointers and tips. He was new to our group, but I trusted what brought him here. His sister and her boyfriend went missing from a summer camping trip. His parents believed they got lost while on a hike, but Trek never did. He couldn't explain why, but he knew they'd been taken. By who he didn't know. Now he had a hunch.

I sat back down and watched Emily wave at the camera. I clicked on our two-way and apologized for not letting her move. "All done for now. Thanks again for letting me use you."

She laughed. "No problem. Anything to keep me out of the modifieds building. Use and abuse away."

I didn't blame her for that one. Very few people wanted to help Dr. Falino, Paul and Stanley.

"Ready for breakfast?" I asked her.

"We'll meet you there."

I hadn't eaten anything since our last meet up with Emily and Braden the morning before, but I wasn't really hungry, which was very unusual for me.

"Looks like you've really gotten a handle on the controls," Preston said, leading me through the room.

I gave a quick wave to Trek, and he flashed a smile before returning his attention back to the monitors.

"Getting there," I said, as we walked into the hallway. This was one of the most barren and isolated areas of the property. It verged on depressing. Everything was dull and grey: the walls, the carpet, the furniture. It matched my mood at the moment.

Preston patted my shoulder as we walked outside. Fog still hung low in the air, and the breeze from the ocean sent a shiver through me. Exhaustion teased at me, but I shook it off.

"I want to focus on the drones a bit more. I really think that could be our least expected attack. If we manage to take out their drones, we could really screw with their strategy. I know we plan on having guys on the ground to shoot theirs down, but I think if we can figure out a way for our drone to take out theirs, it would be a lot better. The fewer people who become unintended targets, the better," I said, our footsteps crunching on the gravel path between buildings.

Preston opened the door to the cafeteria, and I welcomed the warm air as it splashed against my face.

"I know Braden was working on something like that. The issue is weight distribution of the weapon. The drones we have are built for surveillance so there's a lot of problems that come with what you're thinking."

I nodded and slid into the seat across from Emily who was talking intently with Braden. A few open boxes of cereal were set on the table, along with milk, bowls, and spoons.

I reached for Cinnamon Toast Crunch and sprinkled it my bowl and splashed it with milk.

"Nice choice," Preston said, taking the box from me and emptying it into his bowl.

"Thanks. This and and Honey O's are my favorite."

The sweetness of the first bite put my hunger in overdrive. Apparently it wasn't that I hadn't been hungry, I'd just been too focused on memorizing the controls.

"What are the chances that we could mount weaponry on the drones we already have?" Preston asked Braden.

Braden twisted his lips and blew out some air. "The models we have wouldn't work, but that's not to say we couldn't get some to do the trick. They're not a hard thing to build."

"So we'd have two kinds of drones in the sky?" I asked.

"Yeah."

"I guess that's not a big deal," I said, stirring a few of the squares around in the milk.

"Not really. If anything, maybe it'll make TRAC concentrate on the one that's shooting and not the one that's helping to control the modifieds. It could work to our benefit."

"Interesting thought," Preston said, leaning in his chair.

A gust of wind came from behind, and I turned in my seat to see Dr. Falino heading to our table from outside. She looked like she'd had about as much sleep as all of us.

"Good morning," I hummed.

"Good indeed." She smiled, pulling out an empty chair. "Our first production run finished this morning."

"For what?" Braden asked.

"We told Dr. Falino about Izzy's accident and her ability to heal," I answered. "After a bit of back and forth, she confirmed that Izzy had been receiving a biologic that might have accounted for her newfound healing ability."

Braden glanced at Emily.

"My team had miscalculated how long the process would take before results could be seen. I thought the experiment was a failure, but apparently it was a success," Dr. Falino continued. "We have enough to begin administering doses immediately and should be able to continue production."

Braden's stare lowered to his lap.

"We still aren't certain what it can do to help in older injuries such as yours," Dr. Falino told Braden. "But the only way to find out is to initiate the process and begin administering the biologic."

Emily beamed as she reached for Braden's hand. He slowly lifted his head and settled his eyes on Dr. Falino.

"Who asked you to do this?" he questioned.

"Rebekah asked that I make this a priority," she replied, glancing at me.

"It seems like a powerful tool to have in our arsenal." I smiled.

"That it is," Braden laughed. "Not that I haven't loved my time in this thing."

"I can't tell you how long it will take before we begin to see results. Without seeing when the effects began taking place on Izzy, I really don't know..." Dr. Falino's voice trailed off.

"I don't care if it takes a year. Just knowing I have a shot makes life incredible." Braden grinned.

"Hey, I thought I made life incredible," Emily teased, kissing Braden's cheek.

"You do, babe," he laughed. "You absolutely do."

Preston slid his hand onto my knee, and I glimpsed him smiling.

"Have you thought more about what we spoke about a few days ago?" Dr. Falino asked, her focus landing on me. "It takes very little of the solution that the modifieds are soaking in to create the biologic. I'd imagine we're dealing with the same quantities more or less."

I didn't like how she'd put me on the spot, especially after just sharing great news with Braden. We were at her mercy, but she was at ours as well.

"I've been giving a lot of thought to it, but I haven't made a decision yet." I felt my lips tense as they pressed into a thin line, even though I tried not to appear as angry as I was.

She nodded and stood up from the table. "I'm going to catch a few hours of sleep. Braden, we'll get you started on the biologic this afternoon." Something was hiding behind her look. I wasn't sure if it was about Braden, or because I wouldn't share the information.

"Great. Thanks," he said smiling, as she walked away.

Once she was on the elevator, I turned my attention back to the group. "I'm still nervous about her."

Braden nodded. "That's understandable. She used to work for the enemy, but I'll take what I can get from her right now."

"Completely understand that," Preston agreed.

My eyes flicked from Emily to Braden. I wanted to tell them what Dr. Falino had told us about Gavin and his findings, but I was worried the more people that knew, the harder it would be to make the right choice. Preston respected my decision to keep things quiet until I was ready, but I wasn't sure I'd ever be.

"You know what's been bothering me?" Braden asked.

"Do tell," Emily chuckled, still on a high from the earlier conversation.

"We haven't been able to find out who is controlling TRAC; who's calling the shots?" His eyes locked on mine.

"I never thought that tracking the undead would be easier than tracking the ones who controlled them," I confessed.

"We ran the images from the zombie pit, got identification, but they're not the ones in charge."

"How can we be sure of that?" I asked.

"Those three leave a trail wherever they go. There's too much information about them available. Whoever's running it now learned from Marcus's death. They're definitely behind the curtain. I think they're setting up others as scapegoats."

"Maybe we're looking at it wrong. What if it never was Marcus who was actually running the show?" I asked.

Preston's hand steepled together, his thumbs running circles around each other as he thought about what I suggested. We'd never discussed this theory before.

"I don't know why we hadn't thought of that, but it's certainly a possibility," he said, nodding slowly. "It really is."

"We've been able to pick up a lot of TRAC chatter using the IMSIs. The last twenty-four hours have been almost nonstop. Unfortunately, it hasn't been easy to decipher. They've been talking in some sort of code. We've got guys working on it," Braden replied.

"Interesting." I shoved my hands through my hair and worked the loose strands into a quick ponytail. "I doubt I'd do much better, but do you mind if I take a peek at the transcripts?"

"Be my guest," Braden laughed. "Sometimes all it takes is fresh eyes."

"Or not so fresh," I laughed, feeling the exhaustion from the last several days slowly start to seep in. As long as I kept active, I could shrug the sleep away, but it was these breaks that really dangled in front of me what I'd been missing.

"You want to check it out now?" Braden asked.

"Might as well," I said, nearly bolting out of my chair. If I spent a second longer sitting, I'd probably fall asleep right where I was.

We all followed Braden out of the building and into one across the way. It wasn't the building that held the modifieds. It was a much smaller building, one-story, with more windows dotting the exterior walls. Emily swung open the door and we stepped inside. The space looked like a machine shop. Glossy concrete floors and cinderblock walls completed the look. There were 3D printers, drill presses, screw machines and several other pieces of equipment I didn't recognize. Rows of metal tables were lined against a wall and filled with people working away.

To my right I saw a wall full of items that hadn't been there the day before. I walked over to the shelving units mesmerized by what was in front of me. I picked up a glove out of a box and examined it, struck by the lightness of it.

"We've been making all of our own body armor. We've been using the 3D printers to create gloves, helmets, chest pieces... Basically you name it, and we can create it," Braden said, coming up behind me.

"This is incredible," I whispered, tossing the glove back in the box.

"Plenty more where it came from." He studied Emily and then looked back at me. "The engineers we've managed to recruit have opened our eyes to the possibilities that these machines offer."

"It looks like it." I glimpsed a knife sticking out of a box and peeked inside to see hundreds more. I picked one up and held it up for Preston to examine.

"That's not all," Braden said, motioning for us to follow him down the wall.

We stopped in front of several large crates and my heart beat a little quicker. Braden tapped the wood and smiled.

"Open it up," he said, unable to contain his excitement.

Preston grabbed a metal crowbar that was hanging from a hook and pried the lid off the box. Preston shook his head and began laughing as he removed one of the guns from the crate.

"You've got to be kidding me," I said, unable to

hide my grin.

Ever since 3D printers became the norm, our government put locks on the programing capabilities for the general public. When these machines were first invented, they were considered mankind's salvation. Anything could be printed if the person had the money. Cars, medical devices, and of course, weaponry could all be printed with a costly pattern and a few clicks of a button. The government hadn't paid much attention until the guns began winding up in the wrong hands. It didn't take long before legislation was passed to limit what types of patterns could be purchased and by whom. They also made one software company very rich by implementing software locks on the devices, limiting the 3D printers' capabilities.

"Our engineers hacked the printers," Braden said.

"Engineers?" I asked, my eyes narrowing on him.

He threw up his hands and gave a deep chuckle. "Okay. Maybe I lent a hand."

"Or two," Emily laughed.

Preston handed me the unloaded rifle, and I held what appeared to be an MP5 knockoff, a submachine gun often used by SWAT and other government agencies. It would be a good match for whatever or whoever, we faced.

"It shoots smooth too," Braden said.

"I bet it does." I raised it to my shoulder and couldn't help but feel a tingle as I focused down the barrel. I handed it back to Preston, and he placed it back in the box, securing the lid.

"We're just getting a feeling for what all we can produce and how quickly," Braden said.

We followed him over to one of the desks where three guys were sitting, staring at three screens.

"Have you come up with anything?" Braden asked.

The guy closest to us raised his head, and I was shocked at how young he looked, maybe sixteen?

"There appears to be a correlation with geography acronyms, and the references that a lot of these conversations center around seem to fit that possibility," he replied. "The GIS has all of these acronyms."

"GIS?" Emily asked.

"Geographic Information Systems," he answered.

"Well. I certainly wouldn't have come up with that," I laughed. "Can you give us an example?"

He nodded and slid the page on his screen to read an example. "9 NCAP LANDSAT RTP A LE PEN 48.0781° N, 123.1014° W, which translates to Based on National Center for Aerial Photographs and Land Satellite images real time positioning shows an army is less than or equal to arriving on the Peninsula by zero-nine-hundred."

"Where on the peninsula are those coordinates?" I asked.

"Sequim."

"The day Preston and I went to the city, they

were also in Sequim. What was that...three days ago?" I looked over at Preston and he nodded. "Can you see if you can pick anything up?"

The kid nodded and swiped his pages in the opposite direction, landing on the day in question. He began searching the documents with his finger until he finally found something of interest.

I remained transfixed as he slid to the next page and began reading aloud again and then translating for us.

"Exactly where you were in the city was communicated about forty minutes before you arrived," Braden repeated, shaking his head. "You just happened to stumble into an already planned raid."

"This is incredible," Preston muttered, sliding his hand along the table.

The air between us was charged with a newfound sense of knowledge. This breakthrough eliminated the guesswork. We would be able to locate the exact time and date of the attacks. We would be there waiting for whoever was in charge. Only time would tell whether it was our government or TRAC.

Chapter Twenty-Four

With only a week of training under our belts, we were now preparing ourselves for battle against an enemy we knew far too little about, but we had no choice. Small towns across the state and country were under siege, the same modus operandi for each capture: military rolled in, property was seized or destroyed, and citizens were captured.

We no longer had the luxury of time.

Our network had grown tremendously as mergers among the groups took place, thanks to Ted. We'd been able to remotely share our findings and gain support and funding. Many groups had also run some reconnaissance missions, their findings the same as ours. This wasn't only a problem in Washington. What appeared to be our military had slowly taken over town after town from one end of this country to another.

In the last few days, we'd sent members from our location to the larger staging areas across the country to disseminate information and to train others. Our plan was a coordinated effort across the country to send the message loud and clear to whoever was running the operations.

They were using modifieds as if they had an endless supply. Anyone in the country who wielded even a small amount of power needed to be worried. If they weren't, then they were probably in on it. Reports of mayors, city council members, and even postal service workers being torn to pieces were coming in nonstop.

The most terrifying thing about it was that citizens hadn't risen up against it. They were— for the most part—going down without a fight. Seeing the march on the street, gave me a small amount of hope, but knowing how quickly it ended dissolved much of my confidence for the future, mainly because they didn't understand what they were dealing with.

In Washington, twenty-five of us were going to be at the controls today. We had another hundred who would be covering us in the field, taking shots and holding back troops if needed. From what we gathered using the IMSI data, a beach town about two hours north was the next target. It didn't sound like one of their larger fronts so we decided to use this as our first foray into battle.

I let out a shaky breath and watched as the last few members of our team trickled into the cafeteria. Preston was in the corner discussing with a group some of the last minute details that Braden had received from the IMSI analysis. Preston looked good, in his element. He had complete tactical gear on and loomed over everyone around him. It was a good look for him.

Preston scanned the room, and our eyes locked as that familiar pulse of electricity ran through us. We were about to embark on possibly the most important mission to date. My smile matched his as he strode through the crowd toward me.

"Ready to get this show started?" he whispered.

I nodded and felt the slight touch of his hand on the small of my back. It was just enough to show he cared. Emily was sitting behind me, but Braden wasn't here. He was receiving today's dose of the biologic. Timing was essential with biologics, which depended heavily on the process as much as the content.

Preston whistled loudly and the room went quiet. I studied all of the faces who'd committed to be by our side as we began the fight against an organization that was ruthless. There were mothers, sons, fathers, and daughters standing side-by-side ready to take on the evil that threatened our very existence.

Dr. Falino had already administered the biologic to everyone in this room, who wanted it. We weren't certain if or when it would take effect yet, but we had no choice.

"Thank you all for joining this effort. While we've been tracking TRAC for sometime, we didn't understand their capacity for wickedness in this way. The maliciousness that they have toward humankind is contagious. Like a disease it passes from one power-hungry person to another. We can't allow ourselves to be crushed by them or the threat of violence that they're so willing to engage in. Our plan should notify whoever's in charge that we haven't given up, and we are fully committed to fighting them in any way we can," I said, noticing several heads nod in agreement.

"They treat us like we're bugs to be squashed," a man three rows back yelled. "They took my wife and daughter away from me because of some neighbor's complaint. And for what? To make them zombies?"

The crowd grumbled and agreement spread that we had to do our part to stop TRAC. My concern was the government's response toward us once we interfered. So far, they were willing to listen to TRAC, and they fell right into TRAC's hands, even putting a bounty on Preston and me.

"We need to focus on one task at a time," Preston began. "While we can keep the big picture in our mind's eye, we can't focus on it because that reality is constantly shifting and changing."

"We don't know who we can trust at this point. As we've seen and heard, it looks like the government is involved, to what degree no one knows. It could seem far worse than it is or it could be far worse than it looks. Either way, we need to proceed with caution," I said.

People nodded, mumbling among themselves, and I glanced at Emily.

"Is it true?" A woman asked from the back of the crowd.

"Is what true?" Emily asked.

"That your husband will get to walk again."

"We hope so," Emily said, glancing at me.

"The same technology that has built the modifieds appears to contain several healing properties that humans react positively to."

"I just wonder what it'll do to us ten years down the road," the woman replied.

I nodded my head in agreement. None of us knew, and it was a question I'd asked myself plenty of times. It was the same question I posed to myself about Gavin's findings as well.

"We'll be rolling out of here in thirty minutes. Your assigned team leaders will have information that you can read over on the way to our destination. The modifieds are being loaded into a van as we speak. They've been awake for about six hours, and so far, they've responded to our direction. Remember, everyone is your enemy until they prove otherwise. We can't afford to think of it any other way," Preston told the group.

"What if there's no stopping them?" A man asked, who was sitting in the front row. His hand was entwined with the woman sitting next to him, and he appeared frightened.

"I doubt any of us gave up during the outbreak," I replied, glancing around the room. "Or we wouldn't be here today. We have to tap into the same mentality. We're in survival mode right now and failure can never be an option." I paused and took a step forward. "Some people are out there already fighting, but the majority of the country isn't. They're being ushered into whatever camps are set up, or who knows what. None of us know. We have no communication. Everything our country was built upon is being crushed by an elite few. But when did our world decide to let evil win? Because I didn't get the memo."

People started cheering and clapping as I turned around and looked at Preston. A different vibe cruised through the air, one of possibility. I wished I could capture it and let the rest of the country tap into it.

"One more thing," I said, facing them again and the group hushed. "Our worst nightmare when facing these modifieds is an empty chamber. Stay loaded. Now, let's make this a success today so we can come back and sleep like babies."

I swallowed a preemptive smile and felt the charge running through the air. I didn't know what to expect other than a fight, but I prayed for a first victory, however small it might be.

I scanned the room and felt that the end was getting close. Either way it went, something was going to come to a head. I thought about all the people who'd lost their lives, or who'd been swept up in cities across the country. I couldn't stop thinking about the people who, for whatever reason, didn't feel they could stand up and fight. I was doing this for them, the ones who couldn't do it for themselves. I may have started this fight to defend myself and clear my name, but I was going to help finish it to protect those who could no longer protect themselves.

I wanted the next generation to grow up without fear of disease and war because this generation had been plagued with it. I clutched Preston's hand and squeezed it gently. "I'm going to go find Dr. Falino before we leave."

Preston narrowed his eyes on me and nodded. "Okay. I'll meet you at the van."

I nodded, about to turn around, but he held me back for a split second as he grabbed my hand and pulled me toward him. His eyes fell to my lips and his mouth followed. A deep warmth spread through me as his kiss intensified, and it took everything I had to remember where I was. Almost as quickly as the kiss happened, it ended, and I was left staring at an incredibly bemused man, who finally understood the effect he had on me.

"Enough of that," I teased, and he let go of my hand before I spun around to hunt down Dr. Falino.

"I doubt it." His grin was out of this world, and for some reason it gave me the extra push to make the decision I'd been putting off.

I walked out the door and jogged over to the modifieds' building and swung open the door. The smell had either diminished or I'd gotten used to it. Either way, I still wound up breathing into the crook of my elbow. I spotted Dr. Falino, who was draining one of the empty incubators.

"Hey," I said, removing my arm to be heard. "I've been thinking about what you said, and I understand where you're coming from about needing to develop the acceleration process from Gavin."

She turned a knob and stood up with a tube in her hand. "And?"

"If I give you that information how can I be assured that you won't run to TRAC with it?"

"I ran away from TRAC, I certainly wouldn't run toward them."

"You know what I mean. How can I be certain this information won't get into the wrong hands?"

I counted the beats of my heart as steady as a metronome while I waited for her response. She looked across the sea of incubators and slowly brought her gaze back to mine.

"I guess you can't, but it wouldn't be me who got it there. I have a daughter who I would do anything for. She deserves a better world. She's why I'm here now. I need to make things right."

I let out a deep breath. "Our earth could never sustain what this might do to the population. We can't let this get out. It needs to stay between you and me for now. If this got out, everyone would want immortality."

Her eyes darkened and she shook her head. "You're wrong about that."

"About what?" I asked.

"Not everyone would want to be immortal."

I narrowed my eyes. "You're telling me you

wouldn't want to be immortal?"

She shook her head. "Absolutely not. One lifetime is plenty."

I hadn't expected that response from her, and I wasn't entirely sure I believed it. I crossed my arms and glimpsed the clock. I had about fifteen minutes before I had to meet the group.

"Can you make a batch of it off of Gavin's formula?" I asked.

She nodded. "I should be able to."

Ever since Emily and Braden copied all of the information from Gavin's folder into our database, I'd been a nervous wreck. It had been added to the virtual piles of other data for people to sift through and attempt to make sense of it all. Fortunately, it took the kind of knowledge Dr. Falino had to actually understand the significance of his findings.

"I've been meaning to ask you something about Marcus," I said. Her posture stiffened and her gaze dipped. "Was he actually the person in charge of TRAC? The one really calling the shots?"

"Yes. Definitely. He was the one who barked the orders and delivered the blows if you didn't do as he said." She let go of the tube, and it dropped into a bucket.

"And there was never an inkling that there was someone else orchestrating things?"

She shook her head. "Honestly, I never thought that. I don't think Marcus would have been able to handle someone over him. That wasn't his personality. He was a one-man show."

"Then how is his one-man show thriving so well if he's not here to control it?" I asked, my eyes locking on hers.

"He ran a tight ship. Every person who worked for Marcus was willing to take a bullet for him. I'm guessing his top guys knew his plans and simply had the tools to execute them, but I've had plenty of wrong guesses in my life."

I took a deep breath in, letting it fill my lungs completely, regardless of the lingering odor, and let it out slowly. "All for what?"

"Power is an interesting thing. Some people are crushed under the weight of it and others thrive with it to a fault. They allow it to mold a new person because of it. Very few understand what it feels like to influence entire groups of people. For Marcus, his influence started small but grew quickly. It was like his drug. Authority over others was like his fix, and he was able to pick out others like him, the ones who craved it."

"It's quite a responsibility," I said.

"It should be. It really should be, but unfortunately the people who want it the most are the ones who shouldn't be allowed to gain it, but that's not how it works in this world. I don't know if he was born that way, but that's what he turned into as a man."

"Was he like that during the outbreak?" I asked.

"Long before. He and his brother both enjoyed the possibilities that came with gaining control of situations. It just turned out that one brother was better at it than the other. It's something I didn't want my daughter to have to witness, and I just pray she didn't get any of those attributes. Genetics can go either way." She sighed, her eyes looking a million miles away.

"I keep hoping that love is stronger than hate," I said. "That courage is stronger than fear. That's what we need to take TRAC down. It's got to be fear that's keeping the citizens down."

"You started all of this because you wanted to find out what happened to your husband. Why he was singled out..." her voice trailed off. "Why he was killed."

I nodded, and my eyes lowered to the half-empty incubator. "True."

"If they'd given you an option where you could've kept him alive, even if it meant doing something you wouldn't normally do—"

"I would've done anything I had to do if I'd been given that option," I replied.

"Exactly. TRAC is using the one thing to get the survivors to do things they wouldn't normally do."

"Love," I murmured.

She nodded. "Love. These people are being threatened in unimaginable ways. They're doing what they think they need to do to keep their loved ones alive. Things might have been different a decade ago, before the outbreak, but so few of us have any loved ones left. The ones we do have, the ones we love, we hold onto fiercely."

I nodded.

"Don't give up. Things will fall into place. They

always do," she replied.

"But when their passion is founded on hate, not love..." I stopped myself.

"Then you need to feed off of that. Ground yourself in what you're sure of and maybe that will spread. You're not trying to take over the world, you're trying to save it. That, my dear, is based on love."

"Let's hope that's enough."

"Yes. Let's hope."

I chewed on my lip for half of a second and pulled out a thumb drive the size of my fingernail and handed it to Dr. Falino. My hands were moist from the exchange, but this was one of the only things we had on our side. The ability to stay alive. I'd allowed myself to see a different side of Dr. Falino this morning, and I only hoped that I wasn't fooled by her apparent honesty.

"You have my word that this will not get into the wrong hands," she said, her eyes connecting with mine.

"I guess that all depends on which side of the fence you're on," I said, frowning.

"Pardon?" she asked, slipping the device into her pocket.

I shook my head. "Nothing. Sorry."

"Good luck today," she offered, as I walked through the incubators. "I'll start working on this after I'm done here."

I nodded and waved as I opened the door and spotted Preston who was faithfully waiting by the van. This was it—my chance to fight for those who no longer could.

Chapter Twenty-Five

We watched from the hill as the soldiers surrounded the town. Vehicles blocked all roadways in and out, and barricades had been erected to deter foot traffic, but from the look of things no one wanted to go anywhere. They just obeyed.

Using the binoculars, I focused in on two soldiers who were marching from home to home. First they'd knock; then they'd hand whoever answered the door a flyer, and they'd turn around and leave while the resident slowly shut the door after them. Generally, their expression was one of complete shock. Every so often I'd catch a quick flash of anger or disgust, but it was quickly replaced with fear or complacency. I'd watched this interaction at eleven homes, and out of that many, maybe three registered some other emotion. Three.

I spotted their group of modifieds at the west

end of town. They appeared almost lifeless, as they stood corralled, waiting for the signal. Preston tapped my shoulder and pointed to the other end of town. I quickly swung my binoculars. A soldier had a man on his knees with his hands up. He was probably begging for his life or his family's, and my stomach clenched, afraid of what might come next.

Preston adjusted the camera he'd attached to his vest. Every vehicle and team member was equipped with one.

"Look at the soldiers," I whispered. "Not a care in the world. There isn't one reason they'd look over their shoulder and worry that they'd run into any interference."

"Well, that's about to change." Preston shot me a grin, and I silently chuckled.

Yes, it was.

I handed the binoculars to Preston and clutched my controller.

"It's about to get real," I said, positioning the controller on my lap. I unfolded the screen and saw the camera footage appear. Our drone was live. I'd been searching the skies and hadn't seen theirs surface yet.

"Shit. There's movement," Preston muttered, he eyed the direction of their modifieds.

He quickly began searching the sky for their drone. "Got it. They're up. Looks like it's hovering at eleven o'clock."

I nodded as Preston notified the others, and I slowly began raising my drone from the patch of grass that it had been resting on. The viewpoint in the field was much different than all the practice sessions. I steadied my breathing as the drone lifted higher, and I caught a glimpse of our modifieds. My goal was to stay out of view and direct our modifieds.

"Oh, no," Preston whispered.

"What's going on?" I asked.

"A line of modifieds. They're on the move and headed to the man on his knees."

My stomach tensed.

I quickly flipped on communication with the satellite and began programming the exact codes that I'd spent days memorizing. Our modifieds came into view on the screen. They were deathly still. Our program hadn't started to communicate with them yet.

Damn it.

From my vantage point everyone looked like ants, aggressive ants. The soldiers marched in formation down the street, and one by one the doors began opening and people began spilling outside. They marched down their steps, following the directions from the soldiers, until they stood where they were told. Every so often one would glance in the direction of the man who was still on his knees.

I kept my drone behind a Victorian home. The second story turret provided a nice shield as I let it hover, and my fingers programmed the commands. My eyes continually flicked between my screen and the small figures down the hill.

I focused on the man at the mercy of the soldiers, praying the modifieds wouldn't get to him before I had a chance to get ours to join the show when it happened. The first twitch and shudder of one of our modifieds sent a jolt of excitement through me. I toggled between the satellite image and the image from my drone as the modifieds began to heave their heavy legs forward and wobble slowly to their targets. I skimmed the crowd. No one noticed that there was definite activity coming their way.

It couldn't have worked out more perfect as our modifieds snaked between two homes in the center of town, bypassing the soldiers as our modifieds jerked their way toward TRAC's modifieds. My adrenaline was at an all-time high as I transformed Main Street into a zombie pit, but this time it was our rules.

Before the soldiers even recognized what was happening, two of our modifieds lurched toward the targets. Without a hitch, our modifieds tore the arms off the targets and began destroying them piece-by-piece. I watched in utter disbelief as the onslaught of our modifieds overpowered the situation, devastating their supply. The element of surprise was a wonderful thing.

"Their modifieds are too focused on what they were programmed to do. They're not fighting ours at all," Preston said, as astonished as I was.

He put his binoculars down and grabbed his rifle.

It wasn't until I heard a shrill scream echo between the hills that my hopes immediately shattered. Searching for the source, a wave of nausea hit me the moment I saw a little girl running toward the man on his knees. A gunshot fired into the air to get her attention, but she didn't stop running. She didn't care. She wanted her dad. Her hands were outstretched as she continued to run toward him. The little girl wasn't going to stop until she reached him.

The chaos dislodged the soldiers' plans as orders were barked out, and shots were taken at our modifieds, but it didn't matter. We'd managed to take out at least half of theirs.

"Their drone is still too far out of range," Preston muttered in frustration. Our weapon drone wasn't finished yet. Weight distribution proved to be more difficult than we initially thought so it was up to our guys to get it out of the sky.

I glanced back at the little girl who was hanging on her father's neck as he pleaded for her to follow the soldiers' directions. She was having no part of it. Two soldiers attempted to pull her from her father, but she met them kicking and struggling against their strength. I studied the townspeople. All of them stood as instructed. No one moved. All it might take for some was a vivid, momentary recall of a reimagined death or loss of some sort that led to this paralysis of mind, body, and soul. We needed to break through it.

"This isn't going to end well," I whispered.

Preston gave a slight nod, taking his focus off the drone.

Modifieds seven and nine were closest to the little girl and the soldiers, but I didn't know what would happen if the little girl got caught in between when I programmed the modifieds to target the soldiers.

I watched as she twisted and recoiled from the soldiers pulling on her, and then it happened. Her father bowed his head, her arms slipping freely from his neck as the soldiers dragged her away. Her screams reached the heavens and beyond as I watched helplessly.

A crack reverberated through the air, and my heart seized as I saw her father fall to the ground. Preston took aim and downed the soldier who shot the man. The soldier collapsed on the pavement from the headshot as blood pooled on the cement.

I programmed the remaining modifieds to begin their attacks on the soldiers as Preston continued taking aim at the remaining men. I saw our people surround the sides of the houses just out of view as they awaited our signal. The soldiers' attention had turned to our location, searching the hillside.

A bullet hissed through the air, ricocheting on the large boulder behind us. The ping of another sent a stinging pain through my arm. A fragment of rock dug into my skin as I continued the attack with the modifieds. Preston slid down against the rock and nodded. Getting on my radio, I gave the command. It was time for the larger operation. My eyes landed on the innocent man who lay in the street.

As our team descended on the town, shots rang out as the soldiers attempted to protect their territory. The townspeople didn't flee. Instead, they huddled in groups as our team downed soldiers. The little girl broke free from the woman holding her and ran to her father, sliding to hold him in the street.

My heart ripped in half as I watched her try to roll him over. Two members of our team saw the little girl and ran toward her. Preston kept watch down his barrel to ensure that no one got in their way.

Out of the corner of my eye, I caught one of the soldiers fleeing. He ran down the street toward one of the vehicles when a bullet took him down. He fell forward, and I turned away. My focus centered back on the father and daughter below.

"We've got a pulse," came over the radio.

"Let's hope someone in town is a doctor," I radioed back.

The disarray on the streets below continued. My heart nearly pounded out of my chest. I watched as their last modified was ripped to shreds and relief spread through me right before a bullet zinged into the head of our victor, collapsing our modified immediately.

A sniper from our team positioned herself on the roof of one of the buildings and began taking out soldiers, turning the unity they had into disarray, disarming the cohesion they once had. Madness and desperation began infiltrating their squad. They'd never prepared for a plan B. They'd always counted on victory, and no longer understood what they were fighting for or against.

Preston pulled the trigger dropping a soldier who was running toward our team that was guarding the little girl and her father. I scanned the remaining soldiers. There were only seven left. I pulled back our modifieds, sending them back to their holding place. I didn't want to risk losing any more.

Without warning, the soldiers threw their weapons onto the street, holding their hands above their heads.

Preston's head jerked in surprise, and he glanced over his shoulder.

"Do you believe it?" I asked, puzzled.

He shook his head. "I don't. I really don't."

"Is that the difference between fighting for a cause and just fighting?"

Members of our team quickly restrained the soldiers, checking for other weapons and tossing them in a pile. I stared through the binoculars, watching the expressions on the faces of the townspeople. To say they were confused would be putting it mildly.

"Let's make our way down there," I said, placing the controls down.

"Let's do it."

He strapped his rifle to his back as we climbed down the hill. He hiked with such ease that barely a rock was even disturbed. I, however, did not navigate with such ease, often sliding down patches in order to keep up.

"We've got a nurse with the downed victim," Jerry said. He was the man who'd spoken up earlier this morning. "The victim is the mayor."

I gave a half-nod, refusing to look over at the man and his daughter. Instead, I kept my focus on the cowards ahead of us.

My heart hardened as I got closer and saw no remorse—fear for their lives possibly—but no remorse.

These weren't soldiers.

Preston and I stood about three feet in front of them. They were on their knees, handcuffed and tied to one another. The man on the end spat on the ground, barely missing my shoe. He was stocky and grizzled.

The townspeople were dazed as they slowly wandered back to their homes. I could hear our team trying to calm them down as they led them back to their houses. Some were in tears. Others were angered.

"So you shot that man," I began.

"I didn't shoot at shit," the guy scoffed.

"Right. What were your orders?" I asked, folding my arms.

"Same as they always are," a different man answered, this one frail, skittish.

"And what would that be?" Preston asked.

"We don't have to tell you anything," the puny one said.

"True. You don't, but then you'd be no use to us, but you would prove useful for our undead. I never turn down target practice." I smiled, shifting my weight.

The man eyed the ground in front of him. "We have a list of officials who we must exterminate.

Anyone who doesn't give us trouble, we evacuate."

"To where?" Preston asked, as a train rattled behind us. The man didn't answer until the train disappeared.

"We take them to a quarantine area."

"Quarantine for what?" I asked.

He shook his head. "Don't know. That's just what we do. Then we head off to the next town."

"And you never once asked what happens to the people or the towns?"

"No, ma'am."

Now I was a ma'am. Great.

"Who's in charge? Who's giving you the orders?" Preston's eyes narrowed on the larger man, who was continuously shifting weight from one knee to the other.

"Our squadron leader."

Preston's irritation level was growing by the second as was mine. "And who do they get them from?"

The heavier man shrugged and looked at the woman next to him, who hadn't moved a muscle. She kept her stare straight ahead.

"We don't know."

The tips of my fingers prickled with anger as I stared at these mindless beings in front of us.

"You're willing to kill people for a leader you don't know, and for a cause you've never heard of." Preston's hands fisted into balls.

"Our families were threatened. We had no choice," the female spoke, her eyes shifting to meet mine.

"You always have a choice. You can choose to be a coward or you can choose to make a difference. You chose wrong," I said.

"I took my chances. I did what was right for my family," she responded.

"How can you be so sure?" My brow arched.

"They took them away so that they wouldn't be hurt."

"They took them away to use them," I replied. "Just like they use everyone."

A tear slipped down the woman's cheek.

"You want to know the cause we're fighting for?" she asked, her eyes locked on mine.

I nodded.

"Immortality. Those who stand to the end will receive it. My family will not only be protected, they'll be immortal."

"That's what you've been told?" I asked, swallowing back my anger.

They all nodded.

"Whatever those beasts are, they hold our future," the woman said. "No matter how much we hate them, they are our salvation. There's a woman researcher who's cracked the code or so we've heard."

My blood chilled.

I fell right into Dr. Falino's hands. I spun on my heels, leaving Preston with the group, which I now refused to call soldiers, and dialed Emily's number.

"How's it going?" she asked. "I'd say by the looks of it, pretty good."

That was one of the many benefits of us

recording our attacks.

"Dr. Falino can't be trusted. I gave her the information that Gavin had. The information that you guys scanned into the system. She knew what it was for. I think she's the one running TRAC."

"Oh, no. She took off, Rebekah. She's not on the compound."

"Where'd she say she was going?" I asked, anger pounding through my veins.

"She didn't say. I didn't ask. What information did you give her? What did it mean?"

I closed my eyes as the mistake I made washed over me slowly. I never should've trusted her. I opened my eyes and let out a breath as I glanced at Preston. His gaze connected with mine as the realization now hit him. I hadn't told him that I gave her the information, but he knew.

"Gavin found a way to accelerate the healing process. It changes things. Mightily. It's possibly as close as the human race can get to immortality."

"Could you be wrong?" she asked.

"Always a chance, but I highly doubt it. Spread the word. If she comes back, which I doubt she will...But if she does, don't let on that we know who she really is. We need to stay as close to her as possible."

"That won't be a problem."

I hung up and walked over to Preston. "What do we do with them?"

Preston shrugged. "They're of no use to us

now. Maybe throw them in with the modifieds."

The woman cried out, and I glared at her.

"Let's hold onto them. See if any other information might pop into their feeble little minds," I said.

Preston motioned for some of our team members to come over and watch them, while we walked over to the sidewalk.

"I gave Dr. Falino the key. The final piece of information, I just handed it to her," I said, shaking my head in disbelief.

"Everything we do is based on guesses. Sometimes we guess right. Sometimes we guess wrong. We don't know for sure that it's Dr. Falino."

"I'd like to believe it's not the case, but I think that our reasoning skills are more fine-tuned than that." I pursed my lips together, scanning the town.

Preston nodded and sighed. "I know. I just don't want to believe it."

"Is it over if it's her? If she's the one that's been calling the shots the whole time, wanted the power... Now she's got it and more. Do we just give up?"

"One step at a time," he said, pulling me into him.

"I'd rather go out trying then be imprisoned by these bastards," I whispered.

"Don't go there, babe," he said, shaking his head. "Don't jump to conclusions."

My eyes drifted away from Preston to Jerry who was walking over to us, holding one of the fliers. I stepped away quickly from Preston as he handed it to him.

"No need to hide it from me," Jerry said, smiling. There was a twinkle in his eye that I hadn't seen before and my insides crushed. We'd developed a team based on false hope of victory.

"I see why people complied so easily," Preston said, shoving the flyer into my hands.

I looked down to read it, execution threatened if one merely sneezed or stepped out of line. Horrific photographs of those who dared cross the lines were printed as examples. This was how terror went viral, paralyzing even the strongest individuals. For the first time in a long time, I felt defeated and unsure of what our future might look like.

Chapter Twenty-Six

Dr. Falino hadn't come back yet, not that I expected she would. Preston and I sat at the table with Emily and Braden. We'd decided to keep everything to ourselves and let everyone enjoy this small victory. The current in the air was packed full of enthusiasm and hope for future endeavors as celebrations mixed with rehashing of events.

"I think I'm going to go check out the lab," I announced, determined to prove to myself that I couldn't have been so wrong.

"I'll come with you," Preston offered, sliding his chair back from the table.

"I'd like that," I said, my gaze falling to Emily's.

"You didn't know," she said reassuringly, her hand grasping mine.

I smiled and nodded. I slowly stood up and stretched, trying to force the tears down.

Preston reached out his hand, which I held as

we walked through the cafeteria, stopping every so often for a congratulatory handshake or pat on the back. Keeping the smile plastered to my face was difficult, and the second I felt the cold air smack into me, I dropped it.

The refinery lights reflected off the metal, and the night sky was clearer than it had been all winter. I leaned my head against Preston's arm as we slowly walked over to the modifieds' building. I knew I had to keep it together, but it was hard. Really hard.

Preston pulled on the door, and we stepped inside the semi-lit space. The pale blue glow from the incubators gave off enough light as we made our way to the lab where Paul and Stanley were working away, lights blazing as we opened the door.

"What are you working on?" I asked.

"Finishing up the biologic for the next batch," Stanley answered, using a tiny dropper to disperse a liquid into several test tubes.

"Did Dr. Falino mention anything about where she was heading?" I asked, scanning her workstation for the thumb drive.

"No. She just said she had to attend to something and would be back as soon as she could. She asked us to continue production," Stanley said, placing the dropper on its own holder. He removed the latex gloves and glanced at Paul, who was removing his white lab coat and hanging it on a hook by the door.

"Okay. Sweet," I said, attempting to act nonchalant.

"Any beer left at the party?" Paul smiled and wiggled his brows.

"Should be plenty," Preston laughed, placing his hand on the small of my back.

"Ready?" Paul asked Stanley, who nodded as he tossed the gloves into the trash.

"Have fun," I called out behind them, happy about their quick exit.

I started shuffling through Dr. Falino's papers, spotting notes and printouts that matched Gavin's handwriting. She must have printed some of his notes out. I picked up one of the papers, my hand trembling as I stared at it.

"Gavin died to protect this information, and I handed it over. Just. Like. That." I motioned, releasing the paper from my fingers. We watched it sail to the floor, and all I wanted to do was slide to the floor with it.

"You don't know that it's in the wrong hands," Preston said, running his hands along my arms, turning me to face him. "Besides, she probably plans on coming right back."

"I don't see her here, do you?" I asked, feeling the lump form in the back of my throat. "I failed him, Preston. Twice."

"You didn't fail him," he whispered, bringing me into him.

"But I did." I closed my eyes and felt the moistness behind my lids. I'd managed to jeopardize everything so quickly, and there was no patching it up, no fixing this.

Preston traced his hands along my back as he let out a long breath. "I'm to blame just as much. I trusted her too. I thought she might offer something that could be our answer once and for all. You can't carry this burden alone, whatever it turns out to be."

I took a step back and nodded slowly, my eyes canvasing the room for any sort of clue to her whereabouts, even if it was a feeble attempt.

"She had such a good story about love, hate, power, and fear." I shook my head.

"They often do," he sighed, wiping his hand over his face.

I opened the fridge and saw a couple of vials with the letters GT1 scribbled on the glass. I dipped my head lower and twisted the vials, not recognizing the liquid inside. Who knew what it was in this place. I closed the door and spun around to see Preston watching me intently.

"If our world really is going to come crashing down soon, maybe we should take a cue from the others..." my voice trailed off.

Preston laughed and shook his head, holding out his hand. "You never cease to amaze me."

I reached for his hand, feeling the strength of his grip as he brought me toward him. The blood running through my body warmed as I allowed his touch to fully comfort me.

Looking up at him through my lashes, I took in a shaky breath, knowing what I was about to do. What we were about to do. "Let's get out of here."

His eyes darkened as the desire pulsed between us. The intensity behind Preston's gaze made me feel completely vulnerable. It was something I hadn't felt in a long time, if ever. He flashed a half-smile and swept a gentle kiss along my cheek before leading me out of the building.

Everything felt like it was in slow motion. The cold air wrapped around my body as we almost floated outside, begging my mind to lose the memories from earlier. The door to the cafeteria was open, and people were whooping and hollering celebratory wishes and greetings to each other. A pulse of jealousy ran through me right before Preston stopped and yanked me toward him, catching me completely off guard.

"I'm sorry. I can't help myself," he murmured, as he pressed his body into mine.

My breathing changed as I felt his mouth feather across my neck. His mouth softly traced along my flesh sending a flash of electricity through my world. I ran my hands through his hair, fisting the strands as his mouth found mine.

In his arms, I felt like the rest of the world no longer existed, and in this moment that was what I needed to believe. As I stood buried in his embrace, breathless and wanting, a few whistles from the crowd interrupted our bliss, and I groaned at the distraction. Briefly feigning annoyance, Preston kissed me one more time before we parted, and I bowed before the crowd to an eruption of applause. Pretending was nice, even if only for the night.

Wrapping his arm around my waist, we walked quickly through the group, who continued clapping and cheering. They'd obviously been having a good time with drinks in hand. The warmth of the cafeteria swept over me, and I leaned into Preston as we headed toward the elevator. Quickly climbing on, I turned around and scanned the cafeteria, capturing the moment of celebration one last time before the doors closed. This was how I wanted to remember what we'd accomplished, regardless of what tomorrow held.

Preston leaned against the wall in the elevator. He was still dressed in a black, tight-fitting shirt and loose fitting black cargos, and my gaze traveled along his lean, muscular body as I imagined what I would do to him. Before I realized what was happening he had me pinned against the wall; his hands on either side of me as he leaned in, his mouth only inches from mine. The blood pumped through my body at an unstoppable pace as his eyes fell to my lips. I was utterly fascinated by this man's deliberate attempt to entrap me, and all I could think about was how I wanted more.

More of this.

More of him.

The elevator opened on our floor, but he didn't move. Instead he slowly slid his hands down my arms, keeping his lips only inches from my mouth until his hands rested on mine. I inhaled, trying to catch my breath, but he was intoxicating, and I was left wanting.

A moan escaped my lips as he brushed his mouth along my cheek before taking a step back, blocking the doors from shutting with his foot. He smiled as he locked his hand with mine and slowly brought me forward. His free hand traced along my jawline sending sparks of pleasure through my body as he took me in.

Cradling my chin between his thumb and finger he tilted his head down. Looking in his eyes, I saw the reflection of who I wanted to be. He saw me the way I never saw myself. My breath caught as my lashes fell and his mouth pressed against mine.

It felt as if the world around us no longer existed. I didn't know where I was other than I no longer stood in an elevator. My legs were wrapped around his waist. Our kisses deepened with every thought of loss and love exchanging between us. I could no longer deny the attraction, wondering why I had for so long. I didn't even know how we made it to his room until he pushed the door open, and I kicked it shut with my foot. He chuckled, and the low hum of his voice vibrated our lips, pulling me deeper into a haze of ecstasy.

Preston brought me down to the bed and slowly moved onto me, his thighs straddling my waist as I slid my hands underneath his shirt, feeling the hard ripples of his stomach. Tugging on his shirt, he smiled and quickly pulled it over his head and tossed it on the floor. I couldn't hide my smile as my finger traced his tattoo, the definition of his chest and stomach.

"You're so beautiful when you smile, Rebekah," he murmured, kissing me once more.

My fingers ran along his back, feeling the scars and victories of our life together so far. His lips left mine, and my body immediately begged for more as he slowly lifted my shirt over my head. His touch was deliberate, knowing, but his intent was careful and loving as his fingertips traced along the edge of my bra.

I looked up at the man who'd meant so much to me for so long. My lips were swollen and throbbing from his, but I craved him. His button not in reach, I let out a little moan, adjusting my body under his.

Preston's smile deepened, but he just slowly shook his head, letting his fingers skate across my skin. "I'm not rushing something I've waited so long for."

My body quivered as the words wrapped themselves around me. My cheeks blushed, but I knew I was at his mercy and let myself succumb to his wishes. He began peppering light kisses across my stomach, but I pulled him up to me, directing his mouth to mine as my hands slid to his hips. There was no hesitation as his hands brushed over my skin, and he continued to undress me. The warmth inside pooled at the base of my stomach as we explored each other, his mouth caressing and teasing as I let the sensations run through me.

Preston drew his finger along my stomach, stopping just short of my panties, and this time it was my turn. I shook my head, squirming under him, so that he would follow my near-silent pleas. I wanted to feel him, touch him.

My hands worked his button and zipper, and a bolt of delight shot through me when his body trembled with my touch. His breathing grew ragged as my fingers skated along his thighs to his back.

His kisses deepened, parting my lips in a perfect rhythm as the worlds I'd fought so hard to keep separate connected in a way that I'd never dared to imagine. I shuddered underneath him as my fingers dug into his skin, pulling him into me, and allowing our worlds to finally connect as one. In this moment in time, it felt like all of our problems ceased to exist as he held me in his arms. I dared to imagine another way of existing. For the first time in a very long time, I slipped into a peaceful slumber.

It wasn't until the sun shone through the window with such a blazing vengeance that I even realized how long I'd been out. I pulled the comforter up to my chin and felt the chill of the sheets against my skin as I turned over in bed, expecting to find Preston.

Except he wasn't there.

Holding the sheet around me, I shot up in bed and called out for him. It wasn't like I thought he'd pop out from under the bed, so I'm not sure why I felt the urge to holler. Something didn't seem right. I quickly slid on yesterday's clothes and ran my fingers through my hair. Swinging the door open, I almost smacked into Emily, who gave me a knowing grin.

"About time," she laughed.

I scowled at her but couldn't hold back my smile. "Do you know where he went by any chance?"

"He's not back?" she asked.

"Back from where?" I asked.

"He mentioned that he was going to go on a quick jog and bring you your favorite, Cinnamon Toast Crunch, but that was like two hours ago."

My heart knocked in my chest as I shook my head. "I'll go check in the cafeteria. Maybe he got caught up with someone."

"Okay. That's probably what happened."

Not wanting to look like I was panicking as much as I was, I did a fast walk rather than a slow jog to the elevator. Pressing the button several times too many, I couldn't hop on the carriage fast enough. I pressed the button and tapped on the one to close the door. My mind flashed to the night before and I felt my entire body warm.

The doors opened and my pulse climbed as I saw an empty cafeteria. I ran off the elevator and out the door to the modifieds building. Swinging the doors open, I called for Preston and saw no one. I knew he wasn't in the lab, but I checked anyway. My pulse was pounding in my head and my world threatened to collapse. I knew in my heart that something was wrong.

I ran to the next building and the next, all coming up empty-handed. He wouldn't go jogging for two hours. He wouldn't leave me like that. Not after...

Barely able to breath by the time I got back upstairs, I found Emily. About to tell her there was no Preston, our alarm went off. Our security had been breached.

"Everyone to their stations," Trek commanded over the speakers.

It felt like my world was slipping away from me before I even had a chance to claim it.

"I've got to stay with Braden," Emily whispered.

I nodded.

"Stay safe."

"Men down. I repeat men down at stations one, three, and four," Trek's voice sent chills down my spine. Could one of those men be Preston?

Not bothering to wait for the elevator, I ran down the stairs two at a time until I reached the bottom. I threw open the door and ran outside. I had to make it to the command center. That was my station, and that was my way to see what was going on.

A loud rumble echoed through the air, but I didn't stop running until I reached the building. The door was locked. I needed in. I began slapping the door until someone unlocked it remotely, and I ran down the corridor.

"Sorry. Protocol is to lock the door," Trek apologized.

"I understand," I said, completely breathless. "What's the status?"

"Seven killed. We've got nine vehicles inside our walls."

I searched the video screens, trying to find any sign of Preston and found none. I was afraid to ask the one question that I didn't want an answer to. That was a very important survival lesson I'd learned during the outbreak. Instead, I watched the nine vehicles as they barreled down our road. It was only a matter of time before they arrived.

Chapter Twenty-Seven

I watched as the first vehicle came to a rolling stop, dust billowing from the tires. The other eight vehicles lined up directly behind the first. The passenger door swung open, and a woman I didn't recognize stepped outside. Her small frame was overshadowed by her thigh-high black boots, which covered her tight-fitting khaki pants. A black shawl was looped over her shoulders, and her brown hair was slicked back. Her blood red lips pressed together to form a heart shape even though her expression was stern. She took three steps forward and stared directly into the camera as she rested her hand on her hip.

"I'd like to speak with Rebekah Taylor," she nearly growled.

Trek looked at me, eyes wide, and I nodded for him to flip on the speaker.

"What can I do for you?" I asked.

The woman removed her oversized shades to reveal dark brown eyes. She narrowed them at the camera and sucked on the tip of her glasses before speaking.

"You have something I want, and I'm pretty sure I have something you want. Unless, of course you don't mind if he ends up like Gavin."

My breath caught, and I balanced myself using the table in front of me. I began shaking, unable to believe this was happening again. It couldn't be happening again. This woman didn't have Preston.

Trek released the intercom and spun in his chair to see me. "What do you want me to do? I can sound the silent alarm. We've got guns, Rebekah. We can match them."

I focused on the image of the woman and watched as the driver's side door opened and a man stepped out.

I shook my head. "We can't risk it. Not until we know what we're dealing with."

"We're dealing with someone who doesn't value life," he responded.

"Which is exactly why we can't go out there with guns blazing. If she does have Preston, they'll shoot him before we have a chance—" my voice broke, and I stopped myself.

The images of the night before ran through my mind. I wouldn't fail Preston like I did Gavin. I walked to the wall and began staring at our arsenal.

"You a good shot?" I asked.

"I'm fair."

I nodded. "Fair is perfect. Means you're not too cocky, and you'll offer a nice surprise when you hit the targets."

He stood up and picked a .308 off the wall, and popped in a full magazine. "This ought to work."

I smiled and nodded as I flashed back to the day that changed my life forever. Anger and revenge fueled me, but last night that changed. I had something even more powerful on my side, and I wasn't about to let that slip through my fingers again. I glanced at the screen. The woman was becoming increasingly impatient.

"What's it going to be, Ms. Taylor?" she asked.

Trek flipped on the intercom again. "What is that you want from me?" I asked.

"Don't play coy with me." She snapped her fingers, and the man swung open the back door of the SUV and pulled someone out. He shut the door and threw the person onto the ground. Her wrists and ankles were tightly bound. Blood trailed down her jacket.

"It's Dr. Falino," Trek whispered, his voice picked up by the intercom.

I was certain she'd been in on it, but now I didn't know. There was so much I didn't know.

"Yes. It's Dr. Falino." The woman laughed a brittle laugh, peeking over her shoulder as Dr. Falino remained on the ground, almost lifeless. "Does she give you a clue to what I'm looking for?"

My stomach clenched, and I looked at Trek, motioning for him to turn off the intercom. Dr. Falino could've handed over the formula.

But she didn't.

She could've saved herself.

But she didn't.

"I don't want you to go outside with me. Stay inside and monitor the situation. Let Braden know what's going on and to stand down until otherwise instructed. He'll inform the others. We only have one shot at this."

"Yes, ma'am," he said, nodding.

I shook my head. "Don't call me ma'am. Not yet. You're not that much younger than I am."

He grinned and I nodded.

"Glad that's settled."

I strapped a rifle over my shoulder and checked to make sure my Glock was fully loaded, securing it back in my holster. My pulse was racing, but I was no longer driven by madness and revenge. I saw my reflection in the glass and liked what I saw. My black leathers would compliment this woman's whip-snapping ensemble nicely.

I was a woman on a mission, but this one wasn't filled with pure hatred.

"How old do you think she is?" I asked.

"Is this a trick question?" he asked.

I shook my head and smiled.

"Mid-fifties."

"That's what I think too." I nodded and walked out of the room, readying myself to face whatever was on the other side of the door. My hand rested on the metal handle, and I took a deep breath in and clicked open the door.

I walked through the opening, my eyes

landing on the woman. She was as chilly in person as on the screen.

"You're such a young, pretty thing," she drawled. "He always did have good taste."

I stopped in my tracks, my head snapping up to meet her gaze. The man opened the door on the other side of the vehicle, and my heart began beating so fast I thought I might actually black out. I needed my body to be stronger than my mind wanted to allow.

Her laughter was shrill as I watched the man haul out their next victim. Preston was blindfolded and gagged. His wrists and ankles bound in chain, which differed from Dr. Falino. Hers were rope. His blood-soaked hair made my stomach turn in on itself, and it took everything I had not to run to him and hold him in my arms.

I swallowed the misery that attempted to paralyze me. I would not become like the others. I would not let fear control me. I would not bow down to this woman. I was stronger that that.

I watched as the man threw Preston onto the ground, his body colliding with the dirt. His cheek smacked against the surface so hard, bloody spit flew out of his mouth. I looked back at the woman standing before me, her dark eyes void of any kindness. Her darkness nipped at my soul, reminding me what it meant to be human. Why I was different than her.

"Now would be a good time," the woman called.

"Yes, ma'am," the man replied.

I looked behind the woman and watched as he

kicked Preston swiftly in the stomach. Preston's body curled in pain, but he refused to say a word.

"Now, back to our deal," she said, crossing her arms in front of her.

"I didn't make a deal with you," I replied.

Preston recognized my voice and attempted to raise his head.

Her lip twitched in response to my answer, but she didn't say anything.

My eyes drifted to Preston, and she snapped her finger. The man kicked Preston again. His jaw clenched in pain, and the muscles in his neck contracted, but he stayed still.

"You're a tough one," she said, pacing slightly as she contemplated something. "Tougher than I thought. Maybe I miscalculated."

I stood staring straight ahead. "Miscalculated what?"

"Your love for my son," she said, her eyes narrowing into cat-like slits.

It was like a stab to my heart.

My eyes fell to Preston and slowly rose to the woman who stood in front of me. I didn't have the luxury of insanity. It didn't matter what my mind wanted me to do, I had to stay strong and focused. So instead of screaming, I continued to glare at her.

Responding to my silence, she continued. "Yes, that's right...my son. A little surprised?"

My hand instinctively slid to my Glock. "Tricia Blakely."

"I wouldn't do that if I were you. You have too many questions running through that beautiful, little head of yours." She loved to hear herself talk, and I hated her for everything that was about to come out of her mouth. "I bet you're wondering was this all a set-up? Did Preston ever love you? How did he find you? Did he even have a sister named Sophie? Did he work for TRAC all along? How did he fool you? How did he fool Emily and Braden?"

My mouth was so parched and my lips were so dry as I watched Tricia smile, waiting for my reaction. A reaction I wasn't going to give her.

"Oh come on. Tell me at least one of those questions ran through that mind of yours," she laughed, her voice buzzing with anticipation, but her eyes still lifeless.

"Not a single one," I replied flatly.

Preston's mouth twitched slightly, and I knew none of what she said was true.

None of it could be true.

Her jaw jetted forward, and I scanned her face, looking for any resemblance between Preston and Tricia.

"I can tell you some questions that are running through my mind though..." my voice trailed off.

She rubbed her hands together.

The game of it. She loved the game of it. TRAC loved the game of it.

This was the woman who orchestrated it all from the very beginning, and now she was standing in front of me, willing to kill her own son or anyone who got in her way.

"How do you sleep at night?" I asked.

"Very well." She smiled.

"Have you ever loved someone besides yourself? Have you ever tasted love?" I folded my arms in front of me and arched a brow, waiting for a response.

"With everything I just revealed, you want to ask me about my sleeping habits and love life?" she seethed, slipping her sunglasses back on.

"I think the answers are relevant, or at least your reaction is."

She shook her head and tossed her head back in frustration. I wasn't playing into her game. The man standing next to Preston removed his pistol and pointed it directly at Preston's head. I wouldn't let my body tremble, but my insides quivered at the sight, which fed my determination.

I heard movement on the other side of the SUV and quickly looked over to see Dr. Falino slowly rise to a sitting position, her hands digging into the soil as she propped herself up against the SUV.

Tricia turned around to see what the noise was about and began clapping. "Our lovely Doctor rises. I was hoping you'd awake as we crossed the finish line."

Dirt stuck to open sores on Dr. Falino's face. Whatever they'd put her through would be enough for most to buckle. Dr. Falino stared at me and ignored Tricia, which only infuriated Tricia more. She kicked the ground in front of Dr. Falino, spraying tiny pieces of dirt into her face. A few stuck to her lip.

"It doesn't matter what you inject yourself with, you'll still be an ugly person," Dr. Falino said, now staring at Tricia. "Nothing will change that."

Tricia slapped Dr. Falino with such force that her head hit the side of the SUV with a clunk. Tricia turned to me and walked several paces forward.

"You have what I want. I'll give you Preston if you give me what I came here for," she said. "Enough games."

"After what you said, what makes you think I want him?" It took all the strength I had to utter those words.

"You're an interesting species," she replied.

"It's called human. You should try it sometime."

"It's time," she said, glancing at the man behind her.

He nodded and turned around, motioning to the others who obediently waited in the vehicles.

Every SUV door opened in unison, and my pulse raced as I watched heavily armed men step out of the vehicles. There were dozens of them. If we started shooting, Preston and Dr. Falino would end up dead faster than anything.

"You've been running around with something that could change the course of history, and you weren't even smart enough to figure out what it was," Tricia began. "Your high school sweetheart, now, he fully understood the impact of his findings. I thought we were on the same page, and then he turned on me." A callous laugh echoed into the area, and I fought down the urge to shoot her. "But I took care of him, now didn't I?"

Anger hammered through my body so quickly I could taste it. The taste was bitter and unsettling, but it made it easier to imagine her dead.

A flicker of light in the building cattycorner from where I stood caught my attention. I saw a glimmer of a barrel snake through and rest on the ledge of an open window.

"Since you seem to have no interest in my son, which I don't blame you for, he's more like my husband than I'd like to admit, I'll spare you your life. All you have to do is give me Gavin's research."

I gritted my teeth as I glared at her.

"Unless, of course, you'd like to join my army. I haven't come across anyone quite like you," she cooed.

"I'm fine right where I am."

She started laughing and peeked behind her at Preston. "It just occurred to me. You started this whole adventure by yourself. You don't actually care if you're alone. You have trust issues."

I glanced at Dr. Falino. "I've pretty much gotten over those, but thanks for your assessment."

Preston's mouth twitched.

"The one and only gift I took away from the horrible marriage to Preston's father was his distrust of the government. I detested what I saw during the outbreak. I knew I could change things. I knew they were looking at things all wrong. I mean how could we let undead wander the streets and never ask ourselves, how do they keep moving after they're dead? I knew we needed to study this phenomenon, and the best way to do it was using the government's own system against itself."

"Pretty clever," I said. My fingers itched with desire. I wanted to wrap my index finger around the trigger and pull. "So you befriended Marcus when you were imprisoned by MHA?"

"Something like that." She smiled. "Now let's get back to business. Give me what Gavin had, and I'll give you your life back."

"I don't know what it is you're searching for. I honestly don't have anything from him left. What I had from him, I burned when I learned he wasn't the man I thought."

"You wouldn't be that foolish. You listen to me. I will go to each and every person here until I find the person who will give me what I want. I will kill each and every individual who won't give me what I need. The pattern works pretty quickly. Mark my words there will be someone here that will give me what I'm looking for. The weakest links always break quickly."

"Ungag my son," she commanded, turning to look behind her.

The man quickly took the ball out of his mouth and tossed it on the ground.

"Don't bel—" Preston's words were interrupted by another kick to the gut.

"We don't have what you want or Dr. Falino

would've given it to you," I said, as Tricia turned to face me. "Dr. Falino only returned to help us because she thought we had it. She wanted it for herself."

Tricia knelt down to Preston. "You always disappointed me, son," Tricia said, whipping his blindfold off. "You didn't ever understand what you could become. It's no loss."

Tricia's words made my entire body ache for Preston as he lay on the ground completely helpless.

"He's of no use to me, obviously," she said, glancing at the man. She gave a quick nod, and my hand flew to my pistol.

The crack of the bullet beat mine by a fraction of a second. I watched as the bullet entered into Preston's flesh. My bullet met the flesh of the killer too late. My world spun out of control as I watched the blood pool under Preston's neck, his eyes locking on mine as he uttered that he loved me, his eyes becoming hazy as my heart shattered.

"I love you," I said, pushing back the tears.

"Oh, isn't that sweet. The truth comes out, but it's too late." She smiled, and I turned my pistol on her, but was met by several sets of barrels pointed at me.

"Gavin Taylor won your heart because he was one of the good guys. Just like Preston," Dr. Falino muttered.

Gavin Taylor won...one...one...

My gaze flashed to meet Dr. Falino's right before I turned to the camera, giving my signal.

Gavin Taylor won. one. GT1. There were vials of GT1 in the fridge.

The first shot rang out from the sniper in the window as I dove out of range. My body tumbled onto the ground near Dr. Falino. "Give him the entire vial. It's the only way."

"Thank you," I whispered, feeling liquid heat pump through my body as I ran toward the building that housed the modifieds.

Gunfire zinged through the air in all directions as our team descended on TRAC. A ping stung the back of my leg, but it didn't matter. I was almost in hysterics as I swung open the door and ran to the lab. My pulse pounded in my ears as I opened the fridge and took the two vials of GT1. I tucked them into my leathers, shut the refrigerator, and ran faster than I thought my legs could carry me. The gunfire was insane outside as I busted through the doors and half-ran, half-crawled to the first SUV. Preston was just on the other side.

"Get it?" Dr. Falino asked.

I nodded and scanned for Tricia. There was no sign of her. Crouched as low as I could go, I quickly made my way around the front of the car to find Preston, lifeless on the ground. The pool of blood had seeped into the dirt and that's when I truly realized how important Gavin's discovery was. The healing properties we already had floating through us weren't fast enough. He'd bleed to death before they healed him. The accelerant made life possible in new ways. I slid to Preston and cradled his head on my lap, praying I wasn't too late.

"I'm here, baby," I whispered, attempting to open his mouth. "We've got this."

Wedging my fingers in his mouth, I parted his lips just enough for the vial to fit in between. I grabbed the vial and flipped the rubber stopper out and poured the liquid in between his lips. My heart pounding as the tears filled my eyes. What if this didn't work?

"I love you so much," I whispered, putting pressure on his neck wound, rocking him back and forth as I scanned the area. Most of Tricia's men were lying in their own pools of blood, but she wasn't in sight. Something caught my eyes coming out of the cafeteria. It was Emily standing at the entrance, firing round after round behind us.

Behind her was Braden, standing tall and aiming his rifle in the opposite direction from Emily. I followed the direction of his barrel and saw what he was aiming at.

It was Tricia. She had Trek hostage. A pistol pointed at his temple. She was the last survivor.

"Braden's walking, baby. He's walking," I whispered. I kept his head on my lap, but managed to slip my Glock out of its holster. I had a better shot than Braden. I aimed my pistol at Tricia and steadied my breathing. I didn't want to do this, but I had no choice. I looked down the barrel and felt my world turn into slow motion as my finger pulled the trigger. Preston's mother fell to the ground, her weapon discharging, barely missing Trek.

Trek kicked away her weapon and ran over to us. "How can I help?"

"Give me your shirt," I said, barely able to speak.

He ripped off his shirt and began applying pressure as Emily came running over, her hands covering her lips as tears filled her eyes, but I couldn't handle it. Not yet. I wasn't ready to give up hope. I wasn't ready to say goodbye yet.

"Please cut Dr. Falino free," I whispered. "And see if there are some bolt cutters we can use to free Preston."

She nodded, and I watched Braden slowly and carefully make his way over to us. Every step was a struggle, but he had steps to take and every day would become easier. Preston would've loved to see this happen. I swallowed my cries back and kept stroking Preston's forehead with my hand.

Dr. Falino, Paul, and Stanley were by my side, trying to persuade me to let go of Preston, but I refused. I wasn't ready to let go.

I heard the wheels of a gurney behind us and saw Emily pushing it next to us.

I shook my head. "I'm not ready," I whispered, as Braden cut the chains free.

If only I'd gotten the biologic to Preston sooner, he might've had a chance. I felt the first tear sting my cheek as I felt them pry my fingers away from Preston, and I watched them lift his lifeless body to the gurney. Braden and Emily followed the doctors into the building, and my stare landed on the woman who caused all of this. Her arm moved next to her fallen sunglasses.

I darted toward her as I watched this woman fool death, and I wasn't going to let that happen. Her khaki pants were completely saturated in blood as her shoulder wound trickled crimson. Tricia's eyes connected with mine, but I still saw no humanness.

"Finish me off. You know you want to. That tingle of desire you're feeling, I get that too. That's the tingle of power. Once it spreads, there's nothing like it."

"Your insides are so ugly, hell doesn't even want you," I whispered.

"Possibly true." She gave a weak smile, the color in her cheeks fading.

"Your son did what no one else could. He broke the walls down around my heart, and I'm certainly not going to let someone like you help to rebuild them. Because of the Afterworld, I learned that my spirit couldn't be broken so thank you for that."

She coughed and turned her head. "Dullness is worse than death, darling. You saved me," she smiled, her hand slowly gliding through the slick of blood. "I wouldn't last a minute in prison. It would be like being married to his father all over again."

"Don't get your hopes up. We've got some great doctors on staff. We'll get you patched up and you can learn to love cement walls."

A low, rhythmic hum above startled me. I recognized the pulsing whoosh of blades overhead and scanned the clouds, searching for the source, but I didn't find one.

I glanced back down at Tricia, her lids at half-mast, as the deep rumble overhead became louder and louder. The steady beat of blades made my insides curl. Whoever they were, they were coming for us. Just like they'd taken other towns, they'd take us too. I stared at the woman lying in front of me. Anger filled my body as I thought about TRAC coming to her rescue.

The pulsing of the chopper blades drew my attention away from Tricia as I looked toward the sky, readying myself for one last fight. I unstrapped my rifle and walked away from Preston's mother. Keeping my eyes on the clouds above, I watched and waited until the Chinook came into view. With all of the vehicles, there was nowhere for it to land.

I spotted several soldiers throwing black cord out of the side. They began repelling down the rope. I couldn't see where they touched down. My view was obstructed by TRAC's SUVs. Several people came outside to check on the noise, but I barely looked at them. My focus stayed centered on what was about to unfold.

With my rifle raised, I waited for the soldiers to appear. After what seemed like forever, I saw the first soldier wind through the SUVs. I took the safety off my rifle as my mind drifted back to Preston. Even if I didn't win the war, at least we'd won a few battles together. Our time had come, and I had nothing left to lose.

The soldier stopped walking and stood about

ten feet in front of me. Wearing a helmet, shades, and full tactical gear, I had no chance at seeing who was hiding behind the uniform. It wasn't until she spoke that I felt my knees buckle, but I remained strong and locked them tight.

She removed her helmet and shades, staring directly at me, as she strapped her rifle to her back. In shock, I lowered my rifle slowly and tried desperately to piece my life together.

"It's nice to see you again," Charlotte said, taking a step forward.

Chapter Twenty-Eight

I stared at the modifieds' building as the door busted open, and Emily came running out. She looked at the Chinook, which had retreated over the coastline but still brought enough noise and wind to disorient someone not expecting it. Her eyes locked on mine and her cheeks were tear-stained.

"Come quick," she yelled, before seeing Charlotte.

She stopped running and slowly turned her attention back to me.

"What's going on here?" Emily asked.

I shook my head. "I don't know, and I don't care."

Without even a peek at Charlotte, Emily ushered me into the building.

"Keep her out. Please keep her out," I whispered, not sure what I was about to find.

I ran along the outskirts of the incubators

toward Dr. Falino's lab. Braden was standing outside the doors, leaning against the wall. His head hung in his hands.

"What? What's going on?" I asked, my voice urgent.

"Just go inside," Braden said, his expression void of anything I recognized. "He twitched or I don't know... I've heard of a death rattle."

I pushed the doors open and saw Dr. Falino, Paul, and Stanley standing over the gurney. Blood was everywhere: their clothes, the floor, the wall, and the metal gurney. My body swayed as I attempted to make my way over to them, to him. I wasn't ready to see Preston this way, to say my goodbyes.

I reached for the rolling tray to steady myself. Dr. Falino flipped around to hold it still so I didn't go rolling across the room. My eyes fell to the bloody gauze, scalpels, and other tools I didn't recognize.

And finally the tears began to roll down my cheeks. My cries no longer only for me to hear as my body slid to the floor. The pain crippled me as I felt my body shudder under the burden of loss.

Dr. Falino knelt down beside me, peeling her latex gloves off and tossing them on the floor.

"It's okay. It's gonna be okay," she whispered, holding me close.

"I loved him more than anything on this earth...More than myself. It's not okay. It wasn't okay when Gavin died and it's not okay now. It's never okay. That's how TRAC controls everyone.

This pain is too much to bear. I can't do this anymore," I sobbed.

"You don't have to," she said.

I felt a large, masculine hand slowly caress the top of my head, and my head snapped up to meet Dr. Falino's gaze. She nodded, and a hint of a smile surfaced on her lips.

"GT1 worked. The accelerated properties that Gavin discovered, work," she whispered as I pushed myself off the ground.

The level of emotion that gushed through me was impossible to control as I stared down at the man I loved more than life itself. His eyes were still closed, but his hand traveled along my body, finding my hand.

I bent down and kissed him softly, his lips curling ever so slightly. My hand ran lightly over his matted hair as I took in every single part of him. I wanted to absorb this moment and never let it go.

No matter what we faced ahead, we'd do it together. I was no longer alone. My tears of sorrow traded for tears of joy as the depths of both heaven and hell exposed themselves and dared to rip my soul to shreds.

"I love you, Preston Blakely," I whispered.

He squeezed my hand twice as I ran my fingers along his hairline, trying to absorb that the man I loved was by some miracle alive.

There was a knock at the door and Paul went to answer it. I heard Emily's voice and some back and forth arguing.

Charlotte's voice hummed through the air and

grated on my spirit as I quickly turned to see her.

Charlotte's eyes dropped to Preston, and a look of horror spread across her face. She shook her head. "I'm sorry."

"Now's not the time," I said, between gritted teeth.

"Unfortunately, it's the only time we have," she said.

Preston squeezed my hand, and I let out a sigh, sweeping a kiss against his cheek. I placed his hand alongside his body and walked to meet Charlotte.

I motioned toward the rows of incubators, her discomfort level obvious. Seemed like the perfect place to me.

She took in a deep breath and locked her eyes on mine.

"We've been watching you," she began.

"I gathered that," I replied, crossing my arms.

She nodded. "And we've been watching TRAC."

"Are you planning on doing anything besides watching?" I asked, the anger impossible to hide.

"I know what it looks like," she confirmed.

"It looks as if our government is not only involved, but too cowardly to stop a bunch of ignorant assholes who get joy from tearing families apart and killing all in the name of what a particular few desire."

Charlotte nodded.

"You can't tell me that you don't have the manpower or resources to stop TRAC. What are you?" I asked.

"United States Army."

"Exactly. How did TRAC infiltrate the strongest military force in the world? I just met the woman who led the effort, and she honestly didn't seem like much."

"Preston's mother, Tricia Blakely," Charlotte confirmed.

"So tell me why are you standing in front of me instead of stopping the senseless killings that are happening across the country."

"We needed to know exactly what we were dealing with. What it was that TRAC was after because whatever it was that TRAC was after would be the same thing as what all of the groups are after."

"All the groups?" I asked.

"Tricia worked quickly. She not only tapped into our resources, but she stretched her tentacles globally. She somehow managed to strike fear into the minds of leaders around the world and place small government-like cells throughout the globe. She lured them with hopes of immortality and a future existence of a heaven on earth."

"Why didn't you stop her?" I asked.

"She was like a ghost. We didn't even know who it was we were looking for. We thought we were onto someone with Marcus, but when you took him out of the picture and TRAC just kept growing, we knew we had a big problem on our hands."

I bit the inside of my lip and found myself staring at the endless bubbles in the incubator to my right.

"She lurked in the shadows, gave orders, built structures that seemed impenetrable, and never once allowed her identity to be known. She was stealth, untraceable," Charlotte continued.

"Because she hid herself deep in an MHA facility. No one would think to search for her there, immersed in a government-run facility," I whispered.

"Government run now," she corrected. "That was a vital slip-up on our government's part, and they don't like to admit when they're wrong. We never should've handed over security and administration to a private company. Pocketbooks speak louder than most things in the Afterworld. You, along with many other groups, came onto our radar time and again. But your group was well organized...logical, and you started connecting the dots for us. I'm not sure what drove you to search for answers, but whatever it was is something that can't be developed. You have to be born with it."

I laughed, "I doubt that, but thanks for the flattery."

"I'm just being honest," she said, and I'm sure she thought she was.

I began getting very warm as the information began to settle. Fanning myself, I glimpsed the room where Preston still lay.

"I'd like to go outside," I said, nodding in the direction of the entrance.

"Sure. It's a little stuffy in here."

We walked outside, and my eyes landed on

the empty spot where I'd left Tricia to live or die. I didn't even care.

"Our team is working on her," Charlotte answered my unasked question.

"I hope not too hard."

"This is the problem," Charlotte said, turning to face me. "We need to know what she's done. Who's she's convinced to be on her side. Like it or not, her organization is powerful. She built a weapon, the modifieds, that governments and civilians alike want to get their hands on, but we think she was searching for something more, and my gut tells me you know what that *more* is."

"Can't say that I do."

Charlotte shook her head and lit a cigarette. "Do you mind?"

"If you cared what I thought, you'd have asked me before you lit it."

She took a drag and flicked ash off the end. "Possibly true."

I bristled at Charlotte like I always had and glanced toward the line of SUVs, wondering where this conversation was headed.

"There are countless groups that are after her. You're only one of many, but she wanted you. She was willing to risk blowing her cover just to get at you. That tells me you have something she wants, which makes us want what you have."

"Don't get your hopes up," I muttered.

"Think about what our government can do to you. We put a bounty on your head. We could have killed you at any moment."

"But you said it. I have something you want so

you're not going to do that."

A man's voice barked an order at Charlotte. I tilted my head, trying to find the man behind the voice.

"Those'll kill ya," I replied, as Charlotte crushed the end of her cigarette into the gravel and stood up quickly.

"And my current occupation won't?" She cocked a brow.

I had to give her that.

"General Starling," Charlotte said, saluting the man who seemingly came from nowhere. He commanded respect by purely existing.

"You're dismissed," he replied.

She nodded and backed away.

"I apologize on behalf of Charlotte and the United States Government. She doesn't have great people skills, but she's a hell of a soldier."

A smile dusted my lips, and I steadied my eyes on his.

"I'm due for a cup of coffee. What do you say we head to the cafeteria?" he asked.

Knowing there was no arguing, I followed in silence as my mind tried to wrap itself around this very sticky situation. The few people that were in the cafeteria cleared out the moment they spotted the General and me. We filled our foam cups and took a seat at the table nearest the door.

"Threats don't motivate me," I stated.

"Again, I apologize about that." His expression remained unchanged.

"Charlotte was wired, and I heard your

conversation. What she told you was correct, but the truth of it is, Tricia Blakely managed to disrupt the Afterworld in a way I don't think our government thought possible. She got a head start on us. No doubt about that. As Charlotte said, Tricia was invisible, slithering out of our grasp time and again. When her people started the dialogue with us about you and Preston, we had to listen. We knew it was a setup, but we had no choice. We needed time. We'd already learned from Ron and Josh that you weren't the bad guys."

"What happened to them?" I interrupted.

"They're fine. We hid them."

"Ron's father was turned. I —"

"We know. We've told Ron."

I nodded and took a deep breath in, not wanting any of the coffee.

"It was all a trap. We knew you didn't kill Gavin, and Preston didn't kill his sister. The kidnapping charges, arson charges, everything was given to us by TRAC, but we knew what they expected us to do with the information."

"You were willing to let us be killed on the streets. You continued to play her game."

"I'm not always proud of what I have to do for the greater good, Rebekah. I'm sure you can understand that."

"I saw innocent civilians killed just for marching."

"Our preferred method of crowd control is rubber bullets and tear gas, not lead bullets and grenades."

"Could've fooled me," I replied, crossing my arms.

"It wasn't us, which is exactly what I'm trying to get across. More boots on the ground would've only caused confusion and more terror."

I swallowed my anger.

"So why would you allow TRAC to take so many innocent lives and allow them to siege entire towns..." my voice trailed off unable to understand the countless deaths.

"TRAC had managed to cripple some of our bases. It took us by surprise. Some of our soldiers were working for TRAC. We will never let that happen again."

"You didn't answer my question."

"We didn't want to provide boots on the ground because we'd already lost the trust of the public. TRAC made sure of that, which was why we cut the media channels off at the knees. TRAC had stolen our equipment and some of our soldiers. If we put our soldiers on the ground to attack TRAC, the citizens wouldn't have any idea which side was which, and we didn't want to chance an all-out civil war. We knew the cost in lives would be great, but if we entered too early, our country would have toppled."

I stared at my coffee.

"We have airstrikes set to begin at thirteen-hundred. We've found most of TRAC's facilities and certainly enough to cripple them momentarily, but that's where you come in."

"Where I come in?" I asked.

"We're no longer fighting only for the United

States. TRAC has infiltrated all around the globe. It won't be long before this technology gets into the wrong hands. Before governments see it as an opportunity not the liability that it is. You understand that liability."

I didn't say a word.

"We used to only have to be concerned with an R0 factor." He leaned back in his chair.

"What's the R0 factor?"

"The average reproduction number of an infectious disease. Meaning for each person who contracts the disease, on average, it can be expected that a certain number of individuals will become infected from that one case."

"For instance, measles sat at around an eighteen average for infection rate."

"And the outbreak that changed our lives forever?" I asked.

"The scientists at first claimed it only sat at two, but they were gravely mistaken. They didn't account for everything—meaning life, mistakes, accidental contaminations. When all was said and done, the R0 was actually thirty-one. As we all know, it wasn't until it was too late that we realized what those flu symptoms could turn into. We're lucky there's anyone left in the world."

"And?" I asked.

"We no longer just have to worry about R0 factors. We're facing a war like we've never seen before where humans are used as weapons. It's not the disease we have to worry about. It's the modifieds and the ones who want to control them. That's what we have to be worried about. We need someone like you, Rebekah. What you've created with the little amount of resources and funding you had is miraculous. You handed us Tricia. You created an army of the very things she had."

"It wasn't just me."

"I know. We need people like Preston, Emily, and Braden as well. We need your team to join us, Rebekah. This war has barely begun. I need an answer. I need to know if the United States Government can count on you and your team."

"This isn't only my decision to make," I told him, as I stood up.

"I understand that."

"Where is Tricia?" I asked.

"Being tended to and questioned."

"She won't give you any answers."

"We know that."

"Where has the President been through all of this?" I asked.

"He's been in hiding."

I turned around and walked out of the building, my feet carrying me quickly to Preston.

Emily and Braden were chatting with Charlotte, their expressions far more jovial than I expected. I gave a quick wave on my way to Preston and almost fell over once I opened the doors.

He was sitting up on the gurney, his feet dangling over the edge. The gauze had been changed over the wound on his neck, and other than the dried blood that covered him from head to toe, it didn't look like anything had happened to him.

Preston's eyes locked on me, and he flashed a huge grin, sliding off the gurney.

I hopped up slightly on my toes in excitement and saw Dr. Falino, Paul, and Stanley quickly exit the room as I ran toward Preston.

His arms were outstretched, and I dove into his embrace, inhaling everything about him.

"I love you," I nearly cried.

His hands cradled my face as he took me in. "I love you, Rebekah Taylor."

It wasn't long before I heard the General outside and my moment of bliss was interrupted.

"The military is here."

"I know." Preston shook his head. "Charlotte filled me in."

I bristled at the statement, but was thankful I didn't have to start from the beginning.

"I'm so sorry about your mom," I said, my eyes dipping to the floor. He tilted my head back up and shook his head.

"Don't you dare apologize for doing what's right." He smiled weakly. "I never wanted to see that side of my mom. Maybe that's the real reason I never attempted to get her out of the MHA facility. Maybe on some level I knew that side of her existed and wanted it locked away." He shook his head and let out a deep breath "I just never thought she'd be capable of all this."

I nodded, staring into his eyes. "I know."

We stood holding each other as a few minutes of silence wrapped around us.

"They've asked us to join the cause," I finally said.

"The cause?" he asked. "What's the cause?"

"Doing what's right." I smiled. "I think."

He laughed quietly and nodded. "Are you up for it? Working for the government won't be—"

"No.no.no.no.no. I'm not working for the government," I laughed, shaking my head. "I think at the very least, we deserve our own agency. Besides... I don't trust them."

Preston laughed and held me tighter.

"I'm not kidding," I said.

"I know you're not and that's why I love you."

A knock sounded at the door, and I turned around to see the General walk into the room. He grimaced at the sight of all the blood on Preston but carried on.

"Let us know if there is anything we can do to convince you to join us. I understand it's a big decision." He stared at us, but I didn't respond with an answer.

Instead, I watched the General exit as I leaned against Preston, feeling the steady beat of his heart. This decision wasn't without risk, but by the sounds of it, doing nothing wasn't either.

I felt the tingle in my fingertips begin to spread as I thought about the next chase, but Tricia was wrong. The need I felt growing inside me wasn't for power. It was because I wanted to make the Afterworld a better place.

I spun around and Preston grinned, nodding.

We already knew the answer.

And the answer was yes.

UprisingZ Now Available

No one can be trusted...

Keep reading for an excerpt

UprisingZ Excerpt

Chapter One

"I've never seen anything like it," Preston said, nearly whistling in amazement.

The unnerving sight in front of us sent a methodical charge through me as hundreds of naked undead roamed the acreage below. The electrified fence was the only thing separating the modifieds from us as we stood on the hillside and watched our worst fears come to fruition. We were training our own undead, the modifieds that could change the course of the Afterworld.

Preston looked over his shoulder and crossed his arms in frustration before turning his attention back to the activities below.

"So we did it. We finally woke them up." Preston bit his lip and let out a sigh.

"It's the only way to continue the research on the modifieds," I said aloud, more for my benefit than his. "I'm just glad we were in the field when it began. I wouldn't have wanted to see the process."

It was hard to stomach waking these creatures and bringing them into the world. We'd fought so long to keep the undead hibernating.

"Dr. Falino had better be right." Preston stood up straighter and wrapped his arm around my shoulders.

"I'm beginning to get the feeling there's no such thing as right and wrong in the Afterworld." I leaned my head against him and watched the modifieds wander aimlessly below.

Soon, we'd begin the training.

"Only kill or be killed," Preston muttered, lessening his grip.

I nodded right when one of the modifieds near the fence darted for a group congregating near a guard station. A guard shot a tranquilizer dart at the modified, dropping it almost instantly, and the rest of the undead scattered into the field.

We'd learned a lot over the last month, but not nearly enough to end the uprisings that threatened the globe. It was only a matter of time before the undead were used against humans on a wider scale. While we'd learned about TRAC's influence over the modifieds, we came to find out there were even more facilities conducting research. Whether they were all tied to TRAC remained to be seen.

It was a hard decision, but we knew we needed to expand our research to include the manufacturing of thought in the modifieds. It was the first step in controlling them without depending on outside influences like drones and light sequencing. The only way to begin that phase was to wake them up.

A shiver ran through me as I watched the undead slowly gather around the one who'd dropped to the dirt.

"What are they going to do to it?" I asked, my voice hoarse as I saw a few modifieds slither on the ground toward the unresponsive modified.

"The guards or the undead?"

"Both."

"The guards will cordon off the tranquilized creature from the chopper, and then they will drop down, harness and lift it up to the chopper so Dr. Falino can run some tests."

Within seconds, the shudder of chopper blades roared in the distance and slowly came into view beyond the hills. What looked like a kennel dangled below as the helicopter came closer. The sound of the chopper appeared to scatter the undead away from the sleeping modified as the helicopter hovered above the body.

Fencing lowered around the modified and two of our men catapulted to the ground, quickly fastening harnesses around the undead and signaling for the body to be brought back up.

Minutes later, the helicopter flew away and the undead swarmed the area where the creature was taken from.

The idea of controlling these modifieds was at the forefront of our research. If we couldn't control them, we couldn't use them. Watching a modified act on its own accord told me we were closer than we thought to tapping into consciousness, yet too far away to control it. Dr. Falino needed to uncover why some of the undead became unruly, what drove their actions, and why others seemed unaffected. What worried me more was once we tapped into this next phase of modifieds, would we ever be able to control them? Would we be able to keep the modifieds in line, or would we create our own worst enemy?

"What are you thinking?" Preston asked.

"I'm thinking we're a long way from figuring out how to manage them." I took a step away from Preston and glanced at our truck. We'd been on the road for the last month, jumping from one facility to the next, looking for something that we may never find.

"We can already regulate them . . . guide them," Preston said. "We've proven that light therapy works. That's what we saw in the zombie pits, and we've been able to replicate it time and again."

"It's not safe enough. We can't turn modifieds loose on the streets, praying the lights flash at the right time or the drones don't lose their signal to communicate."

"We've done it before," Preston objected.

"You're absolutely right, but we were able to create the ideal setting. All it takes is for the drone pilots to be knocked out, and the modifieds are uncontrollable . . . or if the signal strength is lost between the transmitter and drone communication, total control will be lost."

Preston nodded and let out a frustrated groan. "I'd rather have something than nothing. I understand what you're saying. I know you're right, but I'm worried we can't get to that next step."

I knew what he meant. We'd managed to win several battles with our modifieds, but the technique was filled with so much risk that there was no way to ensure the safety of the public on a larger scale. Little pockets of success didn't equal an overall win. TRAC still controlled entire cities.

"I do get that. We're behind. Plus, it's been too quiet," I said, looking into Preston's gaze. He looked tired. "They haven't charged any other towns in the last week. I'm worried something bigger is on the horizon."

"I wanted to believe it was because my girlfriend managed to take down the leader of TRAC." He attempted a half-smile, but his gaze hardened. The leader of TRAC had been his mother, a surprise to both of us. "I've also been thinking it's been too calm."

"What if they've already found a way to enhance them biologically?" I glanced across the field at the heavily wooded hillside.

"It's possible," Preston agreed. "If that's our end goal, I'd imagine it's the enemy's too."

"What happens when monster and man unite?" I whispered. "Isn't that what we're hoping for?"

"A beast with human consciousness." Preston rubbed his jaw. Whiskers shaded his skin and darkness shadowed under his eyes. We'd been going nonstop, touring facilities and hoping to find answers that seemed buried beneath the horrors of modern medicine. We were still coming up short. The military had managed to cripple several of TRAC's bases, but we still had too many unanswered questions to succeed, and the streets were filled with confusion and clashing of innocents.

"If that's even possible." I twisted my lips into a frown as I turned away from Preston.

"Have you seen enough?" he asked.

My gaze dropped back down to the field of roaming undead. "For now."

He nodded toward the truck, and a small amount of tension left my shoulders at the thought of getting to the one safe place we had. I liked to be in control, and the truth of the matter was that I felt anything but in control around the undead. Modifieds were resilient, their strength was bone crushing, and they were irrational, driven by something we'd yet to uncover or understand.

"Let's get back so we can unpack, shower, and pack for another tour," Preston said, squeezing my shoulders before turning toward the truck.

I nodded and held in a silent sigh.

I knew Emily and Braden were waiting to fill us in on the latest, but I'd asked Preston to take me here first. I wanted to see the modifieds without endless explanations. Preston was one of the few who understood what these modifieds meant on a personal level. His own sister had been made into one, just as my brother-in-law had been created. Their bodies had been used as vessels for the undead.

Mourning once for a loved one was a heart wrenching and soul crushing experience, but seeing them brought back from the dead and used in a way that was meant solely for an organization to prosper was an entirely different breed of evil.

Not every action had to have a scientific reason behind it. Sometimes, silence was the best explanation and provided answers that only the heart could hear. I needed to be alone with my thoughts as I watched the undead roam freely under our watch. Someone's brother, sister, or wife fell under our control. Dr. Falino explained the bodies were only the vessel, not the soul of the person, but it was difficult for me to separate the two.

I climbed into the truck as Preston started the engine.

"I'm looking forward to a shower and bed," Preston said, smiling as he put the truck into reverse.

"You and me both." I leaned my head against the seat.

Preston slid his hand to mine as we continued down the gravel road toward the refinery we'd turned into our base camp months ago. It was as close to a home as we had.

"Do you think we can figure out a way to lock

the showers?" Preston asked, a smile touching his lips.

"We could just put a sign on the door." I laughed and shook my head. The one downside to the facility was the lack of privacy.

"True." He turned down the road to the main facility.

The chopper that had been in the field only fifteen minutes before had landed, and the modified was being transported to the lab. The buildings were abuzz with activity, people rushing back and forth, shadows dancing in the windows, and steam rising from the smokestacks.

Dr. Falino was following behind the group, pushing the gurney until she saw us driving toward her. She stood and waited for us as the others continued toward the building. Her dark hair had been chopped off into a pixie since we'd last seen her a couple of weeks ago, and her features had softened. Ever since she realized it was safer to bring her daughter back to our base, she'd become happier. Truthfully, her daughter was safer here than anywhere else.

I gave a quick wave and felt a pounding between my temples. It looked like a shower and sleep were getting pushed farther away as Dr. Falino hurried over.

"I don't think she knows we're headed out again tomorrow," Preston said, parking the truck.

"Probably not."

Preston squeezed my hand and nodded

toward Emily and Braden, who charged through the cafeteria doors with a burst of energy. It was also the same building many of us called home and the place I wanted to be, but it looked like Dr. Falino had other plans.

"I'll go get caught up by those two while you talk to Dr. Falino," Preston said, and I gave a quick nod in agreement, mustering enough energy to climb out of the truck. I knew why he was avoiding the doctor.

"Good to see you, Rebekah," Dr. Falino said as Emily and Braden swallowed Preston into their embrace. "Good to see Preston in such good spirits."

"It comes and goes," I said, staring down at the ground to avoid her gaze

Preston asked me not to talk to Dr. Falino about the side effects from the GT1 serum that had saved his life.

"Which is why he is still avoiding me at all costs." She folded her arms, and I brought my gaze to hers.

"I've got to respect Preston's wishes," I told her.

Dr. Falino's mouth turned into a skinny line of disapproval. "Well, I appreciate the samples you sent. You were right about the facility you found in Arizona. The cell age was younger than any we'd encountered so far. It's unnerving."

"So they're still snatching innocents up from the towns they take over and turning them into modifieds." I began walking toward the cafeteria.

"Or they've taken it a step further," she said.

"How so?" I asked.

"I'm running some tests to see if their research is more advanced, possibly even cloning."

"And if that's the case?" I asked, yanking on the door to the empty cafeteria.

"Then we've got a lot of catching up to do. It's one thing to use undead as vessels. The cloned cells of an individual take over the modified, giving them the features from the cloned individual but keeping the strength and resilience of the undead."

"But?" I prompted, grabbing a small carton of orange juice from the cooler.

"But if they managed to clone certain organs from an individual and put them in the undead to function—"

"You mean like the brain?" I interrupted.

She pulled her brows together and shifted her white lab coat. "That's one of my thoughts."

"Only time will tell." I took a sip of the juice and leaned my head back. "If they have that technology—"

"We need to bring in more researchers," Dr. Falino interrupted.

"Finding ones who can be trusted isn't that easy."

"I know." She nodded. "But Emily and Braden had a breakthrough. They're filling in Preston right now, I'm sure."

"What's that?"

"They managed to tap into the undersea cable that TRAC has apparently been using to send data overseas. They've stopped depending on the satellite transmission."

"How in the world did they manage to find the right one?" I asked, feeling the familiar tingle of anticipation that had kept me going.

"They said since the outbreak, a majority of the cables had gone dead, but two days ago, one lit up."

"Game changer," I said, smiling. "And they have no way of knowing that we've tapped into the communication line?"

"Not a clue, but it also tells us that TRAC has facilities all over the globe. I'm glad you'll be here for the next while to help us decipher—"

"Change of plans. We're supposed to meet with General Starling tomorrow."

"Here?" She crossed her arms.

"California."

"Any idea why?"

I shook my head. "I don't plan on telling him about your developments."

"Or Braden's, I'd assume." Her brow arched, knowing the answer.

We might be a step closer to trusting General Starling and his division, but we weren't fully there yet. He had a habit of asking too many questions and not giving enough answers, but they did open the bank vault.

"You look like you could use some sleep. I'll let you know what else I find out about those cells." She patted my arm and opened her mouth to stay something but shut it quickly.

My chin turned slightly. "Something you want

to tell me?"

She let go of my arm and nodded. "It's just nice to have you back."

"It's nice to be back. I only wish it were for longer."

I tossed my orange juice carton in the trash and headed toward the elevators leading to the sleeping quarters.

It felt good to be back at our base camp. Preston and I had been running nonstop over the last month, touring facilities and learning more about TRAC's plans for the undead. As with everything in the Afterworld, the more we uncovered, the less we understood. Undead percolating in solution dotted the globe, and it wasn't clear if TRAC was the only group manufacturing these creatures. But the news about tapping into TRAC's communication line was simply exhilarating. With all the chasing, running, and hiding, it was hard to believe one simple mistake on their part could possibly lead us closer to their plans.

Maybe we'd never need these creatures to rise from the dead. Maybe we could stop it before it started.

I pushed open the door to my room and quickly glanced around before placing my holster on the shelf. Everything was as we'd left it, the bed unmade, clothes waiting to be laundered, and a drawing from Dr. Falino's daughter next to a stack of books on the floor.

Between lack of sleep and so many unanswered questions, I felt unsettled, which was no surprise since no matter where I landed, things didn't feel right. I just hadn't expected it to happen here. This was my one sanctuary.

I let out a sigh and sat in the chair by the window that overlooked the facility. Since the government started funding us, the property had grown tremendously. More guard stations had been built, temporary barracks had been erected, and more support staff had been sent our way, but we still had very few answers. We also had more strangers wandering the grounds, which made me uneasy.

A breeze from the doorway skated across my skin, leaving behind a chill of uncertainty. I scanned the room and hallway for the source of the breeze and saw nothing of concern. My nerves were definitely frayed to bits, and I felt on edge. As simple as it sounded, all I'd been dreaming about for the last twenty-four hours was a hot shower and spending some alone time with Preston.

The general had assigned a unit to tag along with us as we collected evidence from the modifieds to bring back to Dr. Falino. Modifieds were also sent back to her for study. Out in the field, it was difficult to assess if the modifieds we were finding had been advancing or if it solely depended on who ran each facility. That was where Dr. Falino's team came in.

I leaned over and held my head in my hands and gently rubbed my temples. Some days, it felt like we were right back where we started, scrambling to find out how many groups were behind this new brand of killing machine, but now more than ever, I could taste the end. I wanted the end to be near.

Ever since Preston had taken the GT1 solution, we'd noticed side effects that were worrisome, and extreme exhaustion, nausea, and skin rashes were the pleasant ones. I wasn't sure how much longer he should be running ragged in the field.

A shiver ran up my spine, and I sat up straight and looked over my shoulder. The room was empty, but there was an unnerving current running through the air. I was definitely on the brink of madness, imagining things, hearing things, and wishing for things that were impossible. Maybe it wasn't madness. Maybe it was knowing too much.

My throat constricted, and I pushed the last thought out of my mind. I wanted nothing more than to go back to the life that I'd had years before where the biggest issue of the day was sitting in traffic or burning microwave popcorn.

I stood up and stretched, thinking about that last thought. Would I even be able to handle normalcy? I'd been looking over my shoulder for so long, who knew if I'd ever be able to stop running? I wasn't sure I'd ever be able to stop the chase.

I walked over to the bed and mindlessly bent over to pick up the drawing when a grey hand from under the bed clasped my wrist and pulled me under.

UprisingZ is Now Available!

ABOUT THE AUTHOR

Karice received an MFA in Creative Writing from the U of W. She has written over twenty novels, and she has several exciting projects in the works (or at least she thinks they're exciting). Karice lives in the Pacific Northwest with her awesome husband and two cute English Bulldogs. She loves anything to do with snow, and she seeks out the stuff whenever she can, especially if there's a toasty fire to read by.

CONTACT THE AUTHOR

Sign up for Karice's newsletter to receive exclusive FREE novellas, learn about new releases and contests at www.karicebolton.com.

You can also text KariceBooks to 313131 to receive a text from her on release days or follow her on Facebook/Instagram/Pinterest/Twitter @KariceBolton

www.ingramcontent.com/pod-product-compliance
Lightning Source LLC
Chambersburg PA
CBHW051314250626
47155CB00007B/2320